THE AURA REALM

ASYRA'S CALL

MAYA UNADKAT

The AURA REALM

ASYRA'S CALL

MAYA UNADKAT

Copyright © Maya Unadkat, 2021

First paperback edition March 2021

ISBN 978-1-7397034-0-0 (Paperback)

Fourth Edition

Map Illustration by Aryan Durgale

Published by Maya Unadkat

SilverDust Press

for Isha,
for my family
and for all aspiring authors.

non est ad astra mollis e terris

TERRARI KINGDOM

OBSCURI KINGDOM

MAGI

...I
...OM

LYNCHI KINGDOM

THE MAP OF THE AURA REALM

CAELI KINGDOM

CONTENTS

CHAPTER ONE

Home on the Water

Once again, Ellora Artemer found herself staring at the wooden door only a few metres down the corridor from her bedroom. Inside stood the purple-painted walls she knew like the back of her hand, even if she hadn't seen them in years. Nobody had. But she knew that now they would be charred. The walls would be blackened, and the furniture would be damaged. She didn't need to see it to know it. It was an unspoken rule in the Artemer household not to go in there. Not that anybody wanted to, anyway; Ellora's mother would still cry every time she walked past a daisy because they reminded her of the ones painted on those purple walls, and Ellora's father would avoid even looking at the door at all costs, averting his eyes to the floor when he walked past.

Ellora, while she didn't want to go inside, didn't avoid the room. She liked to sit on the floor opposite the plain white door. It reassured her and made her feel safe. It filled the gaps and changes in her life she would never get used to. She could picture every single detail about that room: the white, wooden bed frame; the thick duvet covered in multicoloured spots; the wooden toy chest at the foot of the bed, filled to the brim with stuffed animals and plastic dolls and small cars. It had been eight years since Ellora had last set foot in that room, and yet she remembered it perfectly.

"Ellora, are you finished with your packing?" her father called from downstairs. "We really must be going soon."

"Can you come up for a moment?" she replied, jogging back to her own bedroom and away from the wooden door, before jumping onto her suitcase to squash it closed.

Her father's heavy footsteps sounded muffled against the cream carpeted stairs leading up from the ground floor. He was a tall, ordinary-looking man, thinner than he used to be, but healthy-ish, nonetheless. He poked his grey head through the doorway to her room. "All good, Ellie?" The sound of her father's nickname for her made a bright smile spring onto Ellora's face; it was a nickname she didn't hear very often anymore.

"Almost. Can you help me shut the suitcase?" Ellora's voice was muffled by the bag. She had to keep her arms and torso stretched across it to stop it from springing back up. Her father chuckled at the awkward position she had gotten herself into as he walked over to the bed and zipped up the suitcase. He lifted the heavy bag and carried it down to the car.

Ellora looked around the room once more, silently saying her goodbyes to the familiar white walls and wooden furniture that had hosted her for the past eighteen years. She gazed at her reflection in the oval-shaped mirror that hung over her dressing table. Her chestnut eyes glistened brightly against her light brown skin and long brown hair. She would be back eventually, of course, but for now, it was time to start her 'new journey', as her father kept calling it. Ellora had no huge expectations, but she was still hoping to have fun at her new school (well, she liked to think of it as more of a training academy) for as long as she could.

The car journey was quiet. Her mother's quiet was expected; she didn't speak much anymore. And her father's quiet was a nervous quiet, which Ellora understood. After all, his not-so-little princess was moving away. But Ellora's quiet was mostly due to the nausea she knew was to come when they crossed through the Gate. It was never a pleasant experience for Ellora but coupled with her anxieties for the day, she knew it would only be worse. And then the dreaded moment arrived; she saw the soft shimmering from a distance, but the humming could only be heard when they got closer. She squeezed her eyes closed, bracing for impact. And then it was over. They were in the Aura Realm. And Ellora promptly vomited into the paper bag kept in the car for that very purpose.

Their goodbyes didn't take long. Her mother hugged her. Not a real, warm hug that her mother would have given her eight years ago; more like a shell of a hug. Her father patted her on the shoulder and told her to look after herself. He made her promise to call him when she had the chance before getting back in the car.

Any nausea Ellora was feeling immediately vanished when she caught sight of it, the long stretch of still, unnaturally calm water glistening before her.

Most people from her Fourth School would have been ridiculously envious of her for getting accepted into the best school in the Realm, but that only made her feel worse. It didn't help at all that people kept congratulating her for getting accepted but, guilty or not, here she was, standing in front of the Madori School of Aura.

On this early afternoon in October, the sun shone down brightly, but Ellora still had to clutch her jacket to herself tightly, under the breeze. She looked out at the enchanting building. It was carved from a white marble that sparkled under the sun.

She was dragging her suitcase alongside her when she felt an odd sort of tugging sensation. She looked down, but there was only her suitcase. She felt it again, stronger this time, and dropped the suitcase in shock, her eyes widening as she watched the case fly up and away, towards the castle ahead of her.

She was standing a fairly long way away from the building, but she could easily see a grand set of stairs leading up from the water and to a magnificent doorway.

On either side of the door, she could see two mighty towers — the place looked like a castle fit for a queen. But it wasn't a queen that would be staying there, it was Ellora. And others, of course. She still couldn't quite believe this breathtaking castle would be her home. She felt that feeling again. A feeling of guilt. A feeling that told her she was a fraud by showing up here, a liar.

She could see some students introducing themselves to others, and others catching up with those they already knew. Further away, the sounds of parents sobbing their farewells to their children, who would be in their First Form, like Ellora, could just about be heard over the sounds of excited chatter from the older students.

The whole building looked like it was floating on top of the ocean, which was sparkling a beautiful, turquoise colour. But it was a bit of a mystery, to all of the youngest students, like Ellora, how exactly they were supposed to get inside. Would a bridge appear? Or would a path rise up from the ocean floor?

Ellora noticed some movement from the corner of her eye and turned her head to the right just in time to see an older student, who looked to be maybe two or three years older than her, walking straight towards the water. All eyes were on her, as she continued to walk directly on top of the water, and towards the castle.

"I should have guessed it", Ellora muttered to herself, "the water is enchanted". She was, after all, in the Madori Kingdom.

She watched in awe with the other First Formers, as more students followed. And then, she was walking on the water too. She had gone to school in this Kingdom for years, but she still found these little things amazing.

As she approached the castle, she noticed the smaller details. She saw water trickling gently down the towers, creating tiny ripples in the water below, and closed her eyes for a second to listen to the calming sound. Intricate little carvings in the marble looked like Doran – the ancient language of the Madori Kingdom, which had died out hundreds of years ago.

And at the bottom of the stairs, almost as if guarding the castle, was a statue of Arellia. It was really only a chiselled block of stone, but Ellora was surprised at how realistic it looked. Her hair was long and was curled realistically around her face. Part of the stone reflected the colour of the ocean, and its blue eyes seemed to almost sparkle. She really did look like a goddess.

Ellora could remember stories about her from one of the books her parents would read to her at night when she was young. Arellia had been the Founder of the Madori School of Aura, one of eight founders and schools.

A shiver ran down Ellora's back and she felt slightly light-headed. She steadied herself on the bannister and took a breath, continuing up the stairs again after a moment.

A feeling of guilt hit her again when she walked in, but she shook it off; she was here either way, so there was no point in feeling bad about it. And with that internal reassurance, she finally stepped through the unnecessarily large copper doors.

The entranceway itself was similar to a large atrium, with stone floors and blue-coloured walls.

Directly in front of her were a small set of double doors, which Ellora could see led to an outdoor area. To the right of these doors was a very wide staircase with an extravagant bronze railing leading upwards.

To the left was a set of huge doors, almost big enough for a giant, and to the right were similar doors, but these were open. Ellora walked over and peeked into what looked like a never-ending library. She wanted to come back later with Belle, her book lover of a best friend.

At that exact moment, as if on cue, Ellora felt a tap on her shoulder, "Elle, we absolutely need to check out this library later!"

Ellora turned and felt relieved as soon as she spotted the golden hair that belonged to her best friend.

"Bee you have no idea how happy I am to see you." She hugged Belle tightly, before stepping back from her, feeling immensely relieved. Belle's green eyes were filled with warmth and reassurance.

Ellora recognised that Belle must also have been feeling nervous, as much as she didn't show it, since she had donned her favourite black cashmere cardigan – one Ellora recognised as a sign of comfort, as well as a confidence boost, for Belle.

She saw Dan's brown hair and handsome features appear behind Belle as he stepped towards Ellora and greeted her warmly with a quick hug, which she returned. "Nice to see ya, kid." He smiled cheekily.

"Don't call me 'kid'!" Ellora stomped her foot on the ground childishly and the three laughed warmly, instantly feeling more relaxed.

"I just heard from one of the guys back there that the Madori Mistress is about to speak to us," he gestured to a vague area behind him, before wrapping his arms around both of their shoulders and leading them a short way down a burgundy carpeted corridor, and through a door that the other students seemed to flow through.

She smiled warmly at the pair as they stood towards the back of the large room before looking up to see a young woman, who couldn't have been more than thirty years old, walking in front of the crowd that had gathered. This was the leader of the school — Madori Mistress Oriel Delow, Ellora recalled. The leaders of the schools, like Oriel Delow, were all required to have an especially strong affinity for the Aura school they would lead.

She walked with such poise that it almost looked as though she was gliding through the air. However, when talking to the First Formers, an air of authority could be felt radiating from her. In her eyes was a determination so strong, it was almost aggressive.

"Good afternoon, everyone," she began, her voice somehow strong and delicate at once. "I'm pleased to welcome you all to the Madori School of Aura. I know some of you may be tired from your long journeys, so I won't keep you for very long.

"As you all know, there are six different Auras. Madori." Ellora heard a gasp from behind her and turned to see an old-looking, grey-haired man, who had been standing on the side of the room, move his hands in a large arc around his body. Water gushed from his fingertips as they moved, and a large arched shape made entirely of water was formed, hovering in front of him.

"Incendi," Oriel continued, as the man standing to the left of the first one lifted his left hand, palm up, with a bright, colourful ball of fire hovering over it.

"Caeli." Next was a brown-haired woman who, with a small twisting motion of her wrist, created a small but powerful tornado-like gust of wind below her, lifting her into the air where she remained, floating a meter from the floor.

"Terrari." With delicate fingers, the dark-haired woman who was next in the line coaxed a tall sunflower to grow directly from the carpeted floor in front of her.

"Glassi." A white-haired man was next, and in one thrust of his arms into the air, the entire wall behind him was encased in a white, glittering layer of ice.

"And Ferri." Finally, at the end of the line, there was a tall, large man who smiled kindly at all of them. With a gentle wave of his fingers, a dozen butterflies manifested from thin air and came to rest upon his arms.

Ellora watched in awe at all of them, unable to tear her eyes away. She had never seen a demonstration of so many Auras at once, and certainly none so beautiful. She had only seen Aura used for practical reasons, like lighting a hob or filling a glass with water.

"Each of you will discover an affinity for one of these Auras as the days go along," Oriel continued with her speech, interrupting

Ellora's train of thought and drawing her attention to the front of the room once again. "But I would like you all to remember that you will not be practising your Auras straight away. Like all arts, and as you have just witnessed, Aura can most certainly be an art form, it takes time and patience. You will begin by working on harnessing and controlling your skills."

She proceeded to explained to the First Formers how to find their rooms and that girls would not be allowed in the boys' corridor and vice versa. She also told them about the Welcome Dinner they would have that evening. "I look forward to seeing you all later." She finished her announcement.

As the other people around the trio moved in many directions, rushing out of the room trying to find their rooms, Ellora focused solely on staying close to Belle, unwilling to lose her in the confusion. She also wanted them to locate each other's' rooms so they could easily find each other.

Belle reached down and held her hand, giving an encouraging look, apparently able to sense her nerves. Elle smiled back at her, determined to be brave, as they walked towards the staircase together, hand in hand, waving goodbye to Dan, who went to find his own room.

Standing in awe inside Ellora's new bedroom, she and Belle looked around, jaws dropped to the floor, slowly taking in the sight of her new living space. With only thirteen rooms in the corridor, the room was very easy to find.

The walls were painted a beautiful blue-grey colour that reminded her of pebbles, and below her feet was a pristine, white carpet that Ellora imagined could only be kept so spotless using Aura.

On the left was a white door, which led to an incredible bathroom. After poking her head in, Belle reported back to Ellora that it even had a bathtub and was generously spacious, housing two separate sinks for Ellora and her new roommate.

Next to the bathroom were two very large wardrobes that were big enough for them both to walk into. Hearing a sweet voice come from the bedroom door, Ellora and Belle turned around and quickly scrambled out of one of the wardrobes.

"It is cool, don't you zhink?" Ellora heard the slight French accent coming from behind her and turned to see a slim girl with long, curly, ginger hair and a light dusting of freckles across her nose and cheeks standing in front of the bed closest to the door. One glance behind her, at the bed, showed she had already begun to unpack her belongings. "I 'ope you don't mind, but I feel more comfortable sleeping next to zhe door." Her chocolate-coloured eyes looked hesitant, worried her new roommate wouldn't agree.

Ellora glanced around the other side of the room, at what would be her own bed, walked over to it and shrugged off her denim jacket; her side of the room looked slightly more spacious, which she was happy about.

"Not at all. I'm Ellora, by the way." She smiled warmly and held out her hand for the girl to shake.

"I am Melody. It is lovely to meet you," she replied with a bright smile and a quick but firm handshake.

"And this is my best friend, Belle." Ellora introduced Belle, who gave a smile and an energetic wave, which Melody quickly reciprocated, relief clear on her face. Belle was quick to strike up a conversation by complimenting Melody's blouse.

As Melody returned the compliment, a conversation sprung up. Ellora could hear them in the background, as she wandered over to her bed and placed her largest piece of luggage on top; Oriel had told them that their luggage had all already been taken to their student rooms by some of the staff.

The beds were elegant double beds with a small bedside table on the right-hand side of each of them. Next to Ellora's bed was a window, which showed the view of the outdoor area she had caught a glance of when she had first arrived.

From this window, she had a rather beautiful view, as she could see multiple parts of the castle at once, from being this high up. Directly underneath her was a little, stone-paved courtyard packed with tables and benches and Ellora looked out to see the older students gathered in small crowds, catching up with each other. Behind the courtyard, however, Ellora could see a large fountain that looked like it would be a wonderful place to sit and relax, listening to the flow of the water. And, to the left, Ellora could see the sharp marble walls that made up the castle itself. She sighed, content with her new home.

"Elle?" The sound of her name snapped her back to reality and made Ellora jump up a little.

"Huh?"

"I said we should all go to the Welcome Dinner together," Belle laughed at her flustered state.

"Oh. Yeah, of course."

Ellora insisted on accompanying Belle to her own room and helping her unpack. They left the room and turned left, away from the stairs, to find Belle's room. Just as they began to walk, Belle stopped. "Elle, wait. We can find my room later, but we've got ages – why don't we go and have a quick peek around the library? It's the perfect time – it's bound to be empty at the moment." Belle grabbed Ellora by the arm and shook her, looking slightly like a six-year-old begging their parents for sweets. Ellora chuckled at the sight and turned around. "Come on then, Bee," she sighed jokingly, like a parent giving in to supplying their six-year-old with sweets.

They found the library quickly, walking down the four flights of stairs that led to the main entrance hall of the castle and turning left through the arching doorway. "Wow." Belle looked around the room with amazement gleaming in her eyes the second she stepped through the door. The library was filled with a seemingly endless number of bookshelves that went from floor to ceiling, covering the walls from end to end, with an aisle parting the way between the central shelves.

"It's amazing, right?" A voice said fondly. Ellora turned to her left, where the voice had come from, to see a plump young woman sitting behind a dark oak desk. "I love this place, it's like my own personal paradise," she said. "I'm Wendy, by the way, the librarian." She stood up and walked over to them, hand outstretched.

"Ellora. And this is Belle." Ellora shook her hand, offering a friendly smile to the short woman and gesturing towards the tall, blonde, jean-clad figure who had already run down the first aisle of books. "Sorry about that, she couldn't wait to get down here." Ellora chuckled at her best friend's enthusiasm.

"Oh, I completely understand that." Wendy chuckled before turning back to her desk, grabbing a stack of books and heading towards the closest bookshelf on the right.

Ellora weaved in and out of the aisles, looking for Belle before she stopped at the sight of a book which particularly caught her interest: 'Basic Human Mythology: A Timeline'. She looked up to a marking on the side of the wooden bookshelf, telling her the entire aisle was filled with books about Human Mythology.

"Oh, Elle, it's like my dream come true." Belle's voice came from behind her.

"Oh, dear," commented Ellora. "How are we ever going to get you out of here?"

"I think it might be too late for that," Belle laughed in response. "Find anything interesting?"

"Elle, they have so many books! I'm checking this one out for the moment." She held up a small, white book with little blue patterns covering it. "It's a history of the Madori Kingdom. We don't get to take History yet, so I thought I would take a look; they didn't go into much detail last year."

Ellora knew Belle was referring to the General History class she had taken in her final year of Fourth School. She remembered how disappointed Belle had been to find out they didn't explain the History of Aura or the Legends of the Spirits, but she knew that would be against the rules.

The Upper Council were set on the idea that Schools in the Aura Realm should be as similar to those in the Human realm as possible; studying the same subjects in a similar way and so on. They had to make sure each student had a solid knowledge of the Human Realm since most lived there. They even gave their students breaks from school at the same time as in the Human Realm.

Ellora dragged a reluctant Belle out of the library after checking out the book she wanted, to find her room in the First Former girls' Corridor. "Bee, I think there's something I need to tell you," she began as they walked up the stairs. She couldn't shake the guilty feeling she had since she got there, and if there was anyone that could help her, it would be Belle. "I think there's been a mistake. It's about me ... I think there was a problem." She hesitated, wondering how in the Realms she would tell her best friend she was in the Madori School of Aura by mistake.

"What you mean, Elle? What's going on, are you okay? You know you can talk to me about anything," Belle gently reassured her.

"Well, you see, I—"

"Ellora?"

Just as they were climbing up the final few steps, a surprised voice interrupted their conversation. Ellora looked up and froze in shock. "Clara?" she choked out, her eyes glossing over with tears.

She wanted to run over and hug her, but she couldn't seem to move. "Clara?" she heard her own voice whisper. "Is that really you?" Ellora watched as a tear of happiness fell down Clara's cheek, telling her that Clara had missed Ellora just as much as Ellora had missed Clara.

She launched herself up the remaining steps and ran to embrace her old friend. It seemed surreal to both after three whole years of not seeing each other.

"I've missed you," Clara spoke in a steady voice after softly clearing her throat.

"I've missed you too." Ellora finally let go of her, laughing happily and stepped back towards Belle, who had now walked over to them. "What in the Realms are you doing here?"

Ellora looked at Clara, who could easily have been mistaken for another person, now. Her previously long hair had been cut, the waves now stopping just below her shoulders and coloured a darker shade of brown.

"Well, I guess you must be Clara, I've heard so much about you." Belle's friendly voice came from behind.

She had almost forgotten Belle was still with her. She was still in shock about the whole situation; her next-door neighbour of fifteen years, who had had to move across the Realm three years ago, was now standing in front of her.

"Yes, sorry. Clara, this is Belle. Belle, Clara."

"Lovely to meet you." Belle struck up a conversation easily, as usual.

It was when Clara asked Ellora how her parents were that Ellora felt a shiver go down her spine again, like it had when she was walking into the building. She felt cold, suddenly, like somebody had suddenly turned the air conditioning onto its highest setting.

Her world went black, and Ellora felt her body hit something hard, pain shooting through her.

"Run, Ellie. Run!" a voice echoed in her head. She heard it over and over again.

She was panicking.

She looked around, trying to make sense of what was happening, but she could see nothing. Only darkness.

The voice in her head became louder and louder. "Run!"

She felt scared but wasn't sure of what. She tried to run, but she was on the floor. She tried to get up, but her legs wobbled under her weight. She flung her arms around her, trying to find something to hold onto, to help her up, to help her escape, but there was nothing.

Ellora dropped to the floor. "Stop," she murmured at the voices still echoing around her. The words sounded weird from her mouth, weird and weak. "Stop. Stop. Stop." she repeated the word until she found the strength to shout "STOP!"

The voices stopped that very instant.

She opened her eyes to find she was lying on the floor. She looked up into the faces of her friends. They looked terrified.

"What just happened?" Belle asked in a shaky voice.

"I don't know."

CHAPTER TWO

The Roommate

"Ellora Artemer, you will NOT walk away from me!" Belle crossed her arms across her chest and narrowed her eyes into menacing slits when Ellora tried to leave after stating she was tired. "You just collapsed on the floor right in front of me and you think I am going to let you carry on with your day? Absolutely not, young lady." Ellora nearly gave into the urge to crawl away in fear after seeing the look on Belle's face in that moment. At the same time, something in her head told her that Belle was a spitting image of her mum. That thought caused a chuckle, which Ellora swallowed, but the look of utter fear and astonishment on Clara's face was enough to make her burst into laughter.

"It's not funny, Elle." Belle's shoulders and stance relaxed slightly at the sight of seeing her laugh, almost as if it was proof she was safe.

"Seriously, Elle, what was that?" Clara asked as she grabbed Ellora's arms to hoist her up to her feet. "You scared the living daylights out of me."

"Maybe the nerves just got to me," Ellora suggested, although she wasn't sure if she was trying to convince herself or her friends. She was consciously trying to push away the images from whatever that dream was that she had just had. "And you both know how I get when I Gate Jump. I think maybe it all just built up. But I swear I'm feeling alright now," she promised, although neither of her friends looked appeased. Ellora sighed. "Look, I probably just need some food in me." She sounded more convinced than she felt. "And anyway, it's already time to get ready for the Welcome Dinner tonight."

Belle looked at her warily. "I don't know, I still think we should get Mistress Delow," she said, as Clara felt her forehead for a temperature.

"Seriously, I'm good!"

"Fine. But I'm coming straight to your room to check on you once I'm dressed," Belle insisted.

"So am I," nodded Clara.

"Great. Now that you've both essentially signed up to be my bodyguards, how about you get ready for tonight?" Ellora asked with one eyebrow raised. The other two simply nodded and hurried off to get their things.

"Are you sure this dress looks okay?" Ellora was still looking into the mirror, turning to see the back of her dress.

"Yes, Ellora, you look magnifique!" Melody replied, still finishing her makeup.

She was wearing a flowing black dress that reached her knees and was decorated in delicate silver sparkles. This was one of her favourite dresses and it felt silky to the touch. It had actually belonged to Clara before she left and Ellora looked back on the memory of it with a smile. Clara had given it to her because she knew how much she loved it and so she thought it only fitting to wear it again to the Welcome Dinner.

After a few moments of staring at her reflection, Ellora forced her gaze away from her own reflection in the mirror and walked towards her bed to finish putting away the last of her belongings.

Folded neatly and carefully between a set of her navy-blue pyjamas, was a framed photograph of herself with her parents. It was weird to be so far away from them, even though it wasn't much of a change. They hadn't really been a normal family for the past eight years, but they had still stuck together, supported each other.

A knock at the door interrupted her thoughts and she opened it to reveal her best friend. Belle walked in excitedly, looking young, yet sophisticated. She wore a bright red dress that stopped a few inches past her knees, with short sleeves that fell off her shoulders.

"I'm ready!" she almost sang, wearing a bright smile, which almost stretched from ear to ear.

"Someone's excited," Ellora commented with a chuckle.

"Well, we're going to a fancy dinner with nice food and great company – what's not to be excited about?" she asked. "Plus, I'm looking forward to seeing Dan and hearing about his roommate and room and all."

"Oh, of course. *That's* why you want to see him," Ellora teased.

Melody finished applying her mascara and walked over to the pair, wearing a simple, white dress that was cinched at the waist and fell to her knees. "Do not worry, Belle. I am also excited for zhe food!"

When Clara, who was dressed in an elegant green jumpsuit, joined them, the group of girls headed down to dinner and found the First Former dining room with little trouble at all.

The dinner was a lot more formal than they had anticipated, and it was also a lot smaller. Five small, circular tables, with six seats each, were placed around the First Former dining room, which was filled with the joyous sounds of conversations and laughter from the other students. The room was just big enough to comfortably fit the tables without being crowded, and the walls were painted a burgundy colour. There were four big windows on the walls, but no light came through them because the October sky was already dark.

The girls made their way over to Dan, who was already at one of the tables, next to a boy with dark hair. The boy seemed to keep his eyes fixed forward, on a seemingly blank spot on the table in front of him, whilst Dan was frantically waving them over.

Whilst walking towards the table, which was on the opposite side of the hall, Ellora looked at the unfamiliar boy sitting next to Dan. He had longer hair, with wisps that brushed over the tops of his eyes. He was dressed in black trousers and a black shirt, with only the collar unbuttoned and his pale skin looked radiant against his dark clothing and raven-black hair.

As if he could feel her gaze on him, the boy raised his head to look at Ellora. She met his dark, bottomless eyes with her own and froze as she felt a foreign feeling rush down her spine, a sensation like a jolt of energy. She found herself frozen in place, unable to remove her eyes from his, until a bolt of pain pierced her head. She scrunched her eyes closed and grabbed her head to ease the ache, and when she opened them again, it was gone, and the boy was paying no attention to her. She shook her head, tore her eyes away from him and hurried to catch up with the others, who were now a few steps ahead of her.

Taking a deep breath to regain her composure, Ellora sat between Clara and Belle, who had immediately sat down next to Dan. Unfortunately, this left her sitting directly opposite the dark-haired, brooding boy.

After greeting Belle with a quick kiss to the cheek, Dan sent a smile to Ellora, before politely greeting and introducing himself to Melody and Clara.

"This is Hunter, my new roommate." Dan turned and gestured to the mysterious boy sitting next to him, clearly expecting him to greet the rest of the girls at the table. After receiving a pleading look from Dan when Hunter stayed silent, Belle sent a friendly smile to Hunter. "Hi! I'm Belle. This is Ellora, Clara and Melody. It's lovely to meet you."

Hunter shifted his gaze from Dan to Belle before replying with only one word. "Likewise," he said quietly, nodding politely to them all. Ellora thought his eyes lingered on her for a split-second longer than the others.

They looked hungrily at the display of food in front of them; there was a plate of risotto and a bowl of lemongrass soup in front of each. There were also two jugs of icy mineral water, a bottle of cold sparkling water and a bottle of chilled Purple Wine on the table. But what really caught Ellora's eye was the bright red of the Strawberry Juice – an Aura Realm delicacy and one of her favourite thing in all the Realms – resting on the table. "Wow," said Clara. "The chefs must work non-stop in this place."

"I suppose it takes less time to cook when you can control fire and water, no?" asked Melody.

"I guess so," said Dan, distracted by the amazing selection of food.

Hunter was the only one who did not join the conversation Melody had struck up about her parents, the Glassi Aurums. "And my brother Jason graduated from zhis very school!" she told them.

"My sister Kirsty moved to the Incendi Kingdom," Belle answered when Melody inquired about the others' families. "We are very close so I do miss her a lot, but she can't leave her job for more than a few hours at a time." She smiled sadly into her drink.

Ellora tried to cover her frown at the subject of families and was grateful when Clara changed the topic of conversation to food. Ellora had looked away from them, distancing herself from the conversation to focus on her food when she felt Hunter's eyes burning a hole through her. She hadn't looked up, but she could tell it was him; she could almost feel the burning heat of his gaze.

Before she could even think about saying something, Oriel's strong voice came from the front of the dining room. "Students, I trust that you are enjoying the wonderful meal our chefs have made to welcome you to our school." Although she spoke at a normal volume, her voice commandeered the focus of the room.

"'Ow did she even get zher?" Melody whispered to the table. It was true, nobody had noticed her walk across the entire room.

"Classes will be starting in two days' time and your timetables have been delivered to your rooms. I would like you to know that each Student Corridor has at least one Prefect, so if you have any questions or need any help navigating the building, they will be more than happy to help you. I'm sure your Prefects will be coming around to introduce themselves over the next two days.

"For now, I would simply like to wish you good luck for the start of your Madori School journeys, and I hope you enjoy your desserts. I will be seeing you all tomorrow morning in the West Courtyard for your induction." And with a warm, knowing smile she gazed at them for a short moment before elegantly striding out of the room, the skirt of her full-length blue dress floating behind her.

All eyes in the room followed the Madori Mistress as she left the room; all eyes apart from two. Ellora snapped her head back to look across the table at Hunter, who was staring intently at her one more. She frowned, wondering why it was that he kept looking her way.

Ellora's eyes escaped the depth of his gaze when she turned to look at whoever had placed their hand on her shoulder. She saw Clara looking at her worriedly, asking her if she was okay. Ellora reassured her with a forced smile and looked back to the group, suddenly feeling exhausted.

"So, where did you all go to Fourzh School?" Melody's question brought her back to reality.

"We went to Poseidon Fourth," Belle answered, gesturing to herself, Dan and Ellora.

"Poseidon? Isn't zhat 'ere, in zhe Madori Kingdom?" Melody asked.

"Yup," answered Dan. "We've been here a while."

"Well, Dan and I actually live in the Human Realm, in London, and commuted to Poseidon, but Belle lives here. In the South, though," Ellora added.

"Yes," said Belle. "I am very fortunate that my family lives in the Realm, but I do enjoy going to the Human Realm to see these two when I can." She smiled and gestured towards Dan and Ellora.

"Where did you go, Melody?" asked Clara.

"I went to 'ephaestus Fourzh in zhe Glassi Kingdom," she answered. "Et toi?"

"Wow, that's cool! What's it like there? I went to Khione Fourth in the Incendi Kingdom. My family moved there about three years ago and it's always nice and warm," Clara said.

"Wow zhat is so different zhan where I come from. It is so cold back 'ome," Melody laughed.

Ellora glanced at Hunter, once more. Even though he looked quite focused on the plate in front of him, she couldn't shake the feeling he was aware of and seeing everything going on around him.

"'Unter, what about you? Which Fourzh School 'ave you come from?" Melody surprised Ellora, when she tried to involve him with the conversation.

Hunter looked up at her in surprise. "Me?" he asked. "I was home schooled."

"Really? That's interesting," said Clara. "I don't think I've heard of many Aurums being home schooled."

"Yes, well, my parents preferred it that way," he answered stiffly.

"Which Kingdom did you come from?" asked Ellora.

"It's none of your business," he snapped. Ellora frowned.

"Excuse me?" she asked. He stared straight into her eyes. Again. Ellora felt herself getting tired again, so she forced her eyes away from him and looked questioningly at Dan, who merely shrugged his shoulders, confused himself.

Fortunately, Ellora had little of a chance to think about Hunter, or why he was acting like a complete jerk, as they were all distracted when dessert arrived.

Lying on the aqua blue plate in front of her was a single, beautiful slice of chocolate cake. The slice was covered in thick, chocolate frosting and next to it was a perfect scoop of a dark and rich chocolate chip ice cream. Ellora wanted to delve her face into that cake.

The sound of laughter broke her delicious train of thought, and she looked up to see all five faces at the table looking at her, all intrigued by the intense way she was studying the dessert. Dan, Belle, Clara and Melody were all chuckling quietly, and even Hunter's lips twitched in amusement.

She could feel her face burning and averted she her eyes to the table, giggling nervously. "I don't zhink I 'ave ever seen anybody look at cake like zhat," Melody giggled. "But you are right — it looks 'eavenly." She shovelled a heaped spoonful of cake into her mouth and cried a sound of happiness. "Mmmm, it is sooo good!" she said with a full mouth, before shoving another spoonful into her mouth.

Ellora shot her a grateful look and laughed with her, tucking into her own dessert, Hunter completely forgotten.

"Wow, Elle," Clara said, cutting into her own cake. "I haven't seen you look at food like that since the time we had Persephone's Chocolate Bon Bons!"

"Persephone's Chocolate Bon Bons!" Ellora gasped, remembering the magical treat.

"We should get those again," Clara said distractedly.

"Trust me, I've tried! I'm telling you, Clara, I haven't found them *anywhere*," Ellora insisted.

"It's a real shame, Elle, because I swear, I have never tasted chocolate so good in my entire life!"

"What in the Realms are Persephone's Chocolate Bon Bons?" Belle asked.

"Clara and I tried them once, when we were younger, and they were *so* good. They explode when you put them in your mouth—"

"Explode in a good way," interrupted Clara.

"Yes, in a good way, and they were just *so* tasty!" Ellora finished.

"And you never knew what flavour you were going to get – but they were all delicious."

"Oh, yes, there were so many, too – red velvet, mint, chilli, orange, cherry, but my favourite was vanilla," stated Ellora.

"'Unter, 'ave you 'eard of zhem?" Melody asked.

"I think so," he replied distantly, his attention clearly fixed on the food in front of him.

"Elle, I saw they have some Human games in the common room. I think they've got a foosball table! Fancy a match?" Dan asked across the table, cutting through the awkward silence that had lingered after Hunter's vague answer.

"Oh, you're on, mate. Loser has to get the popcorn for movie night." Ellora leaned back against her seat and crossed her arms over her chest smugly.

"Guess you'll be supplying the popcorn then," Dan replied with an equally smug look.

"In your dreams," said Ellora.

"Hey, why don't you guys ever invite me to play foosball with you, too?" Belle gave a playful glare at the pair.

"Well, Bee, let's be honest … you're a bit of a sore loser," said Ellora.

"I am not!" Belle squealed.

"And you're rubbish at foosball," Dan laughed as Belle swatted him on his arm, before laughing too.

"Ooh, movie night? What are you going to watch?" Melody asked enthusiastically.

"Probably some sort of action film," said Ellora.

"Or a horror," Dan suggested.

"Nope. Absolutely not. I couldn't sleep for like three months after the last one," Ellora laughed.

"They've had this little tradition of theirs for almost three years now, their movie nights; once every two weeks," Belle explained to the rest of the group, all of whom, besides Hunter, seemed interested.

"Yep, we've never missed one. Isn't that right, kid?"

"Daniel Pinter, you're only two months older than me; stop calling me 'kid'!"

"Whatever," Dan chuckled at her glare. "You guys want to come?" Melody and Clara nodded their agreements. "Hunter?"

"Oh, that's okay. You go ahead – I need to finish unpacking anyway."

"'Unter you should come!" said Melody.

Noticing the look on her boyfriend's face, Belle also encouraged him to join them.

"Thank you, but really – it's okay. I'm getting tired anyway," Hunter insisted.

"Next time then." Belle smiled politely.

CHAPTER THREE

A Shadow

M elody had insisted on helping Ellora up to her room and at the moment, she was glad for it. She had gotten a headache when she was playing with Dan and had insisted on going up to bed. But it had all suddenly become worse.

"I think I had a little too much Purple Wine," she said, breathing heavily as she attempted to pull herself up the bannister. "Maybe it just didn't sit quite well." She knew, however, that something was not right. She glanced briefly at Melody, who frowned worriedly but said nothing on the matter.

Finally, the girls made it up to their room. "Ellora, are you sure you are okay?" Melody asked gently, but Ellora could barely hear it; the words sounded like they were being spoken through water, they sounded so muffled and far away. Without giving a response or even bothering to change out of her dress, Ellora dropped straight onto her bed.

She was running.

She didn't know where she was going, but she knew she couldn't stop. "Run, Elle," the voice demanded. It was even louder now.

She was going as fast as she could and getting tired, but she knew she had to keep going for some reason. She was running up a set of stairs. Something was behind her; she had to escape it.

The stairs were never-ending, it felt like she would never reach the top. The staircase was wide and had a bannister she used to help pull herself up, but she could only just about reach it, as it was above her head. She frowned at the sight of her hand, which looked a lot smaller than it normally did, but had no time to dwell on the subject, as she continued to clamber up the stairs.

She ran into a room, a bedroom. She didn't recognise the bedroom, but it felt familiar, somehow. There were loud, slower footsteps on the staircase, coming after her. They were loud, but not heavy. Like heels tapping against stone. The steps were slow, unrushed, but coming closer all the same.

She knew she had to hide, but where? Under the bed, perhaps. They would easily find her there, but she didn't know where else to go.

The footsteps were getting closer and she slid under the bed and crouched down in the corner. The single bed above her was positioned against the wall, so she pushed back, lying on her side and hugging her knees tight to her chest.

The footsteps stopped.

It was as if the whole world had stopped. Everything was quiet. It wasn't the usual, loud quiet that filled the air — with the hum of electricity in the walls and the lights, with the wind blowing against the windows, with birds chittering outside. It was silent. She could hear nothing; the air was still, the animals were silent, the world had frozen.

She could hear her own breathing; her heart was beating as loud as a drum.

How did she get here?

Her heart was beating faster and faster and faster.

What was going on?

Should she be going to check? No, her instincts told her to stay where she was and clutch at her knees harder still.

The silence was sickening. She didn't think she could feel more terror than when she was running up the stairs, but she was wrong.

But the most horrific part was not knowing, not knowing what was going on, not knowing where she was, not knowing who or what was out there…

An intense, high-pitched scream suddenly cut through the silence.

She covered her ears with her hands. The sound was surrounding her, enveloping her, engulfing her; it was coming from everywhere. The floor was shaking, and it felt as though the walls were about to fall apart.

"STOP!" she screamed out repeatedly, begging the sound to cease. "STOP! STOP!" She felt like the piercing sound would split her in half; her head was pounding, her ears were ringing, her eyes were clenched shut in pain. Her whole body was trembling, and she could do nothing to stop it.

She saw movement, a shadow outside the door. The disfigured shape was growing bigger and bigger, getting closer and closer. She had to get away, she had to stop it from finding her.

It stopped moving.

It turned, as if it had noticed her presence. She held her breath.

After a moment of holding her breath hoping the figure would leave, another high-pitched scream pierced the air.

It was too much.

"STOP!"

CHAPTER FOUR

The Caeli Prefect

"Ellora! Ellora, come on." This voice was different; familiar, friendly. "Ellora, open your eyes!" Had it just told her to open her eyes? What was going on? Where was that voice coming from?

Her face felt wet. She felt water trickling down her skin and wetting the collar of her top. It was cold, freezing cold.

She had no idea what was going on.

She could no longer see anything, but she felt different; she was in a different place. She remembered the voice that had told her to open her eyes and did so.

"Oh, thank the Spirits, she's awake," the same voice spoke again.

"Do you zhink we should still summon for Oriel?" Another voice asked.

"Let's see how she's feeling, first."

Her surroundings became clearer as she blinked. Hovering above her was Belle, holding an empty glass.

Ellora jumped up to sit on her bed, where she must have been lying, feeling a cold sensation envelop her face, neck and upper torso.

"I knew that would work." Belle stood over her, putting the glass down on the bedside table before placing her hands on her hips, mimicking a heroic pose, with a jokingly proud smile gracing her lips.

"Belle?" Ellora questioned. Becoming even more aware of the cold feeling as it continued to travel down her body, she snapped her eyes to the empty glass. "Did you just throw water on me?" Ellora asked angrily.

Sensing the anger in her voice, Belle sat down on the bed, next to Ellora, with a worried look, but before she could explain, Melody began. "Ellora, you were screaming and crying in your sleep and I was trying to wake you up but you just seemed to be getting worse and so I called Belle and she came and she couldn't wake you up eizher and so she zhrew water on you, but I was really worried about you and it was really scary and I am just glad you are okay and you are okay right? Because you seemed really scared and I did not zhink you were okay and —"

"I'm okay, Melody. Thank you. And I'm so sorry for scaring you," Ellora said honestly. She had noticed that Melody rambled when nervous. She walked over to her and hugged her reassuringly.

Realising her clothing was still soaking wet, Ellora removed herself from Melody and walked over to the wardrobe to change from her pyjamas into a fresh outfit for the day; after that, she knew she wouldn't be able to get back to sleep.

Belle followed her to the wardrobe, as Melody walked over to the bathroom to get ready for a shower. "It was weird, Bee. It wasn't... a normal nightmare, it felt different. It felt real," Ellora told her as she changed from her wet, oversized pyjama top and into a plain white shirt tucked into a black skirt, layering a cardigan on top.

This would be their new uniform until they discovered which Aura classes, they had an affinity for. Once they found out, they would be expected to wear a small crest reflecting that Aura on the left of the shirt.

"Well ... you were in bed the whole time, so we know it *wasn't* real, even though it felt it. Maybe it was just a vivid nightmare?"

"Well, a really vivid nightmare, but yeah, you're probably right, Bee," Ellora said. Before she could think so, say anything else, a loud rumble from her stomach sounded. "Well, I don't know about you guys." She looked around at her friends all still in pyjamas, "but apparently, I'm starved. Anyone else for breakfast?"

"Mmm, yes sounds fantastique, I 'ope zhey 'ave 'oney Cheerios," Melody said in her gentle voice, poking her head out from the bathroom.

"Cheerios? Melody I thought you lived in the Glassi Kingdom. I didn't know they had Cheerios there," Ellora laughed.

"Zhey don't! I discovered zhem one day on a 'oliday to the 'Uman Realm wizh my parents. Zhe Gate in zhe Glassi Kingdom leads to France, and I suppose Cheerios are really popular zhere," she chuckled. "I 'ave been looking for zhem ever since."

"Well, all I need is coffee," groaned Belle, covering her face with her hands. Ellora could see the sleepiness taking over her. "I can't believe it's 6.15 in the *morning* and I'm awake," she yawned.

They all agreed to meet again in the corridor after getting ready, as Belle was still in her pyjamas. Ellora had suggested they meet in 10 minutes, but Belle was not happy with that. "I need time to shower!" She had insisted and Ellora had relented.

So, Ellora sat on her bed while Melody got ready in the bathroom and thought about her nightmare. She couldn't help feeling like it was something ... *more*. Trying to distract herself, she picked up one of her old, favourite books. After all, they had already decided that it was nothing.

"So, when do we find out which Aura class we're in?" Belle asked Melody, who they came to realise knew more than the rest of them, when they sat around the breakfast table on the morning of their first day of lessons. They had kept to their usual seats.

Ellora noticed Belle smile brightly over her shoulder, and turned to see Dan entering the room, followed closely by Hunter, who seemed to be walking over to an empty table. Realising this, Dan grabbed Hunter by the shoulder and dragged him along to their table. Nobody other than Ellora seemed to be in any way affected by Hunter's presence, so Ellora tried to ignore the fluttering and uncomfortable feeling in her stomach.

Apart from at meals, Ellora hadn't really seen Hunter around the building in the two days before classes started. She spent a lot of time in the common room with her friends, but Hunter was never there.

There was one time, at the library the morning before, when she had walked directly into him at a right angle because they both had their heads buried in their books. Hunter had helped her up and had stared curiously at her before walking straight past without a word.

"My brozher told me zhat we will find out soon, but I am sure everyone finds out at different times. For example, Belle, you might 'ave a lesson today in Madori Aura and discover an affinity. If zhat 'appens, you will officially be a Madori Aurum in training," Melody replied.

"Most people will discover zheir affinities in zhe next two or zhree days, but it takes some people a week!" Belle, Clara and Dan looked as if they couldn't wait to start and discover their affinities, but Ellora couldn't help the nauseating sensation in the pit of her stomach.

"What if... What if we don't find out in a week? I mean, what then? Would we just get kicked out?" Ellora asked reluctantly. All heads turned towards her in confusion, but she kept her focus on Melody to avoid suspicion. She didn't want them to know the truth; that she was at the Madori School of Aura by mistake and never should have been accepted.

Before anybody could question her, Melody replied and Ellora shot her a grateful look, "Actually, zhat is a good question. Even zhough zhat 'as only ever 'appened once in zhe 'istory of zhe Aura schooling, zhere is actually a protocol. Jason said 'e learnt about it in 'is 'Aura Politics' class when 'e was in Fourzh Form.

"If someone 'as shown no signs of an affinity wizhin a week, zhey are temporarily placed in zhe Madori Aurum training programme, and at zhe same time 'aving to take extra training with zhe School Masters so zhat zhe person can 'ave all available opportunities to discover and present zheir affinity. But I wouldn't worry about zhat, Elle. Zhe Madori Mistress is personally in charge of 'o gets accepted to zhe school and she's never wrong. You will be fine," she said the last part with a reassuring smile.

Ellora noticed Hunter from across the table, deeply engrossed in the plate of food in front of him. It seemed like he was paying no attention at all to the conversation and to the rest of the table, but something told Ellora he was completely aware of everything going on.

Ellora mentally shook her head of the thought and sent a carefree smile to the table before changing the subject to their new lessons. "So, what class do you all have first today? I have Caeli Practical," she said, reading from the timetable she pulled from her pocket.

"We have Madori." Belle gestured to herself and Dan.

"I 'ave Terrari," said Melody.

"Me, too!" Replied Clara.

"'Unter, what do you 'ave first?" Melody asked. All eyes turned to face him as he looked directly into Ellora's eyes.

"Caeli."

Hunter disappeared before breakfast had finished without a word and without waiting for Ellora, who was going to the same place as he was. She rolled her eyes in frustration and walked out of the dining room with her friends, with promises of meeting in her room after the first class, before they had to part ways.

Ellora looked at her timetable to discover that her class was being held outside. It made sense. After all, Caeli Aura was the Aura of air.

After finding the door to the West Courtyard, she walked through it to see around six other students, who she didn't know, standing around and talking in smaller groups.

It was surprisingly warm, for the Autumn, and Ellora had to remove the sweater she had put on in the morning. She heard a familiar voice and turned to see two students walking out into the courtyard. She recognised the short, slim girl as Hazel, Clara's roommate, and the other brown-haired girl she was talking to was Leia.

Ellora had met them both on her second day at the school, in the common room. She remembered that they both came from the Incendi Kingdom. "The Gate there leads to O'ahu, an island in Hawaii," Ellora remembered Leia mentioning it was where she had been born and raised. She had been completely fascinated by the warm island, as the Gate in the Madori Kingdom led to London, where it rained constantly.

Leia spotted her and waved her over happily, while Hazel smiled timidly. Ellora walked over to them. "I'm so happy to see a friendly face," she said.

"Us, too," said Leia. "I saw your friend back there, a couple of minutes ago. The one with dark hair who doesn't smile or talk much."

"Ah, that would be Hunter," she laughed at their description before lying and telling them she should probably find him so he wouldn't be alone.

Amongst the crowds, she spotted the raven black locks that could only belong to Hunter. She was torn. Half of her wanted to turn around and forget about the dark-eyed, mysterious boy and spend the class with her friends. But the other half knew she should try to make the effort because, like it or not, Hunter was Dan's roommate, and she loved Dan like a sibling. It seemed like he didn't have many friends at the school, and she wasn't being very friendly herself. After a moment of hesitation, she decided to join him.

Hunter was leaning against a pillar with his arms crossed over his chest, looking at a door on the other side of the West Courtyard. He seemed so deep in thought, so serious.

It occurred to Ellora that, in the two days she had known him, she had not once seen him smile. She had seen him frown, of course, and she had seen him try to hide a laugh, but never a smile; she had never seen him look happy.

"What are you looking at?" she asked when she approached the expressionless boy. His head turned to look at her before turning away to look at the door again.

"So now that your friends are all gone, you decide I'm good enough to talk to?" His smooth voice was expressionless.

"Well, forgive me for trying to make conversation," she snapped at him.

"Have you considered that maybe I don't want to speak to you?" His voice kept its low pitch as usual, but this time Ellora could hear a hint of anger in his tone as he looked directly into her eyes. "I certainly don't need your *pity*."

Momentarily surprised by his response, Ellora gathered her thoughts and opened her mouth once more, determined to form a friendship with Hunter no matter how stubborn he was being. "Hunter, I don't pity you. But I *do* pity Dan for being stuck with you." She narrowed her eyes at him, and he narrowed his eyes in return. "Look," she grumbled, finally breaking eye contact and crossing her arms, "you are my best friend's roommate. So, like it or not and I know I do *not*, we will have to talk."

"Except you're scared of me." Ellora was surprised at his response and scoffed in reply. Hunter lazily raised an eyebrow before leaning only one inch closer to her. He lowered his voice so that only she could hear him. "Well, Artemer, maybe you should be." His aggressive tone of voice caused her to stumble back unwittingly. Surprisingly to Ellora, Hunter seemed proud of this reaction.

But Ellora squared her shoulders and lifted her chin ever so slightly before replying, "And just why would I be scared of you, Hunter?"

"Well, I should have thought that you would know there's more than meets the eye in this Realm," he spoke without even a glance at her; his eyes were once again focused on the door.

Just as she opened her mouth to ask him what he meant about that, a voice from behind her made her jump. "Hunter! Fancy seeing you here." The voice was smooth and deep, definitely male.

She turned around when Hunter shifted his gaze from her to a spot over her left shoulder. Standing behind her was a tall boy who looked a few years older than her. He had shaggy, light-brown hair and was smiling warmly at both of them.

"Mason," Hunter acknowledged emotionlessly. "What are you doing here?"

"I've been asked, as a Prefect and a Caeli Aurum in training, to help Mistress Maywether by demonstrating the Domination technique to your First Form class. This first week of classes is only for First Formers, so I was free to help out." His smile didn't falter as he looked over at Ellora.

"I'm Mason Ozuko. It's a pleasure to meet you." He held his hand out to her.

"Ellora Artemer. And the pleasure is mine." She shook his hand in return and smiled shyly.

"Ellora. A beautiful name for a beautiful lady." He sent her a dazzling smile and Ellora felt herself blush. "You know, I need a partner for the first part of this demonstration. Would you like to join me?" He looked hopefully at her.

"No." Hunter stepped slightly in front of her, shielding her from his gaze. "Sorry, Mason, but Ellora has already agreed to be my partner." His voice kept its smooth tone. "So why don't you get lost and leave us alone."

Ellora looked at him in shock, mouth open.

She just couldn't make sense of the boy; one moment he was telling her he didn't want to be friends, and the next, he was refusing to let her leave his side. She glanced up at Mason just in time to glimpse the disappointment on his face before he plastered on a smile. "No problem. I'll ask Mistress Maywether to help me. I hope to see you again, Ellora. Hunter." He smiled at Ellora before sending a polite but colder nod to Hunter and walking away to the Caeli teacher.

"Hunter," Ellora snapped quietly. "Why would you do that? I thought you didn't want to be friends." She felt angry for some reason. It wasn't because she wanted to be Mason's partner, but because of Hunter's weird behaviour and mixed signals.

"You shouldn't hang around with a guy like that."

"Really? 'A guy like that'? What does that even mean, Hunter? A nice guy with nice hair, who actually *smiles*? No, you're so right, Hunter. I should stay here with you — a guy who doesn't even want to talk to me." She was whispering furiously, gradually becoming angrier. "You're not my... my... you're not my anything, Hunter! You don't get a say in anything I do."

"Actually, by a guy like *that*, I meant the spoilt Prince of *Misting* Japan." She could hear the anger seeping into his words and looked up in surprise at his swearing; he had always seemed too composed around her to get this angry.

"The Prince of Japan?!" Ellora gasped.

Something in Hunter's face changed, but she couldn't understand why. "Is there an issue with that?" he challenged.

"Issue? Why would there be an issue? I just didn't know royalty attended this school."

"There are a lot of princes and princesses here. We even have a queen – Queen Stana Amberly of Canada. Most of the royal families in the Human Realm are Aurums, so of course they would end up in the best Aura school."

"How do you even know that Hunter?" Ellora asked.

"Irrelevant," he answered mysteriously.

"Wait, so princes and princesses and... queens... are sent here without any guards or protection or anything?" Ellora asked, now more curious than angry. "Who rules over Canada if its queen is here?"

"Ellora, look around you. Look at where we are. We are in what is essentially the safest building in the Realm, to learn about our powers. Do you really think anybody here needs protection from other students?" He stared at her like she was stupid. "And Stana can quite easily get to Canada if needs be."

"But what about people who *aren't* students?"

"If somebody unwelcome found their way in here, I would be entirely unable to tell you how. It's just not possible." His blunt and tone towards her was frustrating Ellora.

"Well... that doesn't... you still can't tell me who I can or cannot be friends with – whether or not they *are* the Prince of Japan."

"Do whatever the Realms you want, Ellora... But for now, you're stuck with me. I promise the Spirits that I will leave you alone after these next two hours," he seethed.

"Fine." Ellora marched towards the group forming around Mason and Mistress Maywether.

"Fine." Hunter stormed past her to be just slightly ahead of her, hands in the pockets of his black trousers. "And just for the record, I have *great* hair."

CHAPTER FIVE

Missing Friends

"Ellora, are you okay? You 'ave been pushing around zhat cottage pie for a few minutes, now."

Ellora looked up. "I'm fine Melody, it's just that the table feels so empty tonight." she looked around at the three vacant seats. "I *almost* even miss Hunter."

Ellora hadn't seen Belle since the breakfast and was missing her comforting presence. She had wanted to tell her all about *Prince* Mason and his gorgeous eyes. Besides, Belle was more accustomed to the Aura Realm than she was, and she was hoping to find out how she was supposed to react around royalty.

"What *is* it with you two?" Clara asked.

"What?" asked Ellora.

"You and Hunter!" Clara replied.

"There *is* no 'Hunter and me'!"

"Well now, that's just not true, Elle." Clara smiled smugly, as Ellora's face, which was now turning pink from the bombardment of questions. Plus, she did think Hunter was quite good looking, even though she hadn't seen a personality to match.

"She is right," added Melody. "You are definitely *not* just friends."

"No, I agree with you there – 'friends' is not a term I would use to describe my relationship with him."

"Aha! So, you admit there is a relationship!" Shrieked Clara.

"No! Stop putting words in my mouth!" Ellora laughed to hide her embarrassment. Unfortunately for her, it didn't work.

"Oh, really? Then why have you gone bright red?" Clara smirked.

"I have not!"

"Well, you might not like 'Unter, but it does seem as if '*e* might like you," Melody said.

"Oh, trust me," Ellora laughed sarcastically, "Hunter does *not* like me." She quickly felt the need to change the subject. "So, do either of you know what affinity Dan has? I don't remember which lesson he was in," said Ellora.

"I think he had Incendi."

"I suppose that makes 'im an official Incendi Aurum in training zhen," Melody said.

"You know, I thought it would be a bit more fun to watch someone discover their affinity. I thought something cool would happen," said Clara.

"Yeah, I know what you mean. Like with Hunter in our Caeli lesson this morning – we were just doing our exercise and trying to make the leaves on the tree sway and then Mistress Oriel came and walked over to him. She just told him to go with her and that was that."

"But, you know, I *am* glad zhat we will all be in zhe same class from tomorrow – zhey said zhere's only enough of us left for one group and I am not complaining," said Melody.

The girls spoke through the rest of dinner, discussing which of their classmates had discovered their affinities. When dessert arrived, Ellora told them she needed to go to the library and would skip that night's chocolate mousse. Melody looked happy at this revelation when she realised it meant she could have an extra helping of chocolate mousse.

She left the dining room and turned right towards the stairs which led down to the library when she heard voices. "I saw you," a female voice said. Ellora walked further and spotted a head of familiarly shaggy, brown hair, just slightly shorter than Dan's. "Mason, you shouldn't do this to her. One of them will find out eventually," the voice continued.

"Hey! Mason!" Ellora called as she walked a few steps towards him and saw he was standing with a blonde girl with grey eyes who looked his age. Ellora recognised her as the Prefect on her own corridor, Julia.

"Oh, hi Julia." She sent her a smile. Ellora decided, even though she *knew* it hadn't been her fault, that she would apologise for Hunter. And, maybe, she and Mason would be able to go for a walk in the cool evening air. "Listen, Mason, I just wanted to apologise for Hunter's behaviour earlier. He was out of line and —"

"It's fine; that's just how he is. I took no offence by it. You should get going; you'll want to rest up for your second day of classes tomorrow." He cut her off and turned to walk away from her, Julia following, after sending Ellora a smile.

Ellora frowned. He had spoken to her as if he was a prefect doing his duty and she was just a child asking for help. Or maybe, she frowned harder, like he was a prince dismissing a subject. And then he had just walked away from her. He hadn't even smiled – in fact, he had barely even looked at her.

She forced herself to walk up to her room, so she could change into some more comfortable clothes before going down to the library. Maybe he was upset with her because she hadn't been his partner. Or maybe she should have curtsied. Or called him 'Your Highness'. Ellora groaned inwardly. Or, maybe, she was just feeling overwhelmed by the drastic changes to her life and the fact that she was, possibly, going to get kicked out of her dream school.

She decided not to dwell on it any longer and walked down to the library in her jeans and her thick jumper. She wanted to do some research on the Test that had got her into the school in the first place.

She knew, for a fact, that her Test didn't look like everybody else's. Her Test had turned brown, like the people who got rejected, and not silver, like everybody else in the school; she'd seen it for herself.

She walked through the shelves in the library, looking for a section on ... well ... she didn't actually *know* what she was looking for, but she was sure she would know once she found it.

She continued walking past bookshelves until she noticed a section labelled 'Aura School History'. She knew that would have what she needed. She looked through the shelves until a small, dusty old book caught her eye. Golden letters were printed on the brown spine, which read 'Ancient Traditions of the Aura Schools'.

She pulled it off of the shelf and flipped through the handwritten pages to find what she was looking for. She flipped past a page entitled 'Upper Council Training' and another with 'Winter Solstice' elegantly typed across the top, until she finally found the right section.

THE AURA TEST

THE AURA TEST IS AN ANCIENT TRADITION CREATED BY THE FOUNDING UPPER COUNCIL MEMBERS. ALTHOUGH THE MEMBERS COULD SEE THE AURA AND ESSENCE IN A PERSON SHOULD THEY WISH, THEY CREATED THE TEST AS A METHOD OF TESTING MULTIPLE PROSPECTIVE STUDENTS IN A SHORTER AMOUNT OF TIME.

THE TEST REQUIRES THE EXAMINEE TO PLACE THE TIP OF THEIR FOREFINGER INTO A POT FILLED WITH A SPECIAL INK, MADE FROM THE ORKA BERRY FOUND IN THE GLASSI KINGDOM, WHICH TAPS INTO THE PROSPECTIVE STUDENT'S ESSENCE SUPPLY. THE EXAMINEE THEN PLACES THEIR FINGER ON THE MIDDLE OF A BLANK PIECE OF PARCHMENT. THE INK WILL THEN SPREAD OUTWARDS, FROM THE MIDDLE OF THE PARCHMENT, CREATING A 2-DIMENSIONAL IMAGE OF THE ESSENCE IN THEIR BODIES.

IF THE ESSENCE SUPPLY IS STRONG, THE PRINT MADE BY THE STUDENT WILL TURN SILVER.

IF THERE IS LITTLE OR NO ESSENCE, OR THE ESSENCE SUPPLY IS WEAK, THE PRINT WILL TURN BROWN AND THEY WILL BE REJECTED FROM THE SCHOOL.

THERE ARE RECORDED CASES OF PRINTS TURNING OTHER COLOURS, SUCH AS WHITE, BLACK AND GOLD. IN THESE CASES, THE UPPER COUNCIL MEMBER OF THE SCHOOL ANALYSED THE PRINT AND MADE THE DECISION THEMSELVES.

Ellora sighed. That hadn't helped her. In fact, it had told her that her Essence was weak.

She was leaving the library when she heard a familiar voice. "When can you get it?" asked Dan in a hushed voice.

"Soon. But you have to be patient. This takes a lot of planning." That was Julia's voice, Ellora remembered from earlier.

"Okay, but the sooner the better. It's stressing me out," said Dan.

Ellora wanted to ask what they were talking about, and why they were even talking to each other; there was no reason for them to even know each other.

But, before she could say anything, Melody walked up behind her. "What are you doing?" she whispered.

"What? Nothing. What are you doing?" Ellora replied.

"Looking for you. Clara and I found Belle and we are all going to watch a movie in 'er room with 'er roommate. Will you come?"

"Oh. I just have to—" Ellora turned to look at Dan and Julia, but they were gone. "Sure," she said, confused.

Ellora's eyes shot open. She sat up, feeling disoriented, as if she had been spinning around. Again, she heard a familiar voice, only this time it was telling her to hide.

Unlike previous times, this time Ellora recognised her environment: the darkness, the still air. She knew she must have been dreaming again.

When she looked around her, she realised she was under something big; the bed she had hidden under during her last nightmare. She heard low thuds that sounded as if they could be footsteps, and they seemed to be getting closer. She pushed herself as far back as she could in fear.

It wasn't real, as she kept telling herself, only she couldn't explain why everything was so vivid. She could feel the cool brick wall pressed against the skin on her back through her dress. She could smell smoke, something burning. She could hear the loud footsteps getting closer and closer to her.

It's just a dream, she repeated the mantra in her head trying desperately to believe it. No matter how hard she tried, couldn't help holding her breath, so as not to make a sound as the dark figure inched towards her.

Just as the figure approached the bed, Ellora heard a new voice she couldn't recognise. The voice was gentle and made her want to close her eyes and rest her head on the ground. It became stronger, but never louder; the feminine voice kept its light tone. She felt it surround her like it was coming from every direction.

She felt her fear melt away as she felt the voice encompass her like a shield or a cosy blanket. She noticed the figure had stopped advancing and was frozen. She knew, then, that she would be okay.

As she felt the soft voice putting pressure on her eyelids, she obeyed and closed them, suddenly feeling really tired.

And then, she was floating. She was sure of it, but either way, the new pressure on her eyes meant she couldn't check. The singing voice became quieter, or maybe it was just getting further away. Ellora suddenly realised that it was actually *she* who was slowly drifting away, and she welcomed the warmth that flooded her mind.

"Well, I guess it's just the two of us," Clara whispered to Ellora, looking around. They were the last two at the table without a big, coloured crest pinned to their shirt. They were the last two in the entire First Form dining room without one. It was Thursday now and everybody else had discovered their affinities, leaving just Ellora and Clara in class, as official training would start on Monday.

Belle had told Ellora of all the time she had spent in the library and all the books she had found while Ellora was in class. It went without saying that Ellora was very jealous. She also felt herself getting more and more anxious as the days went by because she knew the day was coming when she would be called into Mistress Oriel's office and asked to leave.

"I guess so. But it was nice to see Melody get so happy about her Ferri affinity; she told me she's always had plenty of pets when growing up so I guess it makes sense that she would be good with animals." Ellora felt proud of her roommate.

"I wish I'd had a pet when I was younger," said Clara.

"Um, you *did* have a pet when you were younger, Clara. And look how that turned out," Ellora laughed, digging into her chicken pesto pasta.

"Hey, that fish didn't count!" Clara laughed, too.

"Why not? Because you forgot to feed it for six weeks?" Ellora joked.

"Listen, I was six when I had Fluffy!" Clara chuckled.

"I will never understand how you came to the name 'Fluffy' for your goldfish. But that's not actually what I was talking about. Remember the leitock we 'rescued'?"

"Oh, my Spirit I forgot about that!" Clara exclaimed. "That thing was so cute and fluffy."

"Yeah, I'm surprised you didn't cuddle it to death," laughed Ellora.

"How did we even get that thing to my house?" asked Clara.

"Remember? We were on our way home from Second School, and we were walking to the Gate Stop ..."

"Oh, and I saw the poor thing lying under a tree! It was too hot and I think that was the day we learnt about leitocks, and about how they need a cold climate to live in."

"Yeah, so you smuggled it through the Gate in your backpack and put it in the fridge," laughed Ellora.

"Well, it worked!" Clara was laughing too, holding her sides.

"And you cried so much when your mum said we couldn't keep it."

"I had already named her and everything!"

"And then we had to get my dad to help us bring it back to his Realm. And Ophelia was upset because..." Ellora cut off her sentence and looked back down to her food, smile wiping off her face.

"I can't believe it's been eight years, already," Clara said. "How are your parents coping now?"

"The same," Ellora sighed.

"It must be hard," Clara whispered.

"So, tomorrow's Friday." Ellora pointedly changed the subject.

Yep." Clara went along with it. "We won't be outsiders after tomorrow — we'll be in the official training classes with everyone again on Monday," she said casually.

Ellora couldn't blame her for not being worried; *she* wasn't the only one at the school by mistake. Ellora felt a pang of guilt through her body. She was familiar with this feeling now, the guilt; the feeling she shouldn't be at the Madori School of Aura; the feeling she was living a lie; the feeling that her sister's death was all her fault.

There was nothing much she could do now; she was here. She would wait for tomorrow evening when they would all discover she was a fraud. For now, she would eat her pasta and drink her lemonade. She would enjoy the panna cotta that would be served for dessert and she would laugh and talk with her friends. She would enjoy it all for now, because after tomorrow, nothing would be the same again.

It was the last lesson of the day when it happened. Ellora and Clara had been in their Terrari class in the East Courtyard. Like the Caeli class, this class was held outside. It made sense to Ellora, as this was the best way to access the Earth and Terrari Aura dealt with the Earth.

The courtyard looked like an almost exact replica of the West Courtyard, apart from the stone slabs that covered the floor of the East Courtyard, rather than grass in the other, and the marble statue of the founder Arellia in the centre, rather than an oak tree.

Ellora had been focusing on a lily when it happened. She had been trying to force the lily to grow taller when Oriel entered the room and walked over to them. Ellora's heart pounded in her chest. Surely, Oriel was going to tell her she knew she was a fraud. Or that she had found an error and Ellora had been admitted by mistake. She didn't want to be kicked out.

Or maybe... Ellora's heart leapt into her throat. Could it be possible that Oriel would tell her she did have an affinity for Terrari Aura and that maybe she did belong at the school?

Ellora had all but forgotten about the girl standing next to her until Oriel spoke. "Clara, your affinity has been declared. Please come with me."

Ellora walked over to her bathroom and rested her hands on the cool, marble surface of the counter. She took a deep breath, before turning on the tap and splashing her face with cool water, trying to remove all signs of the tears from her cheeks before dinner.

Why had she let this happen to herself? She should never have come to the Madori School of Aura. She should have stayed home and found a job in London. She could be a baker or a librarian.

She wanted to talk to Belle, or Melody or Clara about what was going on. She wanted to tell them everything about how her admission was a mistake, that they were wrong to let her in. She was no Aurum — just an ordinary girl whose Aura Test had failed. Her Print had turned brown, not silver like an Aurum's Print would have.

She had seen it herself.

Something had clearly gone wrong when the Test Guard had congratulated her and given her admission papers. She tried to tell him he was wrong, that her test had failed, but all he said was: "Look, I don't see your Print. I only see the results that the Upper Council send me, and your results say you've been accepted to the Madori School of Aura."

She really had tried to explain that she didn't belong here, but the Test Guard hadn't listened.

Wallowing in a train of her own thoughts, Ellora had almost missed it; a knocking sound. Immediately, Ellora switched off the tap and walked slowly out of her bathroom. She prodded along the white carpet in her black socks to the middle of the room.

The sound was coming from the door; someone was knocking.

"Ellora Artemer." Oriel stood in front of her when Ellora opened the door. Ellora looked at her standing in front of her in her jeans and figured that she could dress however she liked out of official Aura School hours. However, something still told her that Oriel was here for official Aura School business. "If you're not too busy, I would love to have a conversation with you in my office," she spoke calmly and smiled at Ellora.

Ellora stood in her doorway, unmoving before she realised she was expected to respond. "Oh, uh... right, of course. Let me just put on some shoes." She turned and crossed the room frantically, slipped on a pair of black trainers and returned to the door to follow Oriel.

"Please, Ellora, do sit down. Would you like some tea?" Oriel spoke again only when they reached her office. It was quite plain. It was a fairly large room behind an oak door in the corner of the library, which Ellora had only had the chance to see once before classes had started. The walls were painted a navy-blue colour and the desk was made out of dark mahogany. Oriel's chair behind the desk was a black leather chair and on the other side of her desk were two black leather armchairs. Resting against the wall to the right side of the desk was a long, black sofa and against the opposite wall, long cabinets were made of wood that matched the desk.

Ellora took in the sight of the room, watching as Oriel mixed a blend of herbs that looked unfamiliar to Ellora. She chose the armchair on the right-hand side, as Oriel filled the teapot lying on her desk, with water that poured out of the palm of her left hand. She waved a gesture with the same hand, heating up the water, before adding in the herbs.

The smell of lavender filled the air, and Oriel handed Ellora a teacup before taking her own and sitting in the other armchair. "What is this?" The tea smelt unfamiliar but comforting to Ellora.- "It's one of my own blends, primarily based on lavender. I find it calming; don't you think?"

"Oh, um, yes." Her eyes darted between Oriel and the cup in her hands.

"I'm sorry," she blurted out.

"Come again?" Oriel looked at her, confused.

"I'm sorry, Mistress Oriel. I know I'm here by mistake. It was an accident. I told the Test Guard! But he wouldn't listen to me. And now I'm the only one without an affinity and I didn't know what to do, but I can't help but feel bad and now you're going to kick me out and—"

"Ellora, what are you talking about? You're not here by mistake." Oriel scrunched up her eyebrows in concern. Apparently, Melody wasn't the only one who rambled when she was nervous.

"But... I thought you called me in here to tell me I had to leave and go back home," Ellora whispered, her eyes quickly filling with tears as the feeling of guilt came back, again. She blinked back the tears and cleared her throat, taking a deep breath and forcing her eyes up to look up at her Madori Mistress.

"Ellora—"

"It's Elle. All my friends call me Elle."

Oriel smiled. "Elle, then. I wasn't planning to kick you out of the school. I know you must feel frustrated. That's actually why I wanted to talk to you and why I brought you here. Do you know how your Aura Test is examined?"

"Well, I know the Prints turn different colours; I read that earlier in one of the books in the library," Ellora said, "but I don't know how you examine them."

"Well, after the ink had spread and your Print is captured, it's sent to me so I can see your Essence. It's very rare for any of us to get this wrong; I can see how it runs through your veins and in your blood; it's in your bones and in your skin and I can see it. I remember your print, Elle, I remember your Essence. You definitely belong here; you are not here by accident."

"What? What do you mean by Essence?"

"It's the base of your Aura. You see, some people, like you, have Essence in their body. Certain triggers — like the exercises you have been doing in your Aura lessons this week — cause this 'Essence' to manifest itself as 'Aura'. When this happens, the Essence in your print changes colour. I can feel this change, because once I see the Print, I am connected to it. Take your friend Belle, for example. The second she entered that Madori classroom, the instant she entered the environment, I felt the change in her Essence, as it became Madori Aura. I could see it turn blue in her and on her Print, but I didn't need to; I could feel it," she explained patiently.

"But what if you were wrong? What if my Essence never evolves?" Ellora was still panicking, even after Oriel had explained to her that she was definitely in the right place.

"I'm not, Elle. I see something different in your Essence, something I've never seen before. But I know you will go far, Elle. And you will find your affinity soon. I just know it."

After draining the last of her tea, Ellora left the office feeling tired. Tired and overwhelmed.

Ellora was walking around the West Courtyard, where her first lesson at the school had taken place, where everything had changed. After her conversation with Oriel, she had had no desire to go back to her room; she just wanted to be alone and think for a while.

She kicked a pebble across the ground of the courtyard, enjoying the clinging sound it made against the stone in the silence. Suddenly, she heard another sound ringing through the courtyard. It sounded like a splash – like someone jumping into water. She looked around her, searching for something that could have made that sound, but she saw nothing.

As she looked around, the moon shone brightly on a dark oak door in front of her. This was the door she had seen Hunter looking at a few days ago in her Caeli lesson.

She walked towards the door and raised her hand to twist the doorknob. Before she could try it, she heard a sound coming from the opposite side of the courtyard.

"Ellora!" A familiarly smooth voice called her name. She turned around to see a certain handsome Prefect, and Prince, walking towards her. "Ellora," he said, sounding surprised. "Don't bother with that door; it doesn't open."

Ellora frowned. "What do you mean it doesn't open? I could have sworn I heard—" the splashing had stopped.

"What are you even doing out here? I was hoping to find you after your meeting with Mistress Oriel." Mason and Ellora walked across the courtyard, to the door Mason had come from.

"Well, I wanted some air and — wait. You know about the meeting?" Ellora stopped walking and looked at Mason.

"Yeah, I mean, everyone knows about it; you're only the second student in history who hasn't discovered their affinity in their first week." He looked sheepishly at her, under his shaggy brown locks.

"Yeah, I guess I can't expect it to be a secret; an outlier like me," she whispered the last part as she started to walk again, closely followed by Mason.

"You're not an outlier, Ellora. Well ... I guess you are, but that's not a bad thing! You're just different. In a good way, I mean. You're just ... an exception." He smiled. "Actually, Ellora, the reason why I wanted to find you was to apologise." This caught Ellora's attention. "I was sort of horrible to you the other day. It's just that Julia was worrying me. She's been... different lately and I feel like something's going on with her that I can't quite figure out. Anyway, I know it's no excuse, but I was just feeling frustrated and I didn't want to take that out on you. I guess I didn't handle the situation in the best way. Besides, when I saw you walking out here after your talk with Oriel, I thought you might like some company. Anyway, before I talk your ear off, could you forgive me?"

Mason was looking down at Ellora, clearly nervous. She was surprised; she didn't think guys like Mason got nervous. Especially around commoners or strange First Formers like her. Ellora sighed in disbelief. "Of course, I forgive you." She blushed slightly before they walked through the door. Was she even *allowed* to reject an apology from a prince? "And my friends call me Elle," she added with another blush.

"Elle. Well, I like you, Elle; you're different."

After her chat with Mason, Ellora was feeling a bit better but still couldn't bring herself to go upstairs and face her friends. She would have to tell them about her conversation with Oriel eventually, but for the moment, it was the last thing she wanted. What she wanted was a nice, hot drink.

She snuck quietly down to the kitchen, thankful that she hadn't run into anyone on her way. She made her drink quickly and topped it off with as much whipped cream as she could possibly fit into the mug and decided to stay where she was for a while. There were small, wooden tables on the edge of the kitchen, and Ellora sat at one of them with her hot blue mug in hand.

She hadn't realised how much time had passed with her staring into her mug, but when she finally took a sip, her hot chocolate was only lukewarm, and Ellora decided she would go to the library to find more information about their affinities before heading up to her room. She poked her head through the doors to make sure Wendy was no longer present; Ellora knew she would have her head for bringing a drink into the library.

She walked quietly down the centre aisle and cried out in shock when she barrelled straight into someone else from the side. She looked up with wide eyes, straight into Hunter's face and saw his eyes narrow.

"For the love of the Spirits!" he shouted, jumping up to his feet.

"We really need to stop meeting like this," she joked before noticing where she had spilled her drink. They both looked down in horror at his ruined shirt. "Hunter, I'm so sorry. That was a complete accident!" Ellora answered, standing up with her hands extended in a surrendering gesture.

"Well, maybe if you were looking where you were going you wouldn't have spilt your entire cup of...whatever this is, down my shirt!" he accused through gritted teeth, his eyes glowering down at her. Ellora hadn't quite noticed before this moment how tall he really was.

"It's hot chocolate. And you don't have to be so rude – I apologised, didn't I?" Ellora said sharply.

"Your apology won't get this blasted stain out!" His voice was becoming louder with every sentence.

"Well, Hunter, maybe if you weren't sneaking around like that, I would have heard you were there!" Ellora raised her own voice to match his.

"I was *not* sneaking around."

"Could have fooled me," Ellora snapped before storming away before he could say anything else. "NOW I HAVE TO GO AND MAKE ANOTHER HOT CHOCOLATE!" she all but screamed in frustration over her shoulder.

CHAPTER SIX

The West Courtyard

M oving into the winter, the temperature dropped quickly. Ellora knew her friends had almost started to regret not applying to the Caeli School of Aura instead of the Madori School of Aura; it was always warm in the Caeli kingdom, no matter the time of year.

Ellora had to replace her skirt with trousers on the days of her outdoor lessons and had worn tights, even indoors.

In her Incendi Theory class, Ellora was writing about the advantages of Incendi Aura in healing, when she dropped her pen. When she bent down to pick it up, she felt the prickling sensation of eyes on her. She turned and caught Hunter looking at her, *just* before he looked away. She frowned. This was the third time this week she had caught him staring at her.

She shook her head and looked down at the glass she was writing on. But feeling his stare again, she turned, intending to demand what it was that was just so interesting. But when her eyes locked onto his, she froze, her eyes widened in fear. She could see anger in his eyes, anger like she had never seen before, and she had absolutely no idea why.

Ellora gasped as his eyes narrowed only slightly, and a sharp jolt of pain exploded through her skull. The pain became more and more intense the longer their eyes were locked. She wanted to look away but couldn't, the pain getting worse with each torturous second.

Just when she thought she couldn't handle it anymore, when she thought she would collapse from the pain, just as suddenly as it had begun, it stopped.

Hunter tore his eyes away from her and turned around, leaving Ellora looking as pale as snow and gasping for breath. Immediately, Belle rushed to her side, as Ellora gripped the edge of the desk to keep her jelly legs from collapsing under her weight.

She just felt tired.

Ellora groaned, wincing at the pain when she tried to sit up.

"Here, drink this." She heard Belle's soft voice from nearby and felt a cool glass touch her fingers. She forced her eyes open to see a glass of water in front of her and swallowed it greedily; her throat felt like it hadn't been used for days.

"You were screaming," Belle told her in an accusing voice.

"Hmm?" Ellora was trying to get her eyes adjusted to the light when she noticed she was in her own bed.

"You were screaming," Belle repeated.

"What happened?" Ellora asked.

"You collapsed in class, Ellora Artemer! Master Rainclarke let me bring you up to your room, and I got you into bed, and you fell asleep and you were *screaming* in your sleep!" The words rushed out of Belle's mouth as if on a deadline. "You tell me *now*, young lady, what is going on!"

"First of all, Bee, I'm pretty sure I haven't been drinking, but at the moment, I feel like I've got the worst hangover in the history of Aurakind. So, if you could *not* scream at me, that would be greatly appreciated. And second of all, I honestly don't know what happened... Hunter was looking at me and... I just don't know."

Ellora felt a shiver run through her bones when she remembered the sensation, but she sighed in relief as Belle came to hug her, knowing she must have looked as shaken up as she felt.

Ellora layered on two grey cardigans and a thick black coat on a Thursday night before heading out of her room and towards the West Courtyard. She was very fond of visiting the courtyard at night when the inky sky was clear, and the moon was glowing softly, when she could count each individual star as they shone brightly over her.

On this particular night, Ellora was going to meet Mason, who was lounging under Ellora's favourite tree, knowing it was where she liked to spend her free time when the weather allowed. In her Caeli Theory lesson earlier, Mason had, once again, been asked to help Mistress Maywether with a demonstration and had slipped her a note on his way out, asking to meet her at 9 pm this evening by the Oak Tree.

Of course, Hunter, who had been instructed to work with her and Belle, had scowled at the dopey grin on her face. But, by now, Hunter knew better than to tell her not to associate with Mason. She let him glare at her for the remainder of the lesson, not even caring, but she did avoid eye contact as she grinned and fingered the note she had hidden in her pocket.

She walked down the stairs, now, wondering what Mason had planned for them. She knew the Winter Ball was only a week away; it was all everybody was talking about. Even Oriel was excited – she had told Ellora countless times about her plans for the evening and how happy she was that she'd brought balls back to the Madori Kingdom.

Ellora was distracted by the idea of going to the ball with Mason, when there was a loud creak of a step just below her. In the silence of the corridors this time of night, the sound was amplified and almost seemed to echo. She wondered who else would be wandering around at this time. Students were usually socialising in the various living rooms right now. She assumed it was one of the other girls trying to sneak down to the kitchen, like Ellora or one of her friends would do sometimes in search of a movie snack.

A flash of black caught her eyes in her peripheral vision, and so she stopped her steps and peered over the bannister to see none other than Hunter Nash.

Hunter turned towards the library and Ellora made an instant decision to follow him. She was curious, actually, about why in the Spirits he was sneaking around in the evening. Deciding that Mason would forgive her for being a few minutes late, especially given how accommodating she had been the last time when he had been a full ten minutes late, she crept behind him and into the library. After a conversation with Belle, Ellora had learned that princes and princesses were mostly treated the same as anyone else in the Aura Realm; they weren't special here.

The door was open, so she peered in to see if she could spot him. It was possible that he was only there to check out a book.

Entering the library, she nodded to Wendy, who was still sitting at the desk, reading. She looked down the first two rows of books and, after being unable to spot Hunter anywhere, glanced down at the silver watch she was wearing as she debated whether to leave.

"Is there any particular reason you are following me?" Hunter's firm voice drawled from behind her.

Ellora jumped in surprise. "Don't do that! You scared me!" She shrieked as she looked over at him, leaning against a bookshelf across the aisle, with his arms crossed over his torso, looking at her uninterestedly with one raised eyebrow. "And just *why* would you think I was following you? I wanted to check out a book."

"Oh, really? I must apologize then. But please, do tell me, which book were you intending to check out from *those* shelves? Because I could have sworn that those books are only for the Fifth Formers?" His voice was even and Ellora spotted an amusement in his eyes when she blushed at being caught.

"Whatever, Hunter. I don't have time for this. I've got people to see."

"Of course, you do. Why else would you be stalking me around the library?" He was clearly trying to fight a smile as he turned towards the shelf and opened the book he had picked out.

"Insufferable," murmured Ellora before huffing and hurrying out of the library; the West Courtyard was on the opposite side of the school.

"I'm so sorry I'm late, Mason," Ellora said as she emerged into the cool air of the night.

Mason sent her a small smile as he walked over to her. "It's alright, Ellora. Don't worry about it."

They walked quietly over to the oak tree, Ellora nervously playing with her fingers, and sat on the orange blanket Mason had laid out for them. "So, why did you want to meet me here tonight?" Ellora turned to face him and crossed her legs.

"Well, for one, I wanted to give you this." He pulled out a single red rose from where he had hidden it on the other side of the tree. Ellora gasped and beamed up at him.

"Mason, where did you get this? Roses don't grow in the gardens here."

"No, but as a Prefect, I can leave the school, remember?"

"I thought that was only on weekends."

"Yes, but Oriel needed something from the Main Land today, and she asked me and Julia to go and get it for her. I made a quick stop for you."

"What did she need from the Main Land?"

"A few random materials for some work she is doing to the castle. I think she wants to restore some of the guest rooms. Anyway, that's not important. Normally she would place an order for things like that, but she said she needed it right away, and — anyway, that's not relevant. The other reason I wanted to see you was because we haven't had the chance to talk in a while. I wanted to know how your training is going. Has Oriel said you're any closer to discovering your affinity?"

Ellora explained the little progress she had made in discovering her affinity, the frustration she felt in her Aura Practical lessons with her class and in her private tutoring sessions. She told him how much she enjoyed her theory lessons for each Aura and loved hearing about the cool things her teachers could do with their Auras. Her instincts told her, however, to leave out the extra practise that Oriel had decided Ellora should with Hunter in their spare time.

"You know, I really like Master Rainclarke. I think he's my favourite," said Ellora.

"Master Rainclarke?!" exclaimed Mason. "You've got to be the only person in the history of the school who's said that. He's so strict."

"But he's fair," Ellora defended.

"He's mean," Mason laughed.

"But he's a great teacher," insisted Ellora. "I really like his lessons. And in our private tutoring, although he pretends to get all annoyed at me for not being able to do anything, he's really patient. He understands. He can tell I get annoyed at myself, but he just keeps going. It's like he just understands how difficult it can be to feel so ... different. It's nice having someone who understands you."

"Mason!" A tall, blonde-haired boy with a thick German accent ran out into the courtyard. "Mason, haf you seen Mistress Patel?" he asked. Ellora recognised him when he got closer; Henry Fischer, a First Former who had come from the Glassi Kingdom and who was quite good friends with Melody.

"Henry? What's going on?" Mason asked.

"I vas in charge of checking zhe greenhouses tonight before I vent to bed, and I vent to check everysing and I just knew somesing vas off," he said. "Eett ees zhe strawberries! zhe strawberries are dead! Zhey haf all died."

"Dead? How could they die?" Ellora frowned.

The door opened again, and Hunter ran through. "Did you find her, Hen— Oh. Mason, Ellora." Ellora watched, as Hunter's eyes glanced over them, narrowed slightly, and looked pointedly away.

"Hunter ees helping me," said Henry. "I hafe not found her yet," he said when he turned back to Hunter.

"Don't worry. We'll find her," Hunter said reassuringly.

"Let us help!" said Ellora.

"No," Hunter answered quickly, refusing to look at them. "That's not necessary," he said, before walking out with Henry behind him, without a word.

"So, what 'appened with Mason? 'Ow did it go? Where did you go? Oh, my Spirit, is zhat rose from 'im?!" Ellora chuckled, as Melody bombarded her with questions the moment she stepped into the room.

"We just sat in the West Courtyard and talked for a bit more than an hour. I haven't had a chance to speak to him in a couple of weeks, so it was really nice. And yes, the rose is from him," she added.

"Zhat is so sweet!" Melody squealed excitedly, as Ellora changed into her baggy and comfortable pyjamas. "And?"

"And, what?" said Ellora.

"Zhe Winter Ball?"

"It... it didn't come up. Listen, Melody, I'm sorry, but I'm a bit tired, so I think I'm just going to head off to sleep. Goodnight."

Ellora knew that Melody must have realised how tired she was. Otherwise, she wouldn't have let her off without giving any more details.

"Night night," Melody replied sweetly.

"Thank you." Ellora thanked the angel that had rescued her from that horrid place. "Thank you," she repeated. "Who ... Who are you?"

"Elle, it is me. It is Melody." Ellora heard a soft voice speak to her, but she couldn't process it.

"You sing beautifully." Ellora smiled, eyes still closed. Her own voice was heavy with sleep. "Thank you for saving me. Okay, I'll sleep now. Goodnight."

Ellora woke up with a jolt. She looked over at Melody , who was running over to her. "Elle?"

"Melody?" Ellora asked, finally awake. "Melody ... it was awful," her voice trembled.

"What 'appened, Elle?"

"The shadow almost got me, Melody. I almost saw its' face. If that even *was* a face. It... it almost got me but ... but ... but I got away. Something — someone saved me. I saw a burst of blue light just as the shadow got to the bed. I heard this voice, Melody, it was singing to me. It sounded almost like a lullaby, but it wasn't singing words. More like just a tune. Like it was kind of humming, I guess. I don't know. I've heard it every time the shadow has gotten close to me. But why does this keep happening, Melody?" The fear was written plainly on Ellora's face.

"It seemed really scary, Elle," Melody said, rubbing Ellora's back comfortingly. It was 2.27 am, according to the grey clock sitting on Ellora's bedside table.

"I'm so sorry, Melody. I really didn't mean to scare you," Ellora whispered apologetically.

"I know, Ellora, zhat you would never mean to scare me. But I zhink you should know what 'appened because zhis time was different."

Over the past few months of being Ellora's roommate, Melody had become used to Ellora's nightmares and always tried to help her as much as she could, never complaining about how tired she was the next day. Sometimes, Ellora would wake up by herself, and Melody would calm her down and let her talk through her nightmare. Other times, Melody had to wake her up to end her distress. After the occasion before classes had started, she hadn't needed to call Belle, but she still made sure to let her know the next morning.

You were zhrashing about in your sleep and Elle, it was almost as if zhere was somezhing attacking you from above. It was very freaky, zhe way zhat you were clawing at zhe air above you." Melody shivered. "You were saying 'stop, please don't 'urt me'."

Ellora watched at Melody took a deep breath, obviously trying to forget the sight. She could almost see the gears turning in the small girl's head.

"Elle, can you tell me everyzhing zhat 'appened between when you left to meet Mason and when you got back?" Melody's tone was serious, but calm.

Ellora looked at her inquisitively. "Well, I left, I saw Hunter, I met Mason, we talked and I came back, if you want the short version of it all."

"Wait, you saw 'Unter?"

"Yeah, he was sneaking around, and I wanted to see what was going on," replied Ellora. "But honestly, Melody, the boy is *infuriating* sometimes! Sometimes he's horrid, sometimes he's nice and even a bit funny, but can he just make up his mind?! Aaaargh!"

"So, did you argue wizh 'im?"

"Yes. But what does this have to do with my nightmares?"

"Well, last time you 'ad a nightmare was last Wednesday, no? After your situation with 'Unter in Master Rainclarke's class?"

"Oh, you're right!" Ellora started to piece together the links between her nightmares. "And two days before that, I had run into Hunter in the corridor, and he'd basically growled at me to 'watch where I was going' as if it was my fault! And I was angry and then I had a nightmare! Wait... you don't think he could be behind this, do you?" Ellora was panicking; how was Hunter causing this? There was no way he could do this to her. Was there?

"Wait. What about on that first day? Remember how I told you about the situation I had out in the corridor? When I saw Clara? Hunter wasn't there; I hadn't even met Hunter yet." Ellora felt like she was defending Hunter, but that wasn't what she wanted.

"You are right, Elle. It cannot be just 'im. But zhere must be some sort of link. We will ask zhe ozhers in zhe morning. But for now, we should rest. Tomorrow is Friday, but we 'ave a full day of classes and afterwards you 'ave got extra tutoring after wizh Professor Rainclarke."

They both got into their beds, but their heads were turning, trying to come up with a solution to Ellora's dreams.

After a while, Melody gave up and found one of her favourite novels to read. Ellora felt an urge to go to her spot in the West Courtyard and sit in the fresh air for a while. "Melody, I'm going for a walk. I can't sleep and I think some air will do me good. I'm still feeling a bit on edge after that nightmare, anyway," Ellora told her as she wrapped a black sweater around her navy-blue pyjamas and slipped on her pumps.

"I will come wizh you." Melody put her book away, but Ellora stopped her.

"That's okay Melody, you've lost enough sleep because of me for one night."

"Are you sure, Elle?" Melody seemed unconvinced.

"Of course! I'll be back in a bit," she whispered before slipping out into the dimly lit corridor.

She thought it would have been difficult to find her way to the courtyard in the dark, but she had taken this route so often it was now second nature to her. She strolled out into her courtyard and made her way over to the oak tree, settling herself under the protection of its skeletal branches and bundling herself up in her coat. She leaned her head back against the bark of the tree and stretched her legs out in front of her.

The comforting embrace of the icy, December air made her feel safe and as she felt her eyelids grow heavy, she felt herself slowly slipping off to sleep.

A soothing voice called out to her as she was on the cusp of darkness, of rest. "Ellora," it said. Ellora snapped her eyes open at the sound in her ears and looked around. After a moment, she decided she had imagined the voice and allowed her eyes to rest once more.

"Ellora." The voice was louder this time. Ellora jumped up. She definitely hadn't imagined it that time.

"Who's there?" Ellora whispered. Something inside of her told her to trust the voice; it meant no harm to her. She looked around her and, after noticing nothing out of the ordinary, she walked around the other side of her tree.

Her eyes widened as she noticed a soft blue light coming from the bottom of the other door, the door Hunter had been staring at a few months ago.

Something told her to open the door, although she remembered Mason had told her it was always locked. The closer she got to the gentle blue glow, the calmer she felt. She felt protected, safe. Her hand trembled slightly in excitement at what she would find on the other side of the door as she reached out and turned the door handle.

Her mouth dropped open as she swung the door open.

In front of her was a great, blue lake. The moon reflected off the surface of the water, creating the ethereal blue glow she had seen under the door behind her. The water was still, a navy-blue colour with specs of silver glittering in the water.

Small, smooth rocks scattered the perimeter of the lake and Ellora spotted a small grassy area towards the right. She walked over and sat down, still in awe at what she had stumbled across.

She noticed a few tiny ripples in the water directly in front of her, before a small splash echoed in her ears. Ellora stumbled back slightly and fell on her hands as a shape emerged from the opaque water.

The figure smiled majestically at her, as Ellora gulped and choked out one word: "Hi?"

She heard a soft chuckle, only it sounded more like she had thought a laugh, rather than heard one. "You're half right, young Ellora. My voice is in your head, but it is not a figment of your imagination," the feminine voice echoed in her head again.

"What?" Ellora gasped at a loss for words, convinced she must have been dreaming.

She looked at the figure in front of her who had come closer now and whose features were shining under the moonlight. Her friendly yet powerful eyes shone a glossy, light blue colour, and her long, white hair gracefully framed the soft features of her face. She almost looked as though she could be another Aurum, apart from the silver tone that made her skin look as though it was glistening in the light. The closer she got to the edge of the lake, the more clearly Ellora could make out another odd shape where her legs should have been. It almost looked like ... no, it *was* a tail. It was a bright blue colour that reminded Ellora of a clear summer's sky and sparkled with tiny specks of silver glitter.

"Who are you?" Ellora said.

Ellora heard an amused chuckle in the back of her mind. She looked at the magnificent creature in front her and couldn't help but wonder if she should be scared. "No, my dear, you need not fear me." The light voice tickled her mind.

Ellora's eyes widened in shock, as she realised what had happened. "Did you just ... did you just read my mind?" Once again, there was a chuckle.

"No, Ellora, not quite. I cannot invade your thoughts like that." She smiled patiently. The confusion Ellora was feeling must have shown on her face because she heard: "My dear, you were just projecting your thoughts rather loudly."

The more she communicated, the less scared Ellora felt. She lifted herself up to rest on her knees and leant forward towards the creature. When she was close enough, Ellora looked straight into her eyes.

She felt a rush of coolness flood her veins, as a pleasant shiver shot down her spine. Just as quickly as the connection was made, Ellora dropped down to the ground.

She gasped as a stab of pain pierced through her skull. She cradled her throbbing head in her arms, begging for the pain to stop. She felt the harsh tremor in her body ease as she slowly relaxed. The healing, melodic song she had heard in her dreams played in her head and she felt better. A few long moments later, Ellora felt better and slowly, testing, opened her eyes.

"Asyra." The word ghosted past her lips as she sat up, rubbing her temples. "That's your name; I felt it. I felt it right before the pain." The small nod of Asyra's head told her she was correct. "That song, I've heard it before, in my dreams. Well, nightmares. You're the glowing blue light that has been saving me, aren't you?"

"You are right, Ellora; I am Asyra, Spirit of Madori."

Ellora's mouth dropped open. Even though somehow, she already knew it, she still couldn't believe it. The Spirits of the Realm were myths, legends, fairy tales; that was what most people believed. But here, in front of Ellora was the Spirit of Madori. She couldn't believe her own eyes.

"And yes, my dear. It has been I in your nightmares. I have felt your fear and helped to cast away the evil."

Some things were now piecing together in Ellora's mind, but she still had so many questions.

"Please, Ellora, feel free to ask me." Asyra's voice was gentle.

"Oh, right, I guess I'm still projecting. How, exactly, do I stop that?"

"You must clear your thoughts, focus on masking your thoughts and feelings. I believe the humans call it meditation. I'm sure you could find some books in the library to help you."

"So ... I'm projecting my thoughts all the time? You always know what I'm thinking? Wait, does this mean everyone is projecting all of the time?"

"Yes, my dear, most people are constantly projecting their thoughts. But I block you all out; if I didn't, I would go crazy," she laughed. "But you, Ellora, your thoughts are particularly loud, especially when you are in pain. When you are in pain, I can feel it as if it is my own; it breaks through my block. I want to help you, my dear."

"Help me?" Suddenly, Ellora realised that the pain she had felt when looking into Asyra's eyes was familiar. "Asyra, why do I get the same reaction that I just had when I looked into your eyes when

I look into Hunter's eyes? It doesn't seem to happen every time, but when I look at him for long enough..." she trailed off.

"I am not an omniscient being, Ellora. There are some questions I do not know the answers to." The voice in her head seemed firmer than it had been before.

"Oh. Of course. I guess it's not so important," she said with a frown. She knew it *was* important, but it was clear Asyra didn't know. "This place is beautiful," she commented to expel the awkwardness. "Come to think of it, the entire castle is beautiful. Even all of the paintings and the statue of Arellia at the front."

"Yes, well, Arellia was as vain as one can be, but I suppose one cannot fault her on her style," Asyra replied.

Ellora was feeling tired and the air was freezing cold around her; she just wanted to be back in her warm, cosy bed.

"Now, Ellora, could you step a bit closer?" Asyra asked. Ellora stood up from her position on the floor and walked over to Asyra. "As I said, I want to help you, my dear," she said, as she lifted her right hand and rested it on Ellora's forehead. Her thumb swept across Ellora's skin in a wavy motion, up and down and up and down.

Nothing happened.

Asyra drew her arm back away from Ellora. "You may as well sit down." She gestured to the grass on the ground. "Oriel will take a few minutes to arrive."

"Oriel?"

"Don't you have any more questions for me?" Asyra obviously changed the subject and Ellora followed her lead.

"If you're real, does that mean the other Spirits are too?"

"Of course! There could be no Aura without us," she said.

"No Aura?"

"Indeed, my dear. You see, we were born with the Cores of each Kingdom as their guardians, their protectors. We are each connected to our Kingdom's Core and live to protect it."

"The Cores?" Ellora asked, confused.

"Ah, here she is."

The door lightly swung open, and a figure clad in a thick navy-blue dressing gown stood in the doorway. It was 4 am-, after all. "Ellora." The familiar voice glided through the air. "Your affinity has been declared. Good morning, Asyra."

CHAPTER SEVEN

Sweetened Tea

"It's so cool that we can be Madori Aurums together, Ellora." Belle and Ellora were working together on their first official Madori Exercise in their Friday morning class. Their Madori classes had always been in this room after the second week; it was a grey stone room with wooden desks dotted around.

This was Ellora's first class since discovering her affinity for Madori Aura the night before. In front of them, on their desk, was a glass of water. Their task was to create a ripple. It sounded easy to the students when Master Graynor had given them the task at the start of the hour, but already 40 minutes had passed, and nobody had completed it.

"Yeah, Bee, it's definitely a huge upgrade from not even having an affinity. But I still don't exactly feel like it. I mean, does your roommate wake up screaming in the middle of the night, too?" Ellora replied sarcastically.

"Come on, Elle. I know it's hard, but at least you have us to help you. I mean, it would be so much worse if you had to deal with them alone. By the way." Belle decided to change the topic of conversation. "I thought about what you and Melody told me this morning, about your dreams being linked."

This made Ellora's head shoot up at Belle, eager to know what she had to say about one of the many problems affecting her life at the moment. "What if they're caused by your emotions? I mean, think about it; the first time, out in the corridor, you had seen Clara for the first time in, what three years? Spirits, that must have been emotional for you! And then when you bumped into Hunter all those times, you got angry, right? Well, again, emotions. And last night, you were angry with Hunter *and* you were feeling all lovey-dovey about Mason."

"Bee, you're right. Every time I've been especially emotional, I've had some sort of dream or ... or flashback or whatever it was that happened that time outside my room. But why?"

"Hmm, good question. I'll do some research in the library later on today. But for now, budge over — it's my turn." Belle shoved her playfully as she took her place in front of the glass.

Ellora watched as Belle closed her eyes and took a deep breath. She closely observed, intrigued when the stress fell away from Belle's face and her breaths became more even and natural. She gasped when she saw little ripples burst through the glass. Then, suddenly, the ripples ceased, and the water rose from the glass, one droplet at a time, when suddenly all of the water was in the air. "Belle?" Ellora asked, her eyes wide and her mouth open. But her friend failed to answer. "Belle?"

"What is going on, here?" Master Graynor asked as he came over to them.

"I... I don't know, sir. She...just...look!" Ellora waved her hands towards her best friend.

"Belle!" Master Graynor yelled, and finally, Belle's eyes opened, but they were clouded over and distanced.

"Belle Keloa!" Master Graynor's voice was still louder than usual, but he was no longer yelling. "Can you hear me?"

Ellora stared, wide-eyed, at the now empty glass standing in a puddle of water on the desk. She looked back to Belle, who was trembling under the intense gaze of Graynor, who was now towering over her.

As if registering her fear, he stepped away from Belle and turned towards Ellora instead. In a hushed voice, he said, "Please take your friend to Mistress Oriel and tell her what happened. I will excuse you both from the rest of class today."

Ellora nodded wordlessly, feeling too shocked to speak. She walked over to Belle, aware of the other students in her class staring at them, and grasped Belle by her wrist, pulling her out of the room.

"What happened?" a wavering voice hit Ellora's ears when she got to the corridor, reminding her of Belle's presence next to her.

"You don't know?" Ellora was still lost in thought herself.

"No, I just closed my eyes to try and sense the water, in a way. I read about the technique in one of the library's books a couple of days ago, and I thought it might work, maybe."

"Work? Bee, it did more than work. You didn't just create ripples in the glass, you lifted the water out of there. You were controlling the water; no doubt about it, you're a Madori Aurum," Ellora told her, excitement now overtaking the fear.

The two walked in silence to Oriel's office; Ellora's thought engrossed in her dreams and Belle still feeling the rush and confusion caused by the Aura flowing through her.

They stopped in front of the oak door in the library that Ellora had become so familiar with over the past few months. Just as she raised a hand to tap on the wood, the door swung open. "Come in, girls," Oriel said already with her back to them.

"How did you know we were—" Ellora began but stopped short when she heard a familiar faint chuckle at the back of her mind. Oriel sat in her leather chair and sent her a knowing look when Ellora spoke again. "Never mind."

"Mistress Oriel, I don't understand what happened." Belle seemed unfazed by Oriel's seemingly all-knowingness, and more focused on the bizarre experience she had just been through. She and Ellora took their time to explain, in great detail, what had happened from each of their perspectives.

When they had finished their recounts, the girls both stared expectantly at Oriel, who was staring at her mysterious blend of tea in thought. "Well," The girls almost jumped when their Madori Mistress's voice finally came, "it seems to me that you accidentally harnessed all of your Aura in one go. Now, this isn't a bad thing, but I'm not sure if you would be able to do it again if you tried. I will not ask you for now, because I'm sure even if you do not realise it, the Aura also used up quite a lot of your energy so, instead, I will be sending you to bed for the day. But first." She held out a small blue sweet wrapped in clear plastic.

Belle and Ellora exchanged a quick glance before turning back to Oriel, confused. Oriel chuckled a small laugh. "Sugar can be helpful to replenish your energy, as well as your Aura. These are one of my most favourite, sugariest sweets; blue drops."

Belle took the blue drop from her hand and turned to leave before turning back again, looking as though there was more that she wanted to say. "Belle," Oriel spoke first. "I know you're probably worried and confused, and maybe scared, but I promise you there's nothing wrong with you. This is unusual, yes, but it's not unheard of. For now, I want you to go to bed and rest; we can talk tomorrow if you have any questions." She smiled comfortingly to Belle, who yawned as if on cue. "Elle, please make sure Belle gets straight to her room and into bed. You can stay with her for the rest of the school day until your tutoring session with Master Rainclarke."

"What? Extra tutoring? But I've already discovered my affinity. Why do I still need extra tutoring?"

"Oriel." Julia ran into the office, panting. "Oriel, there's something wrong with the fountain by the gardens. I came as fast as I could," she said.

"What's wrong, Julia?" Oriel asked.

"The water is ... just ... gone."

"What? How?" Oriel frowned. "Ellora," she said, turning back, "we should speak later. I need to go and deal with this, and it looks like Belle's about to fall asleep over there." They both looked at Belle, who was standing upright and leaning against the door, yawning.

Ellora dropped the subject and led Belle out of the room.

After making sure Belle was tucked into bed, Ellora took a trip to the library to check out some books on meditation to read in Belle's room while she slept. She had a few hours still until her 4 pm lesson with Master Rainclarke. After choosing two books: 'Meditation to Harness your Aura' and 'The Ancient Human Art of Meditation'.

"Step one: find a comfortable position. Doesn't seem too difficult." Ellora spoke to herself as she sat on the floor and leant her head against Belle's mattress, positioning herself until her legs were extended in front of her, crossed at the ankles. "Step two: close your eyes. How am I supposed to read the rest of the instructions if I close my eyes?" She groaned as she threw the book to one side. "Stupid book," she growled at it.

"It's certainly not stupid, my dear." A familiar, melodic voice sung at the back of Ellora's mind.

Ellora read through the other steps and closed her eyes, focusing on her breath. In... and out. In... and out. In... and out.

Ellora jolted awake at the sound of the door swing shut. "Hi, Ellora! How are you?" Ellora looked up to find Belle's roommate, Violet, a girl with bright purple hair, walking into the room.

"Oh, no. I fell asleep."

She looked at the silver watch on her wrist to see that the time was 3.55 pm; five minutes before she was supposed to start her private tutoring session with the strictest teacher in the school. She jumped up, gathered her library books and rushed to the door. "Violet, I'm so sorry, I can't talk — I have a meeting with Rainclarke. Urm, don't wake up Belle for dinner, she already ate. I'll explain later. Sorry!" she called as she ran out of the room, no time to wait for a response from Violet.

"Good luck with Rainclarke!" she heard Violet call behind her before the door swung shut. She sprinted down the stairs and turned right down a corridor. She was so close; she might even have made it in time if she hadn't bumped into someone in the corridor.

"Oh, I'm so sorry," she rushed out the words, attempting to pick up her books that had scattered onto the floor when she fell.

"My fault," a voice drawled, as she looked up to see a pale hand extended towards her. Ellora felt heat rise in her cheeks.

"Thanks," she murmured to Hunter, as he hoisted her from the ground. She knew she shouldn't have done it, but she couldn't help herself. She felt something inside of her drawing her eyes up to his as they locked eyes, his hand still wrapped tightly around her wrist. Immediately, she felt a pain in her head and winced, clutching her head between her hands and dropping the books once more.

Hunter immediately released his grip on her and bent down to pick up her books, tearing his eyes away from her. As the throbbing in her head subsided, she took the books he was holding out to her from his hands and, without a word, barged past him, refusing to look at him again. She felt drained, as if she hadn't just slept through the afternoon, and struggled to drag her feet across the floor towards black door she associated with the Incendi classroom.

Ellora threw herself into the room and leaned against the door as she shut it behind her. "You're late." A voice snapped at her from the front of the room; Master Rainclarke was sitting at his desk, facing her direction, and reading.

"I know, I'm sorry," she barely pushed her trembling voice across the room to him, but he heard what she had said. Her head was spinning, and her legs felt like jelly.

"Sorry isn't good enough. You need as much practise as you can get to find your— Ellora, are you okay?" Her world went black.

"Ellora?" A voice called to her and she forced her eyelids open.

She looked around in a daze; the walls and ceiling were an unfamiliar shade of white and she could feel something soft under her body. "Where am I?" She groaned, rolling and stretching her stiff neck to each side.

"My office," a deep voice said from her right.

She turned her head to find Master Rainclarke sitting in a chair a couple of meters away from her with a steaming mug in his hand and a worried expression painted on his face. She slowly sat up, to face him, realising she had been lying down on a black sofa, similar to the once in Oriel's own office.

He thrust the mug towards her, silently asking her to drink it, before she gave it a sniff. "Hmm, let me guess: tea with sugar?" She took a guess, based on what Oriel had told Belle earlier in her office.

"It replenishes your energy, I thought it would help." He said, hesitantly.

"Thank you, Master Rainclarke." She was very grateful, and she could see he didn't have much experience in being friendly to his students.

"No matter, Ellora, it is my job as your Incendi Master. Mistress Oriel would like to see you in her office as soon as you are feeling better," he spoke steadily and Ellora found his deep voice calming.

She drained the remainder of her tea, which has actually given her a burst of energy and removed the last traces of her headache, and awkwardly set the mug on the coffee table placed in the centre of the small room. He nodded to her, as she stood and called out another 'thanks' before rushing out of his room.

"Elle, I hope you are okay. Master Rainclarke told me what happened." Ellora immediately relaxed into the black leather chair in front of Oriel's desk at the sound of her reassuring voice.

Oriel had already prepared tea for Ellora, just the way she liked it. The two had been having regular meetings every other day at first, just to see how Ellora was coping with her extra lessons and her busy schedule. The next week, Oriel asked Ellora to come every day for around twenty minutes to talk about Ellora's lessons and if she felt a specific leaning, or connection, towards any of the Auras. After a couple of weeks of the daily meetings, Ellora started staying in Oriel's office for almost an hour each day, drinking tea and just chatting. And now, their company was comfortable, and for that Ellora was grateful. It was like she had her own safe haven in the school.

"I'm fine; I guess I was just tired after last night, well, this morning, and all."

"Yes," Oriel sighed as she poured two cups of tea.

For the first time since entering the office, Ellora looked up at her, seeing a tired-looking woman with deep bags under her eyes and lines of worry creasing her forehead.

"Mistress Oriel ... Are you okay?" Ellora felt uneasy at the fear and stress visible on her face. Oriel was the one they were all supposed to look up to and seeing her on edge made Ellora feel on edge.

"Yes, Elle, fine, thank you. Now, the reason why I called you in here is to talk more about your Aura." Ellora could tell she was changing the subject, but said nothing about it. "You see, Elle, I noticed this before, but I thought it might have been a delay. Even this morning, I doubted that was the case, but now it has been a few hours and I know for sure." She looked up at her as she handed over the mugs.

"Madori Mistress, what's going on?" Ellora felt nervous as she clenched tightly to the hot mug in her hands as if she could draw the warmth from it.

"Well, nothing's *wrong*, exactly. I don't want you to worry."

This made Ellora worry more.

"We just have a slight situation regarding your Aura. Now, this is not usual, but it seems as though you have a mixture of Essence and Aura inside of you."

Ellora blinked at her, face blank. "What? What does that mean?"

"It means that some of your Essence was converted into Madori Aura this morning when you were with Asyra. In fact, I can see the blue in you as we speak. However, some of your Essence has remained Essence. Well, not some of it; most of it," she explained.

"Why? I mean, why has that happened? Why has my Essence not ... transferred? And I still don't understand what that means." Ellora could feel goosebumps popping up on her skin; she was still different to everybody else. She was still an outsider, isolated.

"Elle, please don't worry. I didn't bring you in here to make you nervous; I simply wanted to fill you in; it's not right of me to keep these things from you when it's regarding your own self. You're old enough to know." She reached a hand toward Elle and patted her shoulder comfortingly when she saw her furrowed eyebrows.

"I appreciate that, Mistress Oriel, I really do. Thank you for not keeping this from me."

"It's perfectly normal, Ellora; most people have Essence left in them after they first find their affinity. In fact, I think Belle is the first student I have seen to discover her affinity so quickly and have no Essence remaining. So, as I said, nothing to worry about." Her reassuring smile lessened her Ellora's grip on the mug.

"Actually, I think that as your training progresses in this school, each student harnesses more and more of their Essence to turn into Aura, until it is all transferred. For some people, though, this doesn't happen, and I believe this is because they have more than one affinity," Oriel stated simply. "More often than not, the remaining Essence remains dormant, but when somebody, like you, my dear, have a large amount of Essence, this is not always possible."

"What?! People can have more than one affinity? I didn't know that was even possible. How does that even work? Wait, why don't I know anybody who has two affinities, then?" The questions bubbled out of Ellora's mouth before she could even think to stop them.

The corners of Oriel's mouth tweaked upwards in what would have been a fond smile if she were not so preoccupied with her worries. "You do, Elle. Your friend – Hunter – I believe he will also have another affinity when the time comes; he definitely has enough Essence. And Noah, of course—"

"Noah? You mean Master Rainclarke?! But he's an Incendi Master; how can he have a second affinity?"

"Yes, Elle, he has mastered the Incendi Aura, but he is also a Caeli Aurum." Oriel smiled warmly, happiness briefly flashing on her face. "You see, Elle, it is extremely uncommon, but it does happen in our Realm. We just don't teach it because it really is very rare."

"So ... you're saying that I might have another affinity?" A blank look covered Ellora's face.

"Well, Ellora, all I'm saying for now is that it is a possibility. And that's why I want you to continue with your extra classes. Oh, did Master Rainclarke tell you your lesson has been rescheduled to Monday? It will be right after your extra Caeli lesson."

"Oh, yeah, thank you, Mistress Oriel. Sorry, again, about that. I don't really know what happened," she lied. "Wait, so if Hunter also has Essence, does that mean he also has to have extra private lessons?"

"No. We have a different situation worked out for Hunter; he will stay over the school breaks to try have some extra lessons with the teachers and discover his other affinity if there is another. This is what we usually do with students who have extra Essence, Ellora. You, however, are a bit of a special case. You have quite a bit of Essence in you, more than I've seen before. I think it would be best for you, Ellora, if you find out yours as soon as possible; I'm sure it would be a weight off your shoulders. Hunter has told me he is perfectly fine to wait until the first break."

"Oriel!" A muffled voice stopped Ellora from responding. "Oriel!" The alarmed voice became closer. "Oriel!" The door to Oriel's office flung open and Master Rainclarke burst into the room, panting.

"Ah, Master Rainclarke, we were just talking about yo—"

"You need to come *now*, Oriel." Master Rainclarke didn't let her finish her sentence. He didn't even seem to care that Oriel and Ellora had been talking about him. He was in too much of a panic about what was happening elsewhere.

Seeing the look on his Rainclarke's face, Oriel quickly stood up and rushed the room without so much as a glance back at Ellora. She looked up at Master Rainclarke, not quite knowing whether to stay or leave. "You should probably go to dinner, Ellora. It's almost six anyway." His voice was distant, distracted by the meeting about to take place.

Oriel's words echoed in Ellora's mind as she walked to the dining room. She didn't quite know how to react to what she had been told. She had gone from feeling guilty for being a fraud, not having any Aura, to being told she had *extra* Aura. She found it difficult to believe. She also made a note to ask Oriel about her Print turning brown rather than silver.

Ellora also wondered what it was that had made Master Rainclarke so nervous; she had never seen him look anything other than completely calm or incredibly angry.

She cleared the thoughts from her mind and focused on getting to dinner. She didn't want to think about her Aura, or her Essence, or Master Rainclarke, or anything until tomorrow. For now, all she wanted was to sit with her friends, have a nice meal, with some of that delicious chocolate cake if she was lucky, and crawl into her bed.

Ellora jerked up in her bed, panting for breath. She was covered in a layer of sweat and had strands of her stuck to all sides of her face.

"Elle, are you alright?" Came Melody's sleepy voice from the other side of the room.

"Yes, Melody. Sorry. Another nightmare," Ellora responded when her breathing had finally evened out once more. "Go back to sleep," she said, but it was unnecessary – Melody had already started snoring lightly.

Ellora looked over at the clock to see it was 5 am. Knowing she wouldn't be able to get back to sleep tonight, and she would be waking up in just over an hour anyway, she decided to shower and get ready.

Her nightmare had been worse last night, somehow seeming to last longer than usual, but Ellora didn't linger on it; she tried to distract herself. It was enough these nightmares were taking over her sleep and her brain during the night, but during the day when she had some sort of control, she refused to be affected by them. And for now, she focused on getting ready this morning since she was meeting Mason for a walk around the garden before breakfast.

She was walking down the stairs at 6.45, dressed in a pale grey goat and a pair of black boots, when she suddenly collided with someone walking up the same stairs. "Oh, Mason," she said. "I thought we were meeting by the fountain."

"Ellora! Oh, right, our walk. Um, listen, I'm really sorry, but do you think we could reschedule? I just have something to take care of."

"Oh, sure, is everything okay?" Ellora asked, but by the time she looked back at him, he was already gone. She sighed deeply and decided that she would go for a walk, anyway, since she was already dressed.

When she finally arrived at breakfast, she was feeling cold, despite her layers, and tired. She needed a cup of tea. She took her coat off and headed towards the table but cried out when somebody ran straight into her.

"WHAT IN THE REALMS—" she exclaimed, looking up to see Hazel's horrified face carrying an empty teacup. Luckily, the many layers she had on under her shirt had protected her skin from the hot liquid, but that didn't change that her shirt was completely ruined, and the entire dining room was staring at her.

Ellora looked up at Hazel and saw tears welling in her eyes. She groaned internally, as she knew Hazel was unbelievably shy; she'd never even spoken to Ellora before. Taking a deep breath, she forced herself to speak, thankful when her voice was even and calm. "It's okay, Hazel. I know you didn't mean it. I'll just go up and change." She turned around and hurried out of the room.

Ellora really considered skipping classes for the day — it seemed like today was going to be a bad day for her. But she shook the thought out of her head; how was she ever going to discover her affinity if she didn't go to her classes.

She was taken away from her thoughts when something hit her and she fell backwards into the wall, shoulder-first. "Ow!" She gasped.

"Sorry, Ellora, are you okay?" Julia ran back up the stairs to Ellora. "I'm so sorry – I was in a rush and I wasn't looking where I was going."

"It's fine," Ellora muttered through gritted teeth.

"Listen, if you're hurt, go infirmary." Julia was already rushing down the stairs again, even as she spoke to Ellora. "Sorry again, but I'm in a rush!" she called over her shoulder.

Ellora took a deep breath once more and headed back downstairs. She sighed, looking around before she realised she hadn't been to the infirmary before; she didn't know the way. Slumping her shoulders, she hoped Oriel would be free and available to direct her.

When she arrived at Oriel's office, still covered in tea and tenderly clutching her left arm, things were busier than expected. "I need it now! This could very well turn into a *very* serious situation if we do not prepare properly!" Oriel demanded. Just before Ellora knocked on the door, Mason and Julia sprinted out without even giving her a second glance. Ellora stared after them; Julia had only run past her a few minutes ago so their conversation must have been incredibly fast.

"Mistress Oriel?" she asked, peeking into the office.

"Elle, how are you, dear?" Oriel asked, attempting to be calm, but Ellora could see that her shoulders were tense and there were frown lines across her forehead. "You're covered in tea."

"I didn't want to bother you, but I've hurt my shoulder and didn't know the way to the infirmary. I didn't think I would be able to change my shirt with it being in this much pain."

"Ah, yes, well, normally I would send you to Healer Amare, but it doesn't seem to be broken, so let me take a look." She took the coat from Ellora's arms and helped her down to a chair. She traced symbols in the air and muttered a few words in a language Ellora didn't recognise, then frowned. "Yes, I think it's dislocated."

"Oh, Spirits," sighed Ellora. "This is really not my day."

"Nor mine, Elle." Oriel gave her a sad smile before getting back to work on her arm. "I'm going to warn you, this is going to hurt, but the pain will be over in a matter of seconds. Ready?" Ellora clenched her teeth together and nodded her head in agreement.

Oriel was right; it *did* hurt. But, fortunately, before Ellora could even think about screaming, the pain was over. Oriel prodded her arm, just to make sure it was okay and was satisfied when Ellora didn't cry out in pain. "Thank you," Ellora said with a smile.

For the first time since she had arrived, she noticed the mess around the room. "Woah," she whispered, eyes wide. "When did a hurricane come through here?"

"Um, yes, well, unfortunately, I have a small situation on my hands, but it's nothing I can't handle." She brushed it off like it was nothing. "You should change and head to classes."

I just *can't* do it!" Ellora exclaimed in frustration. She was fed up with these technique tutoring sessions that Oriel had insisted Hunter give her in her very rare free periods, and her day was going badly enough as it was.

"Well, you aren't *trying*," replied Hunter, sounding just as frustrated.

"Oh, *you* try moving a leaf without being a Caeli Aurum."

"It's not about moving the leaf," Hunter said, through gritted teeth, before taking a deep breath in and exhaling. "It's about," his voice was calmer, now, "feeling the energy move through you."

"How do I do that?" Ellora asked, sounding slightly defeated.

"Close your eyes," Hunter instructed. Ellora furrowed her eyebrows in confusion at his request, but at the impatient look on his face, she firmly squeezed her eyes shut. "Relax, Artemer, I'm not going to hurt you." Ellora thought he sounded fairly amused, but she relaxed her body, rolling her shoulders backwards a few times and shaking her head. Imagine, on the top of your head, a purple ball of light." Hunter's voice was so smooth and calming, that Ellora relaxed and felt her troubles from the day melt away. Ellora hadn't even realised she had been swaying on her feet and jumped lightly in surprise when she felt Hunter's hands on the back of her shoulders to steady her. Her eyes snapped open.

"Did I tell you to open your eyes?" Hunter was sounding frustrated again, and Ellora closed her eyes once more.

"Imagine the purple light travelling downwards. Feel the warmth of the colour spread across you, warming you. Do you feel it?"

"I think so," Ellora answered.

"Then keep that feeling and open your eyes. Focus on the leaf." Hunter waited for Ellora to turn back to the leaf. "Feel the energy come to your hands and lift the leaf."

Ellora forced the energy out of her hands and to the leaf but shouted in frustration when it wouldn't move. "This is pointless." Her shoulders sunk in defeat.

"You just don't know how," he said in a surprisingly gentle voice. "Let me show you." Hunter reached out for Ellora's hand, and as soon as he touched her, she pulled her hand back in surprise.

Hunter frowned at her. "I'm not going to hurt you," he repeated. Although his words were harsh, his voice was gentle and Ellora somehow got the impression he was hurt.

"I *know* that," she stated. "You just surprised me, is all."

"Whatever. It's time for lunch, anyway." Hunter stood up quickly and left without looking at her.

Ellora spent her lunchtime sitting by the fountain. After watching Hunter storm off, her fatigue, both physical and mental, had hit her hard. She knew she didn't have the energy to engage in conversation, and the gardens would be deserted whilst everyone was eating.

She didn't know how much time had passed, but when Ellora opened her eyes and saw Belle walking out towards her, the skies opened wide and rain lashed over them.

"Wow, that completely came out of nowhere!" Belle panted and chuckled slightly after having sprinted inside with Ellora.

"I can't believe I have to change my clothes *again*," Ellora grumbled to Belle as they walked up the stairs. "Twice in one day!"

"If I had a little bit more practise, I would have been able to absorb the water from us and we wouldn't have to change right now," Belle sniffled, having caught a cold after getting drenched by the rain in the gardens.

"Trust us to get caught in that," Ellora said. "Apparently, today is not my day – I'm worried about what else will go wrong."

'Don't think like that, Ellie. I hereby grant you a pass from your day of unluck," she joked in a formal, Queen-like voice.

"Thanks, Bee, let's hope that worked," Ellora laughed.

"For the Spirits' sake, Hunter!"

"What in the Realms do you want me to do, Ellora?! I can't make it move any faster, now, can I?!"

Ellora scowled and crossed her arms over her chest, tapping her foot impatiently. Hunter looked over at her with narrowed eyes. "Will you *stop* with that stupid habit of yours! How do you expect me to make the blasted coffee machine work faster?!" Ellora realised she was being a bit unfair, but she was in too much of a bad mood to apologise. She clenched her teeth together and looked away at the ground.

After her second clothing change for the day and now with a bout of the sniffles, Ellora had been looking forward to a hot cup of coffee in the final few minutes of lunch, only to see those infuriating black locks blocking her path.

Ellora was dragged out of her train of thought when Hunter growled her name and thrust something before her. "Here," he said. Her eyes widened.

"What?" She was confused.

"You look like you need it more than I do." Hunter's face remained expressionless, but Ellora thought she saw something in his eyes that strangely resembled worry.

"Th-thank you," Ellora murmured, as she took the hot mug from his hands.

"Yeah, well, you look like Mistfall, so, you know," he replied impassively, but Ellora caught the side-glance he shot her and the way the corners of his lips lifted a tiny amount, and Ellora knew he was trying not to smile.

Ellora shot a fake glare at him but walked away without a response.

CHAPTER EIGHT

The Winter Ball

The days ticked by, and Mason still hadn't asked Ellora to go to the Winter Ball with him. At first, she had been upset, but she decided she didn't mind anymore. After all, most of her friends were going alone, so they decided to go as a big group. Even Hunter had been convinced to join them.

On the day of the ball, before meeting Melody, Belle and Clara to get ready, Ellora had one stop to make. She strolled over to the library, knowing that's where she would find him.

"Hey," Ellora said when she finally found Hunter between the stacks in the Human Fiction area. Hunter didn't reply but nodded his head in acknowledgement. She smiled at his engagement in this book he was reading. She had noticed he was like that often; he would be so invested in something, so interested, so... engrossed, that he would often be distant to the world around him. Although, Ellora could tell he was always, to some degree, aware of what was happening around him.

Their relationship had developed since they had started their private tutoring sessions, and whilst at first, Ellora thought they would be dreadfully awkward, she now looked forward to them. She had learnt to distinguish his emotions, as difficult as it was. His face rarely changed, but he often got an amused glint in his eye when he was teasing her; the corners of his mouth would tweak upwards slightly when he was trying not to laugh; his eyes narrowed ever so slightly when he felt suspicious. It was interesting to watch, interesting to observe.

"Um, so I... got you something," she mumbled. At that, Hunter's head snapped up and he raised an eyebrow in curiosity. "Well, today *is* your birthday, isn't it?" she asked.

"It is," he responded.

"You've been helping me a lot lately, Hunter. And I wanted to thank you. So, well ... here." She held out a small rectangular box covered in emerald green wrapping she had been holding behind her back.

Without removing his eyes from Ellora's face, he slowly reached out his hand and took the box from her, looking down at it uneasily. "Aren't you going to open it?" she asked, slightly amused at the suspicion on his face.

Ellora watched him as he meticulously peeled back the paper, leaving it neat and intact, before folding it and placing it to the side. He looked up at her, almost as if asking approval, before opening the box. Ellora watched him closely, holding her breath. He stared at its contents in silence and Ellora bit her cheeks to stop herself from laughing.

"Well?" she asked, attempting to look genuine. When his silence continued, she added, "you wear too much black."

"This is horrendous," Hunter spit out the words and Ellora could no longer prevent her laughter as a small giggle escaped.

Hunter stared at her in fear. "You don't actually expect me to wear this, do you?" And with that, Ellora's resistance was gone. She burst into laughter, tears flowing freely from her eyes. Luckily, everybody was preparing for the Winter Ball and nobody was around to hear her.

Then, slowly, the corners of Hunter's mouth lifted, and he was smiling. Before she knew it, the smile turned into laughter as she and Hunter laughed together. Ellora clutched her abdomen when the laughter became too much, and Hunter wiped tears from his eyes.

"Elle, zhank zhe spirits, we need to get ready! What in zhe Realms are you two laughing at?" Melody asked them when she came across the odd sight.

Without a word, Hunter lifted a garishly bright pink tie with neon green clouds on it, from the box, sending himself and Ellora into a fit of laughter once more.

"WHAT IS ZHAT?!" Ellora had to fight to avoid losing control once again at the look of disgust on Melody's face.

"It's a joke," she sighed, finally having stopped laughing. "Hunter, that's not your *real* gift." She waved her hand at the gift box in response to the confusion on Hunter's face. "It's a false bottom," she said.

He lifted the bottom of the box and lifted out another, but less garish, tie. It was a simple style in a baby pink colour.

"I wasn't kidding when I said you wear you wear too much black."

Belle had brought along her roommate Violet, and Clara had brought her roommate Hazel, who had brought her friend Leia to Ellora and Melody's room to get ready. All had gathered at around 4 pm, doing their hair and makeup, and were ready to leave by 8 pm.

"Wow," said Clara. "We all look amazing!" There was a round of laughter, as everyone nodded and mumbled their agreements.

All the girls were wearing a dress of a similar style, with flowy skirts. Oriel had told Ellora that that was the general expectation of a ball like this; a very traditional dress. Ellora looked at Belle, whose dress was a beautifully rich dark blue. "Wow, Elle. That silver really suits you, you know," said Belle.

The girls walked down to the ballroom, which Ellora had learned was through the massive double doors opposite the library. They walked through and looked around in awe.

Ellora had never seen such a huge, beautifully decorated room. The walls were painted a light, blue-grey colour, quite similar to the colour on Ellora's walls, and the ceiling was so high up, Ellora was sure there would be an echo in the room if it was empty. There were circular tables on the outskirts of the room, with light blue tablecloths draping each one. Each table was set with fancy blue dishes and gold cutlery.

Delicate blue garlands hung from the walls, and the ceiling had been enchanted to create the effect of water, reflecting the light of the room back into it and creating a gorgeous, glittering effect.

In the centre of the room was a giant dancefloor, where many people had already begun to Waltz. Through the moving shapes, Ellora recognised Oriel in a deep, velvety blue dress, which was swirling around as she danced with Master Rainclarke, who was dressed in a black suit with a tie that matched the colour Oriel's dress.

"You ladies are all looking very lovely." Dan smiled handsomely as he walked over to them. "Belle, would you like to dance?" he asked, holding out his hand and pulling her away.

Ellora looked around, hoping to see Mason but only caught sight of Hunter.

"Looking for someone?" he asked as he walked over to her.

"Nobody in particular," she replied. "You look very nice tonight, Hunter." Ellora fought the smile, but it immediately appeared when she saw he was wearing a black suit with a black shirt and a very familiar tie.

"Thank you. I could say the same about yourself," he replied, the corners of his mouth curving upwards slightly.

"I must say, your tie is particularly dashing," she joked. "Such a lovely shade of pink. Whoever chose it must have extremely good taste."

"She *does* have good taste," he replied, looking her up and down with that familiar twinge of amusement in his eyes. He paused for a moment, and Ellora watched as his eyes narrowed by barely a millimetre. She looked up at him challengingly, but her focus drifted to a point over his shoulder when she heard a familiar laugh. She looked out to see Mason dancing with a girl who looked absolutely stunning. She wore a black, tight dress with white patterns that brought out the colour of her long, silver hair. The tightness of the dress was a huge contrast in the ballroom full of ballgowns.

They looked so elegant dancing together, as if they were made for each other. Even their clothes matched; he was wearing a white suit with a black lapel and bow tie. Her smile was elegant as she looked up and laughed at something he had said. He smiled handsomely down at her.

Hunter, who seemed to have followed her gaze and apparently decided to distract her, courteously offered his arm, which she took, and led her to their group of friends.

"Who's that?" Ellora whispered privately to Melody, nodding her hair towards Mason's dance partner, when she let go of Hunter.

"*Zhat*," said Melody, "is Liviana de Beaumont, zhe Princess of France."

"Why haven't I seen her before?" asked Ellora.

"She's a Zhird Former, so she would not be in any of zhe same classes as us. Plus, Zhird Formers are always going on trips for zheir Aura training, so I would not be surprised if she is not around very much."

"Wow, who is that?" asked Leia.

"She's so pretty," said Violet. Hazel nodded her agreement.

When the song ended, Ellora saw Mason and Liviana bow to each other formally, before he offered his arm to her and led her to the side, where they continued their conversation.

Ellora gulped and looked down to the floor. "Elle, let us go and find our seats," said Melody, in an obvious attempt to distract her. She led her over to the set of tables on the left, looking for their names.

"I knew he just wanted to be friends with me," said Ellora.

"I don't know, Elle. 'E might just 'ave been dancing wizh 'er because zhey are friends. Besides, probablement zhey know each ozher; most royal families in zhe 'Uman Realm spend a lot of time wizh each ozher."

"I suppose."

Ellora, Clara and Melody found their seats at a round table with ten place settings around. Ellora looked for her name, which she found quickly.

All three of them turned around as a sickly sweet voice called out, "Melody, darling!" Melody was instantly wrapped in an embrace from the gorgeous girl who had earlier been standing next to Mason. They kissed each other on both cheeks. "'Ow are you? I didn't know you were 'ere; you should 'ave said."

"Liviana," Melody's reply didn't sound quite as enthusiastic. "You are right, I should 'ave told you. I just didn't 'ave zhe chance."

"Oh, well, your parents should 'ave said somezhing to my parents." Her smile was blinding. Melody's smile faltered, but she made sure to keep it plastered on her face. "And 'o are your friends?" she asked, just as Mason arrived.

"Ellora, there you are," he said. "Oh. Liviana, you've met Ellora then, I assume?"

Liviana's gaze turned sharply towards Ellora. "No, I do not believe I 'ave. Ellora, I 'ave 'eard much about you from our darling Mason over 'ere," she said as she placed a hand on his shoulder.

"Nice to meet you," Ellora said, snapping her eyes away from her hand to look at her face.

"Mason," said Hunter, as he walked up to stand next to Ellora.

"Hunter," he replied.

After a moment of silence, Liviana spoke again. "Well, it as been nice meeting you all. We must all speak more soon." At the exact moment she stopped speaking, Oriel's loud voice came through the speaker behind them. "Welcome to our annual Winter Ball, everybody." She stopped speaking as there was a round of applause. "We have had a few dances already, but I decided we would properly start this night off with a Human tradition." Another applause. "Maybe those of you who have joined us from the Incendi Kingdom will know this one; the Sadie Hawkins dance!" Everybody started bustling around and talking excitedly.

"Sadie 'Awkins?" asked Melody.

"That's the ladies' choice," whispered Clara. "Elle, now's your chance."

As if she had heard what Clara had said, although it would have been impossible over the sound of everybody talking, Liviana smiled directly at Ellora before turning to Mason. "You are my choice, Mason. Will you dance avec moi?"

"Uh ... sure," he said nervously before leading her to the dance floor.

Without thinking. Ellora turned to her left to find the first person she could and grabbed Hunter's arm. "Come on then, Hunter," she said, refusing to wallow in self-pity.

"Ellora, wha—"

"Ladies' choice. Let's dance!" she said, leading him towards the dance floor.

"Oh, Elle! Hunter, what are you guys doing?" Dan's surprised voice came from beside them.

"What does it look like? We're dancing," Ellora replied jokingly.

"Dancing? With each other?" Belle looked confused.

Ellora had no time to answer before the music started again. Ellora looked at Hunter, immediately regretting her decision. She was really bad at the Waltz. They all had to learn in Second and Third school, but she had never been any good. She took a deep, long breath and walked over to him, focusing on not stepping on his toes.

They each bowed and curtsied, as per tradition, before taking up their position. Ellora felt a bit nervous; she had never been this close to Hunter before. When she wasn't busy avoiding him or stalking him, every time they spoke, she got that intense headache. She reminded herself not to look into his eyes.

"Ready?" He was clearly referring to the fact that she had dragged him to the dance floor without waiting for his answer.

Ellora nodded, not even a little apologetic.

He led her in time with the music, as Ellora counted the beat in her head. 1 2 3, 1 2 3, 1 2 3, 1 2 3. She looked up at him and noticed that he had used some sort of product to tame his wild black hair. 1 2 3, 1 2 3. It looked rather silky. 1 2 3, 1 2 3.

She looked around her and smiled when she spotted Belle and Dan laughing. Suddenly, she realised she wasn't counting anymore. And she wasn't stepping on Hunter's feet either. "I'm doing it!" she whispered.

"Well, of course, you are," said Hunter, amused. "Don't tell me you asked me to dance without knowing how," he laughed.

Ellora blushed a bright pink colour. "Well, actually, I'm not very good at the Waltz. But maybe your talents make up for my lack of."

Ellora felt content on the dance floor, talking with Hunter. She felt relaxed like she never had before with him. She felt happy until the moment she spotted Mason and Liviana over Hunter's shoulder, laughing together. Hunter saw her change in gaze and turned to see what she was looking at.

He sighed. "I hope you're not jealous of her, Ellora," he said.

"What? Jealous? Of her? No way!" Ellora spluttered unconvincingly.

"You're jealous that she's with Mason, then?"

"No! Yes. Wait, no. I don't know," she groaned in frustration.

Hunter raised an eyebrow and she sighed. "That's not what it is. I'm not *jealous* of her. I just … I don't know. There's something about her that I really don't like."

"She's a princess," he said.

"Yeah, thanks for stating the obvious."

"No, what I meant was that she is a princess and all princes and princesses are royal… pains."

Ellora burst into laughter, causing some people to turn and look at her, but she didn't care. "Royal pains? Really Hunter?"

"What do you have against Mason, anyway?" she asked.

"He's … I just … know him."

The song ended sooner than Ellora cared to admit she hoped for, and she and Hunter awkwardly bowed and curtsied to one another, before walking back to the table.

"Nice dance?" asked Clara, a smirk on her face.

"Very," said Ellora.

"Hunter, this is Hazel, Leia and Violet," said Clara, gesturing towards the other girls sat at the table. "Girls, this is Hunter." They exchanged polite greetings.

"Who's Xavier Blunt?" asked Clara, reading the only missing name. before he went to take his seat between Hunter and Belle.

"Xavier?" Violet asked. "He's—"

"Violet? I think I'm sitting with you." An Australian accented voice came from behind Ellora.

"This is my twin brother, Xavier," introduced Violet.

They all turned to look at the boy, who took his seat between Ellora and Violet. He was very handsome and had dark skin and muscly arms. "Hi, everyone. Nice to meet you all properly." He smiled.

"Is purple not your style, then?" Clara asked jokingly, pointing at Violet's bright hair colour. Everyone laughed.

"Nah, that's not really my style," Xavier laughed.

When the next song ended, the dancers all took their seats while streams of waiters and waitresses walked in with food and drinks. Ellora took her seat between Hunter and Xavier. "Zay!" Dan cried as he came back to the table with Belle. "You're sitting with us?" At Xavier's nod, Dan smiled and patted the other boy on the back. "We're both Incendis," he explained.

Ellora looked to the other side of the room and saw Mason sitting next to Liviana. Liviana caught her eye and sent her a spiteful smile and wave that could easily be seen as innocent, but Ellora knew she was anything but.

She forced herself to turn back around as food and drinks were piled onto their table. In front of her was a bowl of lemongrass and mushroom soup, which Ellora thought tasted amazing. Belle refused to even try it since she hated mushrooms.

When they finished the soup, the main course of chicken lasagne arrived. Melody, being vegetarian, received a sun-dried tomato risotto instead. They all drank champagne from the chilled bottles on their tables as they ate and talked. Even Hunter was unnaturally talkative today.

"I've got a serious question for you, Xavier. You better answer me truthfully," said Dan, seriously.

"Oh. Sure, man. Ask me whatever," Xavier replied. His voice was confident, although Ellora thought he looked slightly nervous.

"Do you," he said, pausing dramatically as he looked into Xavier's eyes, "play snooker?"

Everybody chuckled.

"Wow, man. You really made me feel nervous there," Xavier laughed. "Yeah, I play a bit, but I'm nowhere near as good as my sister. Foosball is where my real talents lie."

"Violet, you play snooker?" said Ellora. She nodded. "Great, we have to play sometime! It's getting really boring constantly beating Dan."

"I let you win," Dan mumbled as he jokingly glared at Ellora.

"No, you don't, Dan," said Hunter. "I've played enough to know a rubbish player when I see one and you, mate, are pretty bad."

"Hunter, you play too?" asked Ellora, astonished. When Hunter confirmed that he used to play with his father at home, she insisted on playing a game with him. "Next week, come on," she whined.

"If it'll get you to stop begging, fine, I'll do it. But don't cry when you lose."

Ellora was about to give him a witty retort but was distracted when dessert was brought to them. They had a choice between blueberry mousse and crème brûlée. "All the food here is so fancy. I don't know what to choose," she said, thinking out loud.

"Go for the mousse," said Hunter. Ellora trusted him and put the mousse on her plate, which she loved, even finishing Melody's serving because she didn't like it.

"Did you guys hear about the birds?" Violet asked sadly.

"Birds?" asked Belle.

"It was awful!" said Melody. "I cannot believe someone would do zhat."

"Wait, what happened?" asked Dan.

"The pickatoos! They're a type of bird," said Violet.

"Zhey are so cute," added Melody. "Zhey are so small and zhey 'ave got zhese adorable red feazhers—"

"Well, they're cute until you get close to them. I think they're the only birds I know that have teeth!" Violet said. "And they really love to bite."

"But zhey did not deserve what 'appened to zhem!"

"No, they definitely didn't."

"They were killed," Hunter explained.

"Killed?!" Ellora asked.

"Yeah, our Ferri class were studying them and we found them like that a few days ago in the morning," said Violet.

"It was 'orrible." Melody frowned.

"Good evening, everyone. Again." Oriel interrupted them by spoke into the microphone once more. "I hope you have all enjoyed dinner. In a few minutes, the band will start playing again and the dancing will recommence."

"Well, I haven't danced yet. Anyone up for it?" asked Xavier.

"Yeah, I'll join you," said Clara. They both got up and went to take their position on the dancefloor.

"On that note, Belle?" Dan stood up and held out his hand, which Belle took. They walked over to the dancefloor, leaving six at the table.

"Is it just moi, or do Xavier and Clara look like a very cute couple?" said Melody. Ellora and Violet both simultaneously burst into laughter. "What? Why is zhat funny?" Melody asked.

"Well, I don't really think Clara is Xavier's type," Violet chuckled.

"Yeah, and Xavier is *definitely* not Clara's type."

"What do you mean?" asked Leia.

Before either of them could reply, Mason walked over and sat in the chair previously occupied by Xavier. "Oh. Mason," said Ellora. She looked to the other side of the room to see Liviana surrounded by a group of girls, sending her a death glare. This made Ellora smile.

"You want to dance?" asked Mason.

"Oh," she hesitated, turning to look at Hunter, who seemed too focused on his Purple Wine than to notice her and Mason. She shook her head slightly. "Sure," she answered. He stood up and led her to the dance floor just in time for the next dance.

When the music started, Ellora realised it wasn't the Waltz they would be dancing to; it was the Foxtrot. She smiled; she was good at this one.

Ellora and Mason started their dance in silence, neither of them knowing how to start the conversation.

"So, Liviana," Ellora started. "She seems nice."

"She is; I've known her for almost my whole life," replied Mason. "We grew up together; our families are friends. Actually, we used to spend a lot of time in England when we were in the Human Realm. I all but grew up there! My parents still are very close with King and Queen Winnashire, so we had a Gate that led directly from our palace to theirs. I'm sure you know of them?" he asked.

"Of course!" Ellora answered. "The King and Queen of England. How could I *not* know them?"

"Yes, they are rather lovely people," Mason said.

"Didn't they have a son?" Ellora asked, thinking back to her childhood. She would never admit it, but Ellora used to have quite a crush on the prince when she was younger. But after a while, he stopped appearing in the royal photos. The press had reported that the King and Queen wanted him to live a normal childhood. If he continued to be photographed, he would be unable to leave the grounds alone, to go to school, to even go to a park. Ellora understood why they did it, but she did wonder what the boy would be like now.

Mason looked at her with a frown, before his face relaxed and he let out a small chuckle. "What's so funny?" Ellora asked.

"Nothing," Mason replied, still looking amused. "You asked about the prince, did you not? Yes, I would say he is about your age. I grew up with him. That's why I have a British accent, you see. But Liviana spent a lot more time in France than she did in the Glassi Kingdom, her being next in line to the throne and all."

"Oh, I see."

"Anyway, we've known each other forever, but we are just friends." He smoothly answered the unasked question plainly written across her face.

"Are you sure she knows that?" She felt instantly relieved and they both laughed.

Ellora was enjoying the Foxtrot for all of two minutes before they danced past Liviana's table and she caught the words, "As if I would be jealous. He's the Prince of Japan; there's no way he would give a *commoner* like her the time of day!" As soon as she heard the words, she froze. She felt herself go rigid and stopped on the dancefloor.

"Elle, what's wrong?" Mason asked worriedly, pulling her to the side so she could sit down.

"Nothing. I just ... nothing. I'm sorry, Mason, I need to go ... um ... to the bathroom," she said before walking quickly out of the room and towards the stairs. She sat down on the stairs and willed herself not to cry.

"Elle?" Melody's caring voice called out.

"I'm here," said Ellora, glumly.

"What is wrong?"

"Mason is the Prince of Japan and Liviana's the Princess of France."

"Your point being?"

"I'm not a princess! Is he even *allowed* to date me?!"

"Oh, well, now I *know* Liviana 'as gotten under your skin. Really, Elle, you should not listen to 'er. She's just a stuck-up Snorfuffle. Zhere are no rules about zhis sort of zhing, and you cannot let 'er convince you ozherwise. If you like 'im, you cannot let 'er get in between you, okay?"

"I thought you were friends with her," said Ellora.

"*Me*? Friends with '*er*? You must be joking," Melody scoffed.

"But earlier—"

"I know what 'appened earlier. Zhat was just Liviana being 'er fake self. Zhe truth is, Elle, my parents *work* for 'er. Zhey work in one of 'er gazillion castles and so she 'zhinks she is better zhan zhem; better zhan me. But zhere is *no* way I am letting 'er ruin my life. So zhat is why I am ere; I got into zhe best Aura School zhere is, just like she did, except I got in because of me, not because my daddy forced Oriel to let me in. I am going to make somezhing of myself. I am going to get my parents away from 'er nightmare castle and I am going to prove zhat I can be zhe better person," she said, determinedly.

"You're right, Melody," said Ellora, attempting to put a smile on her face but not feeling up for much more socialising. "I'm just going to step out for a breath of air quickly. I'll see you back in there.

Ellora watched as Melody walked back into the dining room and back to the table. Ellora knew she should apologise to Mason, but for now, she didn't want to look for him. She decided to find him later. She took a few moments to collect herself and force Liviana from her mind before joining her friends back at the table.

"Where's Hunter?" she asked Hazel as they arrived back at the table.

"Oh, he left right after you went to dance with Mason. Said he had a headache."

Before Ellora could ask any more questions, Oriel walked over to them.

"Ellora, darling, you look gorgeous!" When she called Ellora 'darling', it sounded so much sweeter than when Liviana had done the same to Melody. "In fact, you all look magnificent." She smiled at them all.

"I hope you're all having a lovely time at your first Madori Ball. You'll come to know as the years go by that I *love* hosting these events regularly, so make sure to have dresses ready," she laughed with them.

"Oriel!" Julia, their Prefect ran over. "Oriel, I think some of the First Years have had a bit too much to drink. Some of the boys are out in the corridor and I can't get them up to bed." She smiled apologetically for interrupting.

"Oh, Spirits. Why does this happen every year?" She groaned.

Luckily, Rainclarke was nearby talking to Graynor. "I'll take care of it, Oriel. Don't worry," he said when he walked over.

"Thank you, Noah," Oriel replied before he left to take care of the students, and she walked over to Mistress Maywether, who seemed to have drunk a little too much.

"Ellora, you look so nice," said Julia with a smile.

"Thanks, Julia, so do you!" she exclaimed at the sight of Julia's lavender-coloured dress.

"Hi, I'm Julia." Julia held her hand out for Dan to shake.

"Dan," he responded as he took her hand.

"Oh, I thought the two of you knew each other," Ellora said, thinking back to the conversation she had heard between them all that time ago.

"Um..." Julia hesitated slightly, turning around to look over at Belle before replying, "No. No, I don't."

Julia looked like she was about to say something else, when suddenly her phone chimed. She looked down and frowned. "Sorry, I have to go. Apparently, one of my friends is also too drunk to get up to her room," she said before rushing out of the room.

Belle frowned. "Dan, why were you and Julia acting like you didn't know each other?"

"What?" Dan's eyes grew wider. "Because we *don't* know each other," he insisted.

"Dan, about two weeks ago when we were walking to the gardens and we ran into Julia, you gave each other a *look*. And she nodded to you. Why would she do that if you were a stranger?"

"A look? And a nod? Belle, I think you're overthinking a little bit." He frowned, but his cheeks had been tinged a light pink colour.

"Last night. Last night, Dan, you were supposed to meet me by the East Courtyard, but I decided to try to find you because you were running late. I *heard* you talking to Julia! You called her an angel." She shook her head and paced a little, her hands on her hips. "I wasn't sure at the time, but now I am – that was Julia."

"Belle, babe, come on—"

"Daniel Pinter, I am not an idiot. You had better tell me the *truth*."

"Belle, you're overreacting!" He exclaimed.

"That's rubbish, Daniel. Tell me. *Now.*"

Ellora watched as Dan hesitated. He looked nervous and he was rubbing his sweaty palms on his dress trousers. Belle's eyes filled with silent tears as Dan remained silent, and it was all Ellora could do not to slap the boy in the face.

"That's it, then," Belle whispered before she ran out. Ellora followed, but before either of them could leave, a scream pierced through the ballroom. Everybody stopped talking, the band stopped playing and the dancers stopped dancing to look at what was going on. Ellora looked over to where the scream had come from to see Mistress Maywether, hand covering her mouth, looking down to the floor. Ellora pushed through the crowd to see what was going on.

It was Oriel.

CHAPTER NINE
Solstice

Everything happened so quickly. One moment, Ellora was standing frozen before Oriel, looking as she laid on the floor, pale and sweaty. Her face was contorted in such a way, that it looked like she had passed out from pain, clutching her head between her hands.

The next moment, Master Rainclarke was crouched in front of Oriel, blocking her from view. And the next moment, she was gone, and the crowd had vanished.

"Ellora?" A gentle voice pulled at her mind. "Ellora?" it repeated.

"Asyra?" Ellora thought loudly. "Is that you?"

"Yes, dear."

"Is Oriel alright?" Ellora asked immediately.

"She will be," answered Asyra. "I need to see you as soon as possible."

"I'll be there tonight. After I check on Oriel." And with that, Ellora erected her mental boundaries, not in the mood for any disagreement.

First, Ellora took Belle up to her bed and sat with her as she cried. It didn't take long for Belle to fall asleep clinging on to her, but Ellora gently lowered her to the bed and left to go to the infirmary.

She knocked tentatively on the door to the private room and poked her head in. "Mistress Oriel? Are you alright?"

"Ellora!" The voice that responded was weak. "Come in darling, please." Ellora crept in and took a seat next to the bed in which Oriel was lying.

"How are you?" Ellora asked.

"Ah, Healer Amare says I'll be fine. I just need some rest. I'll be out of here on Monday." She smiled reassuringly, but the smile didn't reach her eyes. A pang echoed through Ellora, when she realised in that moment that Oriel's smile reminded her so much of how her own mother smiled now; hollow and empty.

"What happened?" Ellora asked, ridding herself of the thought.- "Oh, don't worry about that Elle. What I want to know, however, is how you and I are going to have our tea tomorrow!" Ellora smiled at that, as she thought fondly about all of their tea meetings over the past months.

"I'm sure I can sneak some tea past Healer Amare." Ellora smiled brightly.

The two chatted for a few minutes, but with every second that passed Oriel seemed more tired, and Ellora left her to rest, feeling relieved that she was all right. It was time to see Asyra.

"Asyra?" she called aloud, when she walked to the lake, a cup of well needed hot chocolate in hand. "Sorry, I had to make a stop for this, but I managed to see Oriel."

"Ellora, welcome back." Asyra rose from the water as Ellora settled down to the grass and bundled her coat around her.

"What's going on?" Ellora asked, ready to hear everything.

"Oriel fainted because she felt a great force in the castle." Asyra projected the words directly into Ellora's brain. "Do you remember when I was telling you about the Cores of the Kingdoms? Of the

Auras?" Ellora nodded silently, not wanting to interrupt. "Well, each Core is also linked to its Master or Mistress. Oriel is linked with the Madori Orb. Do you understand?"

"So ... there's something called the Madori Orb, which powers the entire Kingdom and its Aura, and Mistress Oriel is linked to it?"

"So, you do understand. Brilliant. That will make it a lot easier to explain this time around."

"This time? Who else have you told?"

"That doesn't matter, my dear." Asyra had answered too quickly for Ellora's liking. Who had she told? And why wouldn't she tell Ellora? Ellora narrowed her eyes suspiciously, but Asyra spoke before she could insist on being told who else was privy to this secret. "What's important is that the Orb has been taken. That is why Oriel fainted."

"Taken? What do you mean taken? By whom? Why?"

"That is the problem. I do not know who has taken it and I do not know why. What I do know, however, is that the Orb can be used in a very dangerous way if it is taken by the wrong people."

"Well ... what ... who ... why would anybody need it? Who would take it? And what for?!" Ellora stammered out.

"The Orb can only be fully wielded by Oriel, as the Madori Mistress, but another Madori Aurum can still manage a lot of harm. As for why..." Asyra's voice trailed off and Ellora knew that was not a good sign.

"Asyra," Ellora began, "Winter break is starting soon. What if somebody tries to sneak out the Orb?"

"Ah, that's not a problem, dear. I'm sure Oriel has already decided that she will stand by the entrance whilst everyone is leaving. She would be able to sense it if somebody tried to take the Orb away from the castle boundaries, you know, and anybody with enough information to steal the Orb would know better than to take it with Oriel standing right there."

"Why didn't they take it tonight?" Ellora pressed further.

"I am quite certain that whoever took it, *did* intend to take it tonight. They would have been unaware of exactly how much energy it would have taken to remove the Orb, with the amount of protection surrounding it. In fact, I'm impressed they managed to get it out at all."

"*Impressed*?" Ellora spat out the word as if it was a disgusting taste in her mouth.

"There's no need to get upset, Ellora. I am impressed, but that doesn't mean I condone it."

"How will they get it out, then?" Ellora blurted out the question to stop herself from saying anything stupid to the most powerful being in the Kingdom.

"Well, Ellora, the only other way I can think of that would be accessible for students would be the Gate."

"Gate, like between the Human and Aura Realms?" Ellora asked.

"Yes," Asyra answered. "The Madori School of Aura has a Gate Room. The miniature Gates in this room cannot transport a vehicle, like the ones you must be accustomed to, however it can transport one person at a time. There are Gates in that room that lead to different areas of the Human Realm, as well as each Kingdom in this one. Well, and there is one more Gate in there, but that one is sealed on the other side; it is only one-way, and for obvious reasons."

"Wh-which Gate is that?" Ellora asked, almost afraid of the answer.

"It goes to The Under."

Ellora's mouth dropped. "The Under?" she asked. "Like, the place where all the dead people go?"

Asyra replied with a mere "Yes."

"Does it go to the... nicer side? To Paradise? Or..."

"It goes to Mistfall," Asyra answered, matter-of-factly. Ellora swallowed thickly.

"Oh, Spirits... I mean... you... it would be disastrous if they got into the Gate Room!" Ellora was terrified.

"Only Oriel has the key, Ellora, so I see that unlikely for the time being."

"Well ... what's going to happen?" Ellora asked, unsure of why Asyra was even telling her this. And why her, of all people.

"From my lake, there is not much I can do, my dear. That is why I am asking you for your help. You must help me save our Kingdom. Help me, help Oriel. Help us all."

"Why me?" Ellora looked up at Asyra, feeling slightly scared and confused

"Because I trust you, Ellora Artemer."

*

The night before the Winter Solstice, Clara had fought with the kitchen staff to get some hot chocolate with plenty of whipped cream and what seemed like endless amounts of mini marshmallows, four tubs of Moonrock Ice Cream, with massive ice cream scoops in place of spoons and had even brought a tin of Star Cakes that her mother had sent her from the Incendi Kingdom.

Belle devoured the Moonrock Ice Cream in silence, her empty eyes staring at the blank screen on her TV. Ellora had been especially worried about her; she had been having all of her meals in her bedroom since she broke up with Dan and was actively avoiding him, whilst Ellora knew Dan was actively seeking her out to provide her with an explanation. Classes had been cancelled for the week, following the theft of the Orb, and Dan had been going crazy without seeing Belle. Ellora sat next to her now, refusing to leave her side as she drank the hot chocolate and ate two of Clara's Star Cakes.

She loved Star Cakes and hadn't had any in years; she liked how no two cakes would be alike, because they all depended on the stardust they were made from. The first one she ate was sweet and chocolatey, and the next was more like vanilla.

"Did you hear?" asked Violet. "About the leitocks in the Ferri sanctuary?"

"What in the Realms is a *leitock*?" asked Leia.

"Only the cutest animal ever!" answered Clara. "Imagine the body of a penguin from the Human Realm, with the head of a kitten. Absolutely adorable!"

"It sounds...interesting," Leia replied, and Ellora struggled to hold back her laughter at the look on Leia's face.

"It sounds scary," Ellora said when she got her stifled giggles in order, "but when you see one, you'll see how cute they are!"

"What 'appened to zhem?" Melody asked urgently. Ellora was surprised she didn't know since she was a Ferri Aurum herself.

"Well, I spoke to Henry today, and he told me that apparently, the leitocks in the sanctuary went crazy this morning! They were running around attacking each other! The Ferri Prefects had to sedate them, apparently," Violet answered.

"What?!" Melody cried. "But leitocks are some of zhe most peaceful creatures in zhe entire Realm!"

"I know," replied Violet, with a grimace.

"I wonder what happened to make them go crazy like that," added Clara.

On the afternoon of the Winter Solstice, Ellora still had no idea where to start in looking for the culprit. In three days, she and lots of others would be heading home for the Winter Break. That didn't give her a lot of time. She had hoped to make some sort of a breakthrough before most of the suspects left the building.

Despite spending every free moment in the library, Ellora had still not found anything on the Orb and the days were ticking by. She thought that with each day that passed, the thief got closer to escaping. She had gone to all of her lessons; she had gone to her extra sessions with the teachers; she had attended all meals; she had continued to practise meditation; she had seen Oriel daily. And yet, somehow, she had still spent hours poring over books in the library to find the answer. And, yet, she could find nothing.

And now, Ellora was standing in her room, looking at herself in the mirror, and trying to just freeze all of the emotions swirling around her head.

She felt guilty, because she hadn't discovered *anything* about the Orb.

She felt sad, because she hadn't had the time to see Mason, or even have a proper conversation with Hunter, let alone have an extra tutoring session with him.

She felt awful, because there was nothing she could do to help her best friend.

She felt tired. Just tired.

But here she was, standing in front of her mirror in the most beautiful dress she had ever seen. It wasn't a ballgown like she had worn at the Winter Ball a week ago, but the Winter Solstice Celebration was still a black-tie event, so she wore a long, silver, one-shouldered dress. It was a soft silver, a light silver and it matched her deep skin tone perfectly, her brown, curly hair cascading down her shoulders to graze the fabric. Her makeup was simple, but glamorous – gold eyeshadow, thin, winged eyeliner, gentle blush and a delicate lipstick.

She smiled at herself in the mirror, something she always did before leaving the house.

"Wow," Melody said from behind her. "You look ... wow," she repeated. "Très magnifique."

Ellora blushed; she never was very good at accepting compliments. "Wow yourself," she replied. Melody was wearing a beautiful deep green dress that hit her knees. "We ready to go?"

"Yes. Just ..." She paused as she sprayed her favourite, fruity perfume in the air in front of them and they both dramatically and jokingly danced through the mist, laughing with each other. "And now we are ready," Melody said, slightly rolling the 'r' in 'ready'.

They walked down together, having agreed to meet the others in the room that had acted as the ballroom for the Winter Ball. A beautiful sight greeted them as they walked through the tall double doors, with bright chandeliers and long tables filled with pastries and steamed vegetables and risotto and chicken and steak and countless other dishes and the Aura Realm speciality – Purple Wine – and Strawberry Juice and Champagne.

"Hey!" Leia waved the two over to their group and Ellora bumped Belle's shoulder and sent her a smile when she arrived. She also searched the room for Hunter, as he and Dan hadn't turned up to any meals for the past week.

Then, she spotted him. He looked handsome in his black suit and silver tie; she always did think black suited him. He was headed towards them. With Dan.

Ellora immediately put her black purse down on the table and hurried over to the pair as quick as she could in her tall, black stilettos.

"What do you think you're doing?" she demanded, prodding her finger into the silk of Dan's light blue shirt at his chest. "Don't you think you've hurt her enough? She trusted you! She does *not* want to see you. I practically had to force her to come tonight!" She growled at him.

"Elle—"

"Dan, seriously, I want to hear your side of the story, but now is not the time."

"Elle, I need to speak with her."

"Seriously, mate, can you not see how heartbroken she is?"

"Ellora." She stopped immediately when Hunter addressed her, "I think you'll want to hear what Daniel has to say."

Dan didn't speak, but he pulled a long, velvet-covered box from his blazer pocket.

"What's that?" Ellora demanded.

"A gift," said Dan. "For Belle. That's why I was talking to Julia. I asked her to get it for me. It's made of Redmer, a stone enchanted to protect its wearer."

"Oh." Ellora could think of nothing else to say. Luckily, she didn't need to, because Belle was standing behind her.

"I wanted to give it to you sooner, Belle, but the stone is twice as effective if presented to the wearer on an auspicious day. I really wanted it to be a surprise, but when I realised you were serious about breaking things off, I just wanted to explain everything to her. I understand why you've been avoiding me, but do you think you could forgive me? Please?"

Belle immediately broke into tears. "Dan, I'm so sorry," she said. "I'm so sorry, Dan, I'm so sorry. I knew you wouldn't hurt me; I knew it. I just didn't understand why you wouldn't tell me."

"I know, Belle. I just wanted it to protect you. I just wanted to give this to you for Winter Solstice this year. I know you've always loved these crystals and I was finally able to get you some. I should have explained it to you last week, though. This is entirely my fault."

"What do you think?" Hunter asked Ellora, standing next to her and watching her two friends.

"I'm so glad," she sighed in relief. "You have no idea how much it broke my heart to have thought he was cheating on her. And how hard it has been to stay away from him this past week. But you should have seen how much of a mess Belle was; I couldn't leave her. I'm glad he has you, Hunter," Ellora said, as she looked up at him sincerely.

"Yes. Thank you. I'm glad they've worked things out, I mean... they're the perfect couple. Look, they even ended up matching their clothes by accident," Hunter said, pointing out the similarities in colour between Dan's golden tie and Belle's golden dress.

"Yeah, I guess you're right," answered Ellora with a small smile.

"Elle." Another voice interrupted Ellora's train of thought. She turned around to see Mason in yet another beautiful white suit. "I've missed you this past week." He shot her a dazzling smile.

"Oh, please, I'm sure you say that to all the girls," Ellora joked.

"Only the beautiful ones. You know, your smile really lights up the room," he said quietly. Ellora blushed.

"My mother used to say that to me," Ellora replied.

Can I escort you to your seat?" he asked.

Ellora hesitated and looked to where Hunter had been standing beside her just a moment ago. But he wasn't there. In fact, he was behind her, talking to Violet, who was smiling at him and blushing slightly.

Ellora frowned but shook her head slightly and turned back to Mason. "Thank you," she answered.

Ellora sat opposite Belle and between Mason and Hunter and spent the entire meal trying to avoid looking at Liviana and her posse, who were all glaring at her with more hatred than she had ever seen in her life.

She couldn't help feeling a little jealous of Liviana, who was wearing a beautiful black dress with lace detailing across it.

"Hey, you two are matching!" Announced Daphne Darkwater, a girl in their Form who Ellora knew from Fourth school, who was sitting a few seats over.

Ellora looked down at her dress and next to her, at Mason, but she didn't know what Daphne was talking about.

"You and *Hunter*, Ellora." Added Allison Baird, Daphne's best friend.

As if it was rehearsed, Hunter and Ellora both looked at each other's clothes before looking down at their own in perfect sync. When their eyes met for a split-second, Ellora blushed slightly, and Hunter cleared his throat before they both quickly looked away from each other.

"You guys didn't plan that?" Daphne asked.

"Oh ... Um ... No," Ellora said lamely, feeling slightly awkward that Hunter hadn't uttered a single word to her since they sat down.

"If I can have your attention, everyone!" Oriel called from the front of the room and, almost simultaneously, Hunter and Ellora let out small sighs of relief. "I hope you all enjoyed the meal," Oriel said. "I don't want to take up much time. I just have a few announcements. First of all, I want to wish you all a very happy and safe Winter Break, whether you are planning to go home or stay here. And finally, I just want to wish you all a very, very joyous Winter Solstice." And with that, everyone clapped politely.

Ellora excused herself from Mason and her friends, as she headed to the bathroom before the ballroom. She was washing her hands when she heard loud voices outside the door, before it swung open.

"Well, well, look at what zhe cat dragged in."

Ellora groaned at the sound of that voice.

"Ellora Artemer. You looked like you were 'aving an awfully nice time with *Prince* Mason back zhere." Liviana spoke quietly, in her voice she kept low, yet elegant and threatening all at once.

"I was, thank you," Ellora replied politely before trying to get out of the bathroom. One of Liviana's minions blocked her way before she could get to the door.

"Just remember, darling, 'e is a prince. You are nobody. Do not get your 'opes up; 'e would never settle for somezhing like you," Liviana said. "Even if 'e *does* 'ave to spend zhe evening with you."

Ellora narrowed her eyes at Liviana's last statement but convinced herself not to believe Liviana; she was trying to fill her mind with doubts *again*. She took a deep breath and kept her head high. "Well, *darling*, I'm sure if I am the one with whom he wishes to sit, it says more about you than it does me." Even though she had kept her voice steady and confident, as soon as she strode out of the bathroom, Ellora felt like she was going to be sick.

"There you are." Mason put his arms around her shoulders when she found him in the hall. She smiled at him briefly, but the smile didn't quite reach her eyes. "Would you like to go for a stroll?" he asked.

"Oh, um, actually could we go a bit later? I'm just not feeling very well at the moment," Ellora replied. She felt sick to her stomach she was actually feeling envious of Liviana right now.

"Are you alright?" he asked.

"Yeah, I'm fine. Just have a bit of a headache. I just need a drink," Ellora replied.

"I'll go and find you some water."

Ellora sat and looked down at her fingers, playing with the silver ring on her middle finger. The ring used to belong to her mother, and she had gifted it to her when she was very young; ever since Ellora could remember she had been entranced by that ring and her mother had given it to her when she was too small for it to even fit her yet. But now, it fit her, and she twisted it around and around.

"Are you alright?" Hunter asked as he sat next to her. "You're looking pale."

"Ever the charmer," Ellora joked, but Hunter continued to look concerned. "I'm fine, Hunter, really. I just have a bit of a headache."

"Well, would you like me to walk you up to your room?" he asked cordially.

"Thanks, but it's alright; Mason has gone to get me some water so I'm sure I'll be..." She trailed off when she caught sight of Liviana entering the room.

Hunter followed her gaze and frowned, before asking, "Has Liviana done something?"

"Is it that obvious?" Ellora asked. "I just can't stop thinking about something she said."

"Hmm, let me guess – something about you being a commoner or a peasant or just not a princess, like she is?"

"How did you know?"

"Because the girl is a stuck-up snob who cares about nothing more than her crown," Hunter laughed softly, but Ellora could tell his mind was somewhere else, occupied in other things. "Trust me, you shouldn't listen to a single thing she says."

"But how do you know? What if she's right? I mean ... I can't do princess things like carry books on my head or ... ride a horse sideways." That actually attracted Hunter's full attention and made him laugh.

"Look, if Mason turns you down because of either of those things, first of all, he's an idiot because nobody can do those things. And second of all, he really doesn't deserve you. In fact, if things don't work out it would absolutely be his loss, because you are something special, Ellora Artemer. Don't forget that." His friendly smile turned into something a bit more serious, before he stood up and walked away just as Mason reappeared.

"You look a bit better, Ellora," he said, the relief clear on his face. Mason had insisted that she looked better and insisted a bit of fresh air would do her good.

Ellora, somewhat reluctantly, agreed and walked out with him, her hand tucked into the crook of his arm. He led her up staircase after staircase and, eventually, she had to remove her heels to finish the journey.

"Voila," he said dramatically as he opened one final door for her that led outside to a very large rooftop.

Ellora gasped as she looked around her. The tiny little door she had stepped through seemed to lead to an endlessly large space. "This is gorgeous! What is this place?"

"The secret rooftop gardens. It's only accessible to the Prefects, so that we have a place for some peace and since I have invited you, you can see it too. Not many people know about it," Mason replied smugly. "I thought you might like to see it."

"You thought right," she answered before walking over to the edge and looking down at the beautiful sight. They were surrounded by water, of course, but the enchantments made it look, as Melody put it, magnifique.

"This is my favourite part." Mason interrupted her thought and drew her attention to a large wall of white lilies that seemed to glitter under the moonlight. She followed him to the wall only to realise it was the entrance to a maze. "Some of the Ferri Prefects decided to grow it a few years back; they don't get a lot of creative freedom in the gardens downstairs, but here we can all do as we like. And every year, the new Ferri Prefects maintain and add to it," Mason explained, as they began their stroll through the flowers. Ellora looked at each rare blossom in awe.

Ellora turned around to look at him, and there he was, standing only centimetres away from her. He had an intense, warm look in his eye as he bent down towards her. And without thinking, without worrying, Ellora wrapped her arms around his neck and dragged his face down to meet hers. And she kissed him.

It could have been hours, it could have been a mere few seconds, but when the two broke apart again, neither could wipe the smiles from their faces.

"How was the Main Land the other day?" Ellora asked, her hand in his, as they began their second stroll through. "I feel like I haven't been out of this place in years."

"It was alright. Julia and I had loads of things to get for Oriel, so we spent most of our time shopping in really random and out-of-the-way shops, looking for things I'd never even heard of! Like she wanted something called a 'bambonut plant'. What even is that? We couldn't find one no matter where we went!"

"Wow, I wonder why she wanted many obscure items," Ellora said, knowing it must have been related to the Orb.

"I don't know, but I hope she doesn't send us on these shopping trips for too long; I'm exhausted," he sighed, running his hand through his shaggy hair. "We had to leave at 6 in the morning and only came back at midnight. Plus, I had to deal with Julia." He rolled his eyes.

"What's wrong with Julia? I thought she seemed really nice." Ellora said.

"She's great, usually. But lately, she's just been so stressed out. I think something happened with her family. Somewhere near the start of term, she visited some family while we were at the Main Land and since then, she's been ... off. I think her aunt is really sick, or something." He looked sad as he told her.

"Oh no, Mason, that's awful. Poor Julia, she must be struggling."

"I think she is. Anyway, I'll talk to her and see if I can help in some way."

After their slow and barefoot stroll through the maze and a long chat under the night sky, Mason walked Ellora back to her corridor and left her again, after a few more minutes of kissing. Ellora definitely had a wide smile on her face, as she drifted off to sleep. That is, until Melody stormed in, slamming the door shut behind her.

"Melody?" Ellora jumped up in her bed. "What's wrong?"

"Zhe leitocks, Ellora," Melody answered, as if that explained it all.

"What about the leitocks?"

"Zhey are dead."

"Dead? I thought they had all been separated."

"Zhey 'ad been. But somebody killed zhem."

"Somebody?" Ellora was wide awake now.

"Somebody in our school *murdered* poor, innocent little animals!" Without warning, Melody covered her mouth with her hands and ran to the bathroom to throw up. She came back out with tears streaming down her face, and Ellora realised what had happened. The animals had not only been killed, but Melody had been the one to find them.

*

Saturday came, and Ellora left the school side by side with Dan, along with the large group of students also going home. Melody had left earlier, and Ellora was grateful. She was still upset at the scene she had found the night of the Winter Solstice, even if she was pretending otherwise, and Ellora thought a couple of days with her family would do her some good.

Ellora smiled and said goodbye to Oriel who, as promised, was standing by the door and smiling at each student who walked past.

Her journey home seemed shorter than it really was, and whilst she knew she would only be there for 48 hours, she was already eager to get back.

CHAPTER TEN
New Year's

The moment Ellora had walked through the doors of the school, she saw a group of unusual people dressed in oddly coloured clothing walking into the library, presumably to Oriel's office. One woman had been wearing a red suit and one man was wearing a pink blazer. A lady in the orange had looked especially unsettled.

Ellora was confused at the grave and serious looks on their faces, and she made a note to ask Oriel the next time she saw her and went up to her room, where Melody was already unpacking the three suitcases she had taken home. "Spirits, how much did you take home with you?!" asked Ellora from the doorway.

"Elle, you are back!" Melody said as she ran to give her roommate a hug. "I am so 'appy to be back again — zhe Glassi Kingdom was so boring. But at least maman and papa 'ad zhe time away from Liviana's clutches," she said, pulling a face. "Ow was 'ome?"

"Fine thanks," replied Ellora, automatically, attempting a natural smile.

"I zhink zhe ozhers are waiting for us in zhe common room," said Melody, abandoning her bag and leading Ellora out into the corridor.

None of the group realised they had been catching up for so long, until Clara's stomach grumbled. She blushed slightly and laughed, "I guess I'm hungry."

"Well, I am not surprised; you said you skipped lunch and it is already almost time for dinner!" said Melody. And with that, the five headed to dinner. Ellora tried not to think about the fact that she hadn't seen Hunter since she had come back, and instead tried to focus on seeing Mason again.

They walked to the dining room around ten minutes early, at 8.50 pm, to be the first ones to arrive. Dinner was being held late today, due to the travelling. Ellora, being at the front of her group of friends, was the one to open the door. When she saw their jaws drop open, she turned out to see what they were looking at. The dining room was filled with water.

It was like a block of jelly, only it was moving around, like someone had placed a barrier at the door to stop it from flowing out.

"I'll find Oriel," Ellora suggested. "You guys stay here and make sure nobody tries anything stupid." Her friends nodded, and Ellora set off for Oriel's office.

She saw Hunter in the hall and was about to call for him, but he turned around and left before she could. She frowned at him but went to find Oriel without delay. On her way to Oriel's office, she ran past the same group of people she had seen earlier.

"My cow! It took my cow!" cried the woman in the orange suit, as the group walked out of the library.

Ellora continued on, through to the familiar oak door that sat in a hidden alcove. She was about to knock on the door, when she heard voices inside.

"What can I do, Noah?" Ellora recognised Oriel's voice, but it seemed different now, quiet. She sounded scared. "It's my responsibility and I just don't know what to do." Her voice broke and Ellora peeked through the little crack in the doorway to see her Madori Mistress sitting on one of the leather armchairs with her face buried in her hands. She saw her Incendi teacher reach over to place a hand on one of her shaking shoulders.

"Oriel, it'll be okay. We will find the Orb and we will find whoever is doing this to our Kingdoms; they cannot be this careful forever." Ellora thought Master Rainclarke sounded like a completely different person; he sounded scared, too, as he comfortingly patted her shoulder.

"I know, Noah. We'll find them. But if we don't get the Orb back ... the sacred oath—"

"I know, Oriel. I will do whatever it takes to get it back. I will not let you die." Ellora froze. She didn't know that the Orb being taken would lead to her Madori Mistress's death. She felt a small twinge of anger thinking about being kept in the dark by Asyra. And then fear.

"Hey, Elle, what are you doing here?" Mason's voice nearly made Ellora jump out of her skin. She heard shuffling in Oriel's office and prayed to the Spirits they didn't know she had heard them. She took a deep breath to stop her voice from trembling and plastered a smile on her face before turning around.

"Oh, hey, Mason! I was just going to tell Mistress Oriel there's something wrong in the First Form Dining Hall," she said in the most normal voice she could manage. "What are you doing here?"

"The same thing, actually, someone from your form found Julia and I on the way to dinner; I came to let Oriel know."

"Let me know what, exactly?" Oriel and Rainclarke emerged from her office. The only signs of the conversation Ellora had heard were the faint tear marks on Oriel's cheeks; her voice was back to its authoritative, strong self.

"Well ... you should probably come and see for yourself."

And that was how Ellora found herself sitting between Dan and Melody, in the staff dining room, which was now crammed with tables that didn't belong there, along with the rest of the First Form students. Almost.

"Where's Hunter?" she blurted out.

"What?" Dan looked confused at her random question and slightly surprised at the sound of her voice, since sitting at the table she hadn't spoken at all.

"Hunter. Have you seen him this evening? I mean, hasn't he come to eat?"

"Oh. I haven't seen him. He's here somewhere, though; he didn't go home. But he might be sitting with someone else, maybe."

"Dan, when 'as 'Unter ever sat wizh anyone else? I zhink I would actually be worried if 'e did not sit wizh us by now," Melody piped in, between spoonfuls of soup.

"Well, I don't want to worry you, now do I?" a familiar voice drawled from behind them. Ellora froze. She hadn't seen him since the Solstice, and for some reason, she felt nervous. There was also the fact that he had purposefully ignored her in the corridor earlier.

"'Unter! Zhere you are! Ellora 'as been worried sick about you!" Ellora shot Melody the scariest look she could and tried to fight the blush creeping onto her face.

"No, I have not, thank you very much, Melody." The glare didn't stop for a single moment.

"Did you see what happened to our dining room, Hunter?" Belle asked.

"Yeah, it was weird, right?" Clara added.

"No. I didn't see it." His eyes quickly fixed on the tablecloth.

"What? But I saw you there." Ellora frowned.

"You must have been mistaken," he replied confidently after clearing his throat.

"Oh, Belle, before I forget, Elle and I got you a surprise," Dan said, interrupting the conversation to pull a ruby red cardboard box, with a bright gold bow tied neatly on the top to hold it together, out from a bag he had put under the table.

"Don't tell me—" Belle said.

"Yup," Dan interrupted. "Raspberry cheesecake from Aphrodite's." Belle let out a little squeal of excitement.

"Well, actually, it's for everyone," Ellora added with a laugh at how big the box was. "We got an entire cake."

At that moment, Oriel glided into the room.

"Welcome to the staff dining room, everyone. I'm sure you're all aware, by now, of what has happened in your own dining room. I will tell you what I can, for now." Her voice commanded silence and the attention of every pair of eyes in the room. "No, we do not know who has done this, nor why, nor how. We do not believe whoever flooded the room is dangerous, or none of you would be here; we would not risk your lives. The other members of staff here at the Madori School of Aura, as well as the Senior Prefects, Fifth Form students that are here and I, are working to find out what has happened here, and I promise to keep you all up to date. Until further notice, you will all be eating your meals in here. Please, enjoy your dinner and do not hesitate to find me or any of the other teachers for anything you may need." And with that, she walked over to sit at her table, between Master Rainclarke and Master Graynor.

"I wonder why Oriel didn't just remove the water," Belle commented.

Ellora knew the answer – Oriel had told her when she had seen the First Form dining room that whoever had taken the Orb had somehow done this. Even Oriel, the *Madori Mistress*, hadn't had the energy to clear it away. But there was no way she would be able to tell her friends about this without telling them about the Orb.

Luckily, she didn't need to; Violet had run into the room and over to her usual table.

"I wonder what that's all about," said Clara.

"Weird, isn't it? She's usually the first one in here," Belle chuckled.

"You'll have to ask her tonight, Bee," Ellora added.

"Guys, do you zhink 'ooever did zhis is in zhe First Form?" Melody asked. All eyes at the table turned to look at her surprising question.

"What do you mean, Melody?" asked Dan.

"Well, I just mean … Why zhe First Form dining room? Why zhat one in particular?"

"I guess it's a possibility," said Clara. "Plus, this has never happened before and now when we join…?"

"That's creepy … one of our friends could have done this and we don't even know why," said Belle.

"'Ooever it was, it 'as got to be someone who stayed 'ere instead of going 'ome for zhe past couple of days," Melody said.

"Apart from a few First Formers, the majority of people who stayed were Prefects and Fifth Formers," said Ellora, frowning at the sight of Hunter's eyes darting around.

"And teachers," said Melody.

"What, you think a teacher was responsible?" Laughed Belle.

"No way," agreed Clara.

"Have you heard?" Everyone at the sound of Violet's thick Australian accent, as she came to stand between Ellora and Melody at the table.

"Heard what?"

"I overheard some Prefects talking nearby and came running to tell you all — the Orb's been taken! Nobody knows who did it. But that's how the dining room thing happened." The words bumbled out of her without making much sense.

Dan froze, his eyes wide.

"What is zhat?" Melody furrowed her eyebrows at the fear on everyone's faces. Even Clara and Belle looked confused.

"The Madori Orb," began Hunter, "is the core of Madori Aura; the core of the very kingdom itself. The Orb is protected by the Madori Mistress or Master and stealing it would be a very difficult task, indeed. Are you sure it has been taken?"

Ellora narrowed her eyes at him. She wondered how he knew so much about the Orb, considering she could barely find any information about it at all in the library, and all of her knowledge had come from Asyra.

The week passed quickly, which worried Ellora even more; she hadn't told her friends yet about the Asyra and about looking for the Core, and the Winter Break was almost over. Soon, the rest of the students would be returning. She had stayed up to date with Oriel, but even *she* didn't have a clue what to do; this had never happened before.

It was already New Year's Eve, and Ellora and her friends had gone for a walk around the grounds. Ellora had decided she needed a break from her research to look at it again with a fresh perspective.

They were walking past the library when Ellora thought she heard a muffled cry coming from the library. She stopped in her tracks, as the others walked ahead and, sure enough, she heard another muffled sound and a thud.

"Elle, where are you going?" asked Clara.

"I'll be right back," she replied quickly, heading into the library to see if everything was all right. She entered the room and saw absolutely nothing.

She was about to leave, having confirmed there was nothing wrong, when she heard a weird sort of sound. It was a muffled sound, sort of like a moan.

"Hello?" Ellora asked quietly. "Is anyone there?" She crept nervously around the bookshelves, peeking into each aisle when she went.

The sound came again, louder this time. Ellora held her breath and considered running out of there to get help, but she heard the sound once more, and this time, it sounded like whoever made it was in pain.

"Hello?" Ellora asked again, louder this time, as she continued through the stacks.

A thudding sound came from a few bookshelves over, and Ellora went over to see where it was coming from and gasped at the sight of red spots on the floor. She ran over and saw someone lying on the ground, their arm hitting the bookshelf to their left, creating a thudding sound to attract attention and ask for help.

"Oh, Spirits!" Ellora shouted, noticing the large splodge of red on their torso, soaking their previously pristine white shirt. She saw light brown hair splayed across the floor and heard another sound similar to the moans she had heard when she first entered the library. "Eh," said the female voice. "Ellor. Ellora."

"Daphne?" Ellora whispered fearfully. "Daphne?!" she shouted, moving closer to her face to move her hair out of the way. "Daphne! Help! Someone help us! Daphne, you're going to be okay, alright? You're going to be alright," she whispered reassuringly as she sank down to the ground, taking Daphne's head in her lap but being careful not to move her torso, which was still bleeding.

She looked down at her friend's face, sticky with sweat, strands of hair covering her eyes and bloody fingerprints scattered across her cheeks. She looked further down to see Daphne's sleeve had been torn and blood was oozing out from under it. Ellora gasped when she saw one deep gash, starting at Daphne's chest and carving down to the left side of her abdomen, and she looked back at her face; if she looked at the wounds any longer, she would vomit and she knew she couldn't do that right now.

"It'll be okay." She forced her voice to be steady.

Ellora, Belle, Dan and Allison Baird were sitting on the chairs just outside the infirmary. Daphne had been in there for a couple of hours, already, and Ellora had sent Clara and Melody back away since there was no space for all of them and they didn't know Daphne very well, anyway.

Allison was sitting in her chair, her head in her hands and her elbows on her knees. She was silent, but Ellora could tell she was crying from the small shakes of her shoulders. She couldn't blame her.

Belle was sitting next to Dan, her head on his shoulder. She had cried at first when she had run into the library at the sound of Ellora's screams, but she was calm now.

Ellora sat in silence. Well, external silence, anyway.

"Asyra." She sent the message out as a thought.

"Yes, my dear," Asyra responded.

"My friend. Daphne. She's been attacked. I don't know what happened, but she was found in the library, bleeding from her stomach. Has anything like this ever happened before?" she asked, silently pleading for some sort of answer.

"Not that I can recall," she sounded worried. "Is your friend okay?" Asyra asked.

"I don't know."

Ellora remained silent for a while. "Do you think this could be linked with the Orb?"

"I don't know how it could be, my dear, but I will tell you not to rule out any possibilities."

"Maybe she caught someone with it and – well, Oriel told me that if I had found her a few moments later, she would have bled to death. She said I also might have scared away whoever did this."

"Ellora, there is no need to think about such things; you didn't find her a few moments later, you found her when you did. There is no need to think about what might have happened otherwise."

Ellora didn't respond but started her meditation to build the walls around her mind once more. She pictured a huge lake in her mind, and as she watched it freeze from the bottom up, she felt the strong mental wards being erected.

"Dan." Hunter appeared at the end of the corridor, a bag on his shoulder. "What's going on?"

"It's Daphne Darkwater," replied Dan. "She was hurt and Ellora found her."

"Oh, Spirits. Ellora, are you ... are you okay?" he asked. She looked up at him at felt a flutter in her stomach at the worry in his eyes but forced her thoughts back to Daphne. They hadn't been very close, sure, but they had known each other since Fourth School.

"Fine, thanks," she replied.

"Allison," Hunter said gently, his eyes moving from Ellora. "Let me know if there's anything I can do." Allison lifted her head slightly, her eyes burning red from the tears and her face pale. She gave a short nod of thanks before burying her head in her hands once more.

"Well, listen, I heard you were all camped out here." Hunter spoke again after a moment of silence, "so I thought I would check if you needed anything to eat. And I brought you all some water," he said, pulling four water bottles out of his bag and giving one to each, starting with Allison and going down to Ellora. "Have you heard anything about the attack, then?"

"We don't know if that's what happened," Dan answered him.

As Hunter handed the water bottle to Ellora, she looked down at the blue shirt he was wearing and gasped.

"What's wrong?" he asked.

Ellora swallowed. "You... you're bleeding." She whispered so quietly that only Hunter heard her.

She watched as Hunter's eyes grew wide and he looked down at his torso in alarm. "It's nothing," he said, hurriedly buttoning up his jacket to cover up the stain.

"Hunter—"

"Ellora. Leave it," he said before she could argue.

"Daphne is alright," Oriel said, coming out of the infirmary. "She is sleeping, but Allison, you can go and see her." Allison jumped to her feet and ran into the room. "You all should be heading to bed. It's late and I'm sure this ordeal has been draining on you all." She gestured to Hunter, Belle and Dan.

In silence, they and Ellora went to leave, but Oriel spoke before they could. "Not yet, Ellora. I'll need to speak with you first."

"Are you sure you didn't see anybody? Nobody around her or in the library?" Oriel asked Ellora. They had been sitting in Oriel's office for a while, now, and Ellora had already explained how she had found Daphne in the first place.

"Nobody," Ellora responded. "Although, I did think I saw someone before I went in there, which is one of the reasons I did in the first place. I thought someone ran past the door, but it was too fast for me to catch a glimpse. And when I found her, I was too focused on Daphne to look around me; I was just worried about my friend."

"That's okay, Ellora. I'm so sorry you had to experience that; are you alright?"

"I'll be fine, Mistress Oriel, thank you. Did Daphne see anything?"

"Daphne doesn't remember anything at all. We are hoping she regains her memory soon, but it's likely she won't."

Suddenly, the image of red against the pale blue of Hunter's shirt came into her mind. Could it be possible that he had had something to do with this? "Oriel, there is one more thing I should tell you," she said. But then, she hesitated. What if she was wrong? What if she was accusing someone of something so serious, when they were innocent? Not just anyone – Hunter. "Urm, Asyra thinks this could possibly be linked with the Orb," she mumbled.

"Thank you, Ellora. I'll look into it. Meanwhile, would you mind if I walked you to your room?" she asked, standing up. "I don't want you walking around alone at this time of night, especially when something like this has happened to one of my students, your friends, in what I thought was the most secure building in the Kingdom. At least, I used to think so."

CHAPTER ELEVEN
Lucifer

The Winter Break was finally over, and Daphne was up and moving again. "It's nice to see you again, Daphne," Ellora said to the girl when she saw her at breakfast.

"Thanks, Ellora. It's nice to be back. And away from my parents," she laughed. Her parents had insisted on staying in the castle and with Daphne until she was better. "And just in time for the first day back. Woohoo," she said the last part less enthusiastically, but Ellora could tell she really was happy to be back. "Hey, listen," Daphne began, "I heard what you did for me. Thank you. Seriously."

"Please, Daphne, no thanks necessary. Seriously. So, you still haven't got your memory back?" she asked, pouring a box of cereal into a bowl whilst stifling a yawn. Ellora hadn't had a good nights' sleep since New Year's Eve. Every night since, the nightmares had returned and disturbed her rest.

"No. I've tried to remember, but it's just blank."

"Don't worry about it; we'll catch whoever did this." Ellora smiled reassuringly and left her to sit at her table. It worried her that Daphne couldn't remember and that whoever had attacked her was still out there, but she knew it would be no help whatsoever to pressure Daphne about it.

"Elle," said Clara, bringing her out of her thought. "Listen, with all that happened on New Year's, I didn't get a chance to give you this," she said, pulling out a small cardboard box with little holes poked into the top.

"Clara, what is this? You didn't need to get me anything! I didn't get you anything."

"No, that's not why I got it. You've just wanted one of these for as long as I can remember and when I went home, I saw the little guy and I just *had* to!"

"Don't tell me—" Ellora gasped as she opened the box to reveal a tiny little thing the size of an apple. "No way!" she squealed, as she brought the little orange thing up to her face.

"What is it?" Belle asked.

"It's a Penny Pet!" Ellora exclaimed.

"A what?" asked Dan.

"A Penny Pet! They're animals, but they're tiny, look. And this one's a little cat." She spread the palm of her hand, so everyone could see the pet sleeping in the middle, just as he started to wake up and look around. "Hi there, little guy," she whispered in a baby voice that made Clara look slightly nauseous but also humoured.

"OH, MY SPIRITS, 'E IS SO CUTE!" Melody whisper shouted. "Elle, can I 'old 'im?" she asked.

"Of course you can." Ellora gently deposited the cat onto Melody's hand. Melody fed the Penny Pet a strawberry from her pancake stack, as Ellora wolfed down her cereal to take her pet back again. "We're going to need a name," she said.

"Daniel," Dan replied instantly. Ellora shook her head at him before laughing.

"I think you should name him Harry. He just looks like a Harry, you know?" Belle said.

"Hmmm, I'm not sure how I feel about Harry," said Ellora.

"Bella," said Melody. "Or Ginger."

"Pepé," Clara suggested.

"Hunter, what do you think?" Belle asked.

Ellora swallowed nervously and looked up at him, trying to keep her face calm. She focused on the frozen lake. Internally, she was trying to convince herself there was no way Hunter had done anything wrong, but for some reason she couldn't believe he wasn't involved.

"Lucifer," Hunter said.

"Pardon?" Ellora looked confused.

"The cat. I think you should name him Lucifer."

"Lucifer," Ellora repeated out loud. "I like that. Do you like that, Luci?" Her baby voice made a reappearance, as she spoke to the Penny Pet on her hand, who made a content purring sort of sound, before curling up and falling asleep again.

"Well, looks like that's settled," said Clara.

Belle and Ellora had taken a walk on their break, with Lucifer in Ellora's hand enjoying the fresh air. They sat on the bench by the fountain for a few minutes before heading back to Master Graynor's class.

Ellora could tell something was wrong with Belle; she kept fidgeting with her fingers and seemed lost in thought. "Is everything okay?" she asked.

"Yeah, yeah," Belle replied. "It's just, I can't help but feel a bit scared, you know? Whoever did that to Daphne is still out there, and we don't even really know what happened."

"I get that, Bee," said Ellora. "It's weird and it's even scarier to think that the person who did it is walking around these corridors with us." She paused for a moment, considering Hunter and his possible involvement. She shook her head of the thought. "But we're okay. Nothing will happen, I mean, Oriel's got everyone looking out for anything suspicious. And with everyone back now from the break, there's too many people around for anything to happen, anyway. We're safe," Ellora promised.

Belle drew in a breath, about to say something else, but before she had the chance, an odd sputtering and pouring sound suddenly came from in front of them. The fountain had gone completely crazy.

It sprayed water everywhere, all over them and on the plants in the vicinity and on the other students in the area. Immediately, Ellora covered Lucifer with her other hand to protect him, as everybody ran around in a panic to get away from the freezing cold water. On a frosty day like this in January, it was not a pleasant sensation, and they would get sick.

Even in the midst of the chaos of everybody running around frantically around her, Ellora automatically stopped to look around. Somebody who was there must have done whatever it was that had caused the fountain to act like this.

Belle pulled Ellora by her elbow to get her inside, and Ellora finally relented when Rainclarke appeared in the gardens, telling everyone to leave. Ellora noticed Julia, who had been doing her prefect duties also attempt to clear the gardens.

Xavier jogged over to them in the confusion. "What in the Realms just happened?" he asked in his strong accent.

A sharp scream pierced the air, as Liviana walked inside, wringing her dress of the excess water. "'Ooever did zhis, YOU WILL PAY!" She shouted, water dripping from her. Belle and Ellora struggled to stifle their laughs at the sight of the grumpy girl. With sopping wet clothes, her hair ruined and her makeup running down her face, topped with the look on her face, Ellora thought she actually looked quite troll-like.

Liviana looked straight into Ellora's eyes. "Zhis is your fault; I just know it." She stormed away, her followers trailing behind her, equally as wet.

They went back to their class after Belle had attempted to use her Aura to absorb the water from them and make them somewhat dryer. Ellora noticed Hunter's hair was also wet when she passed him in the corridor. "Was Hunter out there?" she whispered to Belle.

"I don't think I saw him. Why?"

"Nothing."

"Hey, you." Mason smiled, as he approached and took Ellora's hand. "I haven't seen you around lately. Been avoiding me?" He grinned cheekily.

"You wish. You won't get rid of me that easily." Ellora smiled and leaned into him slightly and lacing their fingers together. "Feel like walking me to Oriel's office for my meeting?" she asked.

"Well, it would be my pleasure." Mason bowed jokingly. "And I have something for you."

"Oh?" Ellora asked, smiling brightly at her now official boyfriend.

"Ta da!" he called, pulling out a small box from the inside pocket of his jacket. "I saw it in the Main Land over the weekend." As she was opening it, Ellora could see the excitement on Mason's face.

She opened the dark blue box to see a beautiful ring made from a rose-gold band, twining around a small pink stone in the centre. "Oh, Mason, it's beautiful!" Ellora gasped, as soon as she set her eyes on the item. "You really shouldn't have," she said, looking back up to him.

"It was nothing." He shrugged. And yet again, Ellora was reminded that she was dating a prince, and that gifts like these probably *were* nothing. "Well, don't you want to put it on?"

"Oh, of course!" she exclaimed. But on each finger, she tried the ring, and the ring was just too small. On her pinkie finger, however, it was too big. Ellora frowned at the small jewel.

"Doesn't it fit?" Mason asked, brows furrowed.

"Ellora!" Oriel said, walking past them. "Were you on your way to me? We can walk together." She smiled.

Ellora and Oriel came to understand that the incidents – the flooding and the fountain – must have been instigated by whoever had the Orb.

"Only someone with Madori Aura, or Essence, in them can use that Orb. But none of the students are trained enough to harness the energy that comes from the Orb."

"So that must be what's going on. Whoever has it can't control it and they're accidentally setting it off," suggested Ellora.

"Exactly," said Oriel.

"Who is doing this?!" Ellora groaned, slumping her forehead into her palms.

"I know it's frustrating, but you should be focusing on your training. How are your classes going?"

"They're good. I'm not doing as well as Belle is; she's really good at controlling her Aura. But I'm making progress. Thankfully I've caught up to everyone else in the class, now."

"That's good to hear," Oriel said as they left her office to head to the staff dining room for dinner.

Ellora took her seat next to Belle, a few minutes late because of her meeting with Oriel. "Hey," she said, looking around the table. Ellora frowned when she saw that Hunter was missing and looked around the room for him. Ellora turned quickly around at the sound of the heavy door swinging open and the missing member walked in at that very moment, with Rainclarke. Hunter walked calmly over to them and took a seat without a word.

"Where've you been?" Ellora heard Dan ask.

"I was just running slightly late." Hunter's reply was vague and Ellora knew it was on purpose.

Suddenly, Liviana barged in, demanding to talk to Oriel. Julia followed, apologising to Oriel and arguing with Liviana at the same time. "For the Spirits' sake, Liviana! Leave Mason and I alone to do our rounds; you're only getting in the way!"

"Oriel, tell *Julia* zhat I can walk wizh Mason if I would like to."

"Girls, can this wait? It's dinner time and you are causing quite a scene." They looked up to see all of the First Formers staring at them.Ellora felt a wave of nausea sink through her at the sight of Liviana, as well as nervousness. She most certainly didn't want to overhear her obsession with Mason and how desperately she was trying to spend time with him.

Suddenly, Xavier shouted. "Help!" His voice was muffled.

Everyone turned to his table, trying to find him in his usual seat, but he seemed to be missing. "He's up there!" Shouted Leia, pointing up to the ceiling. Everyone looked up to find Xavier floating in some sort of a bubble. He was pounding at the walls that seemed to move like jelly, like the substance Ellora had found in the First Form dining room all that time ago.

"Xavier? How did you get up there?" asked Oriel. "Can you breathe?" She looked confused and worried all at once, but her voice was steady. But Ellora had spent enough time with her Madori Mistress to recognise the slight hint of stress underlying in her voice. They shared a look and Oriel nodded her confirmation she thought this must have been linked with the Orb.

"Yes, I can breathe," he cried. "I don't know what's going on – there's air in here, but I can't get back down!"

"Ah!" Called another voice, belonging to Allison Baird. She was in the air, too.

Ellora let out a little yelp as she felt herself lifting into the air. Her eyes were wide, as she suddenly had to look down to look at her friends. She was standing in this sphere-like thing and could see the walls were made of water; she could see the liquid flowing around. She reached out a hand and tentatively touched one the wall. It was icy cold to the touch and sent a shiver through her, but when she poked and prodded it some more it seemed to stretch.

One by one, people floated upwards, carried in large bubbles, and soon everyone was floating upwards. Everyone besides Oriel and Belle.

"Somebody get me down from 'ere!" A muffled, familiar voice demanded. "Now!"

"For the Spirits' sake, Liviana, calm down!" Julia growled back at her.

"Belle," said Oriel. "We have to bring the bubbles down; somebody else is controlling them, but we have to take over. Whoever is doing this is doing it by accident."

"What do you mean?"

"No time for an explanation now. Just help me get them back down here." she said, as they were all bouncing against the ceiling.

"You can do it, Bee," called Ellora, encouragingly.

Belle nodded her head in determination and focused on the water around her.

Ellora felt relief wash over her when she saw her feet getting closer and closer to the ground. Her stomach lurched like it did when she was on a roller coaster in the Human Realm. When she was finally on the ground, the strange bubble had disappeared and the sounds around her were no longer muffled, Ellora knew she deserved a double helping of chocolate cake this evening.

CHAPTER TWELVE

A Dark-Haired Intruder

E llora was running through the corridor. Again. She was looking for somewhere to hide; somewhere she wouldn't be found, where she could be safe. But there was nowhere else.

She found herself in the same place yet again, huddled in the corner, trying to ignore the screams. There was something different about this night. The screams were different. Familiar.

Suddenly, everything stopped. The screaming stopped. The creaking of the wooden floorboards was non-existent.

Ellora held her breath for as long as she could, afraid to make even a single tiny sound. But her lungs were smaller now, and she couldn't hold it for over twenty seconds.

When she was sure that the sound of her own breathing was the only sound she could hear, Ellora crept out from under her bed. She stuck her head out first, checking left and right, as if she expected someone to be waiting for her. But the room was clear, and she emerged out.

She tiptoed over to the door, which seemed huge at the moment, and looked outside. Once again, there was nothing.

"Ellora?" The weak little voice of a child called her name. "Ellora, help!"

Ellora looked around her, looking for the source of the voice, but she couldn't find it.

"Help!" The little voice squealed from behind her, and Ellora jumped around as quick as she could. She took a few steps down the corridor, but there was nobody there.

She froze immediately, when she heard footsteps behind her, her heart rate increasing until she was sure whoever it was behind her could hear it beating through her chest.

As slow as possible, she turned around, fists balled at her sides and her body tremoring slightly.

She was not prepared for the sight she saw: fire. Fire in the corridor, stuck in time. She didn't know what to do but followed her instincts when they told her to step away. One creak of a step behind her, and the fire moved to life.

The flames roared loudly, blazing their way down the hall. They moved faster than Ellora could even think, jumping around and down towards her.

Ellora jolted up in her bed, panting, a layer of sweat making her pyjamas stick to her skin. She placed her palm over her heart to slow her breathing, as she crawled out of bed and over to the sink to splash cold water on her face. "Frozen lake," she muttered. "Frozen lake." And slowly, her heart rate slowed.

Glancing over to the clock beside her bed, she noticed the time was 2.44 am. She groaned, realising she had only had three hours of sleep that night, an hour more than the night before, but several hours less than she actually needed.

She stared at herself in the mirror. The bags under her eyes were darker than ever, and her frame looked too thin. She knew she needed sleep, and soon. She also knew she needed help.

Ellora knew there was no point in trying to go back to sleep; it would either be a waste of time or end in another nightmare, so she got ready instead.

Her shower was fast, and she dressed herself in sweatpants and a t-shirt. Grabbing her bag, she headed down to the library, where she had spent a lot of time in the recent mornings, leaving Lucifer sleeping peacefully on her bedside table.

It had been a full week since the incident in the dining room, but Ellora still found herself unable to relax, with so much on her mind. She was constantly on edge, constantly looking out for anything, or anyone, unusual.

She sat after picking out another book on Aura Realm history from the shelf. At this moment, the library was empty, and Ellora found a spot in the corner under a window and took advantage of this by sprawling her things across the entire desk, before getting out a book and taking advantage of the moonlight streaming in from the window above her to read.

She felt herself drifting off, when a loud THUD startled her. She looked around suspiciously; why would anybody be in the library at this time of the morning? After hearing nothing more, she shook her head and buried it once more in her book, convinced she had imagined it.

But before she could return to her reading, a clattering of an object followed by a muffled male voice shouting "Spirits!" in pain. She jumped out of her seat. Checking her watch, she noticed it was already 6 am. She decided she would investigate the sound, taking a dim lamp with her, that had been hanging from the wall.

She got closer to the dark door that led to Oriel's office and crept behind a bookshelf to hide herself. Whoever was in there was definitely not her Madori Mistress. Ellora's eyes widened, as she realised whoever it was in there could be looking for Oriel's key to the Gate Room.

In a panic, Ellora turned around to find Oriel, but tripped over her own feet instead and landing quietly on the thick the carpet. A wave of pain travelled through her left arm, and Ellora winced, biting her lip to stop herself from crying out. The last thing she needed right now was for whoever it was in that office to find her.

She stood up just in time to see the door swinging open and a dark-haired figure coming out. *Turn around, turn around, turn around!* She begged the intruder to turn her face into the light so she could figure out who it was and help Oriel.

Unfortunately for Ellora, her wish came true.

Ellora inhaled sharply, stumbling backwards and squeezing her eyes closed in agony when she leaned backwards on her left wrist.

Tears filled her eyes, and Ellora couldn't decide if that was because of the pain or because someone she had trusted with her life, someone she had stood up for had just run out of Oriel's office, holding something in his hand that Ellora couldn't make out.

She swallowed her gasp and covered her mouth with her shaky hands, eyes bulging. Her heart sank into her stomach and she waited for the dark figure to leave before she allowed herself to sink down to the floor, clutching her stomach.

She felt sick.

She waited for a moment, a long moment. It could have been minutes, it could have been hours, but when Ellora finally got over her shock, it was still dark outside.

She had to find Oriel as soon as possible, but she wouldn't be able to wake her; only Prefects had access to the staff quarters, and so Ellora would have to wait until the morning. Then, a thought occurred. She would visit Asyra and ask her to summon Oriel. Ellora headed straight to the West Courtyard.

She burst through the door, into the fresh air of the West Courtyard and collapsed against the wall, still clutching her left arm in her right. She had left her bag and her books in the library, but right now she couldn't care less.

She stood in the cold air, feeling goosebumps arise along both of her arms. The moon lit up the courtyard, and Ellora felt immediately better when she inhaled a gulp of cold air into her lungs.

She noticed a familiar figure, as she walked over to her oak tree, sitting on the nearby bench. She instantly sending a wave of relief through her. "I see I am not the only one who comes here when she needs to think." Oriel's soothing voice sounded different now. She always sounded so confident; so calm. Now, she spoke quietly, her voice barely cutting through the wind.

"Mistress Oriel, I have something I need to tell you; something about the Orb."

Oriel's eyes shot up. "The Orb?"

"Could it maybe be more than one person? Like maybe two people working together?" asked Ellora.

"I guess that's possible, my dear. But I just don't even know where to start." Oriel put her forehead in the palms of her hands.

"Mistress Oriel ... I think I might know what's going on." Ellora drew in a long, shaky breath. "I heard you and Master Rainclarke talking in your office a while ago, and ... I know what will happen."

"Ah. I see," Oriel said with a sigh. "Well, Elle, I'm very sorry you had to hear that, but it's true. When I became the Madori Mistress, I had to take a vow that linked my Aura to the Madori Orb."

"Why? What does that even mean?" Ellora asked.

"Well, you see, Ellora, it's almost like I gave my Aura to the Orb. I draw my energy from it, and the Orb uses my energy to form a connection between us; you could say the Orb is alive. It allows me to sense the boundaries in the castle, the protections."

"So ... if you can almost *sense* the castle, shouldn't you have been able to tell that somebody was taking the Orb?"

"Well, in theory, yes. But, you see, I can sense the boundaries at all times, so I have learnt to switch it off, in a sense."

"Then how did you not know the Orb had been taken?"

"That's the problem; in order for someone to take the orb without me knowing, it had to be someone whose presence would not be unusual in the boundaries. Whoever it was, it was somebody I know well, somebody I trust."

"I think it was Master Rainclarke."

"Noah?" Ellora was surprised that Oriel's brows had furrowed in confusion rather than horror.

Ellora took a deep breath. "I just came from the library. I was in there and I heard someone in there, and I tried to see who it was, but I hurt my wrist and then I saw the door opening and ... it was him," she whispered. She couldn't even bear to look at Oriel as she spoke. "I think he must be working with someone, and I think I know who—"

"Ellora—"

"I really trusted him, and he was my favourite teacher, but I saw him with my own eyes. I heard him going through the things in your office. He must have been looking for the key to the Gate room, so that he could get out! Why else would he be rummaging around in there like that?" Ellora couldn't stop the words from running out.

"Ellora, listen." Oriel's voice was more assertive than before, but she still spoke softly. "Elle, slow down. Come on; sit down Take a breath," she coached her. Ellora hadn't even noticed she had stood up and paced.

"I'm sorry," Ellora said. "I'm not usually like this, but I haven't slept properly in weeks and I don't know what to do and I'm just so tired. Why would Master Rainclarke do this?" she asked sadly.

"Elle. It's alright. It's not him."

"What? What do you mean? I saw him!" Ellora cried.

"He was in there for me." Oriel walked away and came back holding a familiar object. "He was making me some tea." She held up the empty blue teacup.

"Tea?" Ellora asked, bewildered. "Tea?"

Before Oriel could reply, Ellora burst out in laughter. She couldn't hold it in and clutched at her sides, her belly aching from the movements. "Tea!" she repeated, her laughter getting louder. "Ow!" She gasped and clutched her wrist once again.

"Elle?" Oriel asked in concern, taking Ellora's left arm into her own hands.

"I'm okay. I'm sorry," she said when she stopped laughing. "But you have to admit – this is hilarious. I mean ... I ran away from him and I think I actually broke my wrist because I thought he was trying to *kill* you. When all this time, he was just making you tea," she chuckled again.

"Well, when you put it like that." Oriel smiled sympathetically. "Come on; we can talk and get you to the Infirmary at the same time. I don't have enough energy right now to trust myself to fix your wrist safely." She helped Ellora up and held the door open for the two of them.

"Wait," said Ellora, as they began their walk. "How do you know it isn't him? How can you trust him to be in your office like that? I mean, I know he's your colleague, but how can you be *sure*? If the person who took the Orb was someone close to you, how did you know you could let him into your office without him taking the key to the Gate Room and getting out of here?"

Oriel eyed her curiously for a moment before speaking. "Asyra told you about the Gate Room, didn't she?" When Ellora nodded sheepishly, she began her explanation. "Well, for starters, I don't keep the key in my office; I keep it here," Oriel said, as she dug under the thick jumper she was wearing to reveal a small diamond hanging off a chain around her neck.

"*That's* the key?" Ellora asked, astounded.

"It's not a traditional key, but yes, this opens the door to the Gate Room. Without access to that room, there is no way that someone could leave the castle with the Orb without my knowing. Secondly, Noah is not a Madori Aurum, so he would have no use for the Orb."

"Yes, but he might be working with someone else who *is* a Madori Aurum!"

"And thirdly, Elle, Noah knows that taking the Orb away from the Kingdom will slowly, but surely, kill me if it isn't brought back."

"I know that; that's why I was so upset that it was him," Ellora spoke softly.

"Noah wouldn't try to kill me." Oriel was confident and reassuring.

"But how do you *know* that?" Ellora was torn between relief at the fact that her Incendi teacher was innocent and could, indeed, be trusted and the worry of him wanting to hurt her Madori Mistress.

"You don't trust me?" a flash of hurt crossed Oriel's face.

"Mistress Oriel, of *course,* I trust you. I just don't want you to … we can't lose you." Ellora couldn't bring herself to say the words.

"I promise you, Noah wouldn't hurt his wife." She waited, not saying a word, for the information to sink in.

"I understand you trust him, but what — what?"

Ellora opened and closed her mouth wordlessly for a few moments before she could bring herself to speak. "You and Master Rainclarke are married?"

"We are," Oriel laughed.

"But you're so—"

"So much younger?" Oriel gave a small, sad smile as if she received that particular comment regularly.

"Actually, I was going to say, 'so different'," Ellora replied. "Well, I guess it's true what the Humans say."

"And what is it that the Humans say?" Oriel chuckled.

"'Opposites attract'. I mean, think about it, Mistress Oriel: Madori and Incendi," said Ellora.

"Well, I suppose you're right," Oriel laughed. "By the way, Elle, I think you can call me Oriel by now. The Prefects all do, too. Anyway, like I said, Noah wouldn't hurt me, and he wouldn't hurt our Kingdom. You'll just have to trust me on that."

"Don't worry Mis— I mean, Oriel, I trust you. And I trust Master Rainclarke." For a moment, there was a peacefully still silence, before Ellora spoke again.

"Oriel?" Ellora asked, tentatively. "Why are you telling me all of this? Don't you think I could have something to do with the Orb?"

"Ellora," Oriel sighed. "I know for a fact that you have nothing to do with the Orb. I'm sure you are aware or Asyra's abilities to communicate via thought, and I believe she has told you that you are a rather loud thinker." She released a little laugh.

"Yes, but she taught me to meditate to build up my mental walls. She doesn't hear my thoughts, anymore," replied Ellora.

"No, but you let your walls down to talk to her, do you not?" Oriel raised an eyebrow before continuing. "She has skimmed your mind on more than one occasion, Ellora. We know that you have nothing to do with it." Ellora felt some tension ease from her shoulders, as she released a sigh of relief.

"What were you doing in the library at this time, anyway?" Oriel asked Ellora after another moment of silence.

"Oh. I couldn't sleep," Ellora mumbled in response.

"I've noticed you haven't been able to sleep for a while now. What's going on?"

"It's my nightmares. They've just been really bad recently," Ellora sighed. She didn't want to talk about it.

Luckily, she didn't have to because Mason came barrelling around the corner just as they were reaching the Infirmary.

"Oriel, thank the Spirits! You have to come, right away," he panted.

"What's wrong?" Ellora and Oriel asked at the same time.

Mason gave them both an odd look before answering. "It's one of the First Formers. Henry Fischer. I don't know what happened, but one of his friends came to knock at my door. I think he saw something, or — I don't know." He looked scared.

"Elle, you should go to the infirmary," Oriel said quietly, so Mason wouldn't overhear. Ellora considered arguing with her and insisting on joining her, but the throbbing in her wrist was getting worse by the second. "I'll come and check in on you as soon as I'm finished, but don't leave without me; I don't want anyone walking around alone." And with that, she walked away, following Mason back to the boy's corridor.

"Hi, Healer Amare." Ellora greeted the healer when she entered the Infirmary.

"Ellora. I don't think I see anybody else around nearly as much as you." Healer Amare chuckled from her seat behind her white desk. She was a chubby woman who Ellora had never seen wear anything other than her blue scrubs and her white Healer's coat.

Ellora looked around the room at the two rows of three empty beds draped in pristine white linen and chose one close to the door to sit on. The room smelt like lemons, not real, fresh lemons like the ones Ellora's mother used to grow in the garden when she was young, but a chemical sort of smell. At the back of the room, on the right, was a little cubicle made of frosted glass, with a white door and to the left of the small room, was a kitchen area that held some sugary items to replenish Aura.

"What have you done, then?" Healer Amare walked over and asked, noticing the way Ellora was gingerly cradling her left wrist.

"I don't know, but I think it might be broken." Healer Amare took her wrist carefully in her hands and nodded silently.

"This will hurt," was all she said before closing her eyes and moving her hands across Ellora's wrist. "Malakono, malakono, malakono," Healer Amare chanted. As soon as the words were said, Ellora felt a warmth spread across her arms.

"Malakono, malakono, malakono," Healer Amare sung the words once more. This time, the feeling was warmer and Ellora felt her muscles relax. After the third chant, however, the feeling became more intense and Ellora clenched her teeth to stop herself from crying out when she felt as though she was being scalded by hot water. The fourth chant made the heat ease, but the fifth chant caused the warm feeling to disappear altogether and suddenly, Ellora felt like she was frozen to the very bone. The icy burn was even more painful than the heat.

The sixth chant, however, was the worst; Ellora felt the bones in her arm pull apart from each other, pressing against her skin from the inside, just before they slammed into each other and reconnected. Ellora couldn't stop her scream then.

And then, as the chant was said a seventh time, the pain was over. Ellora wiped her forehead and realised she had been sweating without even realising it.

"I must say," said the Healer, "you did a lot better than some of the other First Formers."

"How do you mean?"

"There was a boy who came in the other night," Healer Amare replied as she put some salve on Ellora's arm to help with the bruising. "I mean, he had a broken arm, *and* he was bleeding, so it was a bit harder for him..."

"He was bleeding?"

Healer Amare looked up curiously but nodded.

"Did he, by any chance, have dark hair?" Ellora's voice was now but a whisper.

"Yes," the Healer responded nonchalantly. "A nice young man, if you get past the fact that he doesn't speak much."

Ellora looked up at the kind lady. "Was it Hunter?" she asked.

Healer Amare looked at her with a smile. "Yes, that was it! Hunter."

Ellora felt a pang in her chest. "Was it that night that I found Daphne?"

"Actually, I think it was. A bit earlier, though. In fact, I must have discharged him only a few minutes before Oriel brought the girl here."

In that moment, Ellora immediately decided to talk to her friends; they had to know what was going on.

CHAPTER THIRTEEN
The Madori Jewel

"Hang on, you're telling us that the Madori Orb was stolen," began Clara in a whisper.

"And if it gets it out of the Kingdom, Mistress Oriel will die?" Belle continued.

"And zhat Mistress Oriel and Master Rainclarke are married?" Questioned Melody.

"Oh, and let's not forget that behind a mysteriously locked door in the Caeli courtyard, there's a massive lake with a *mermaid* living in it," Clara whispered.

"Yeah, pretty much." Ellora realised just how ridiculous it all sounded.

"We need to tell Dan. Plus, he might be able to help us," said Belle.

"And 'Unter," added Melody.

"No, you can't tell them!" the words rushed out of Ellora's mouth. She panicked. She hadn't wanted to fill her friends in on her suspicions about Hunter, especially because she had no proof and wanted so very much for it to be wrong, but it meant she needed an understandable reason for keeping him and Dan in the dark.

"Tell us what?" Dan spoke, as he bent to kiss Belle on the cheek, Hunter following behind him.

Ellora cursed inwardly. "Oh, Spirits, it's all ruined now!" She plastered a smile on her face as she looked up to see Dan and Hunter taking their seats at the table. "I figured out a new chess strategy I wanted to try out on you. I thought I could finally beat you at a game. It's called the 'Fool's Mate'. Have you heard of it before?" She had, actually researched some new chess openings in the library hoping to take Dan by surprise.

"I haven't, but I look forward to seeing it in action. I'll probably still beat you, anyway." He stuck his tongue out at her.

"In your dreams, mate." Ellora stuck out her tongue in response. She looked over to Belle, who was frowning at her, wondering why she was lying to her boyfriend, but Ellora just sent her a reassuring smile that said: 'trust me'. Ellora knew she would have to find some reasonable excuse later to stop her from telling Dan. If Hunter really was the thief, who knew what he could do if he found out Dan suspected him?

The heavy doors swung open once more and everyone turned around. Through the doors walked Oriel, with a pretty girl, who Ellora hadn't seen before, following behind closely. Her skin was only a few shades darker than Ellora's own.

"Good morning, everyone." Oriel spoke just at the entrance to the room. "I have a quick announcement to make before you all carry on with your breakfast." The small girl behind her stepped around to stand next to Oriel, who put her hand on the girl's shoulder. Ellora frowned. "This is Ilisha." Oriel smiled. "She is a transfer student from the Caeli School of Aura who will be with us from now on. I trust you will all make her feel welcome."

Oriel's announcement was short, and when she turned around again to talk to Ilisha, everybody continued on with their breakfast.

She looked curiously at the girl, who was now walking confidently over to Violet's table with her head held high and a firm smile on her face. She smiled at Violet, Hazel, Xavier and Leia, who were the only four sitting at the table. Ellora watched her make her introductions.

"She is really pretty," said Melody, interrupting Ellora's thoughts. Ellora only replied with a hum before forcing herself to eat a bowl of cereal, as well as two slices of toast with butter and jam and a cup of coffee. She didn't normally eat as much, but she had a big morning ahead of herself and she knew she would need her energy. She also fed Lucifer little pieces of toast.

"Hi, I am Ilisha. It is nice to meet you all." Ellora froze when she heard that coming from behind her. She tried her best to chew the piece of toast still in her mouth, before swallowing and turning around.

"Hey," said Belle. "I'm Belle. It's so nice to meet you; It's so cool that you come from the Caeli Kingdom, what's it like there?" she replied enthusiastically.

"Why is it zhat you 'ave a British accent if you come from Caeli?" Melody asked curiously.

"Well, the Caeli Kingdom is really nice; it's always nice and warm," she answered Belle with a smile before turning to Melody. "And whilst my family is Indian, I actually grew up in London. We only moved to the Caeli Kingdom about two months ago."

As Ilisha replied that she was from India, although her accent was so incredibly subtle that none would have ever guessed, and continued making her introductions, Ellora looked at the people around her on the table. She definitely wasn't liking how Hunter seemed to hang on to her every word.

She supposed she couldn't blame him; Ilisha seemed like an intriguing person. And she was pretty; very pretty. And she had really nice teeth. And nice hair. Ellora frowned.

"I love your hair; it's gorgeous!" Ilisha said, interrupting Ellora's thinking.

"Oh. Thank you." Ellora smiled politely yet unenthusiastically. "I'm Ellora." Her instincts told her to be careful around this strange girl. She met her eyes and felt a shiver travel through her. She grimaced at the bitter cold feeling and narrowed her eyes slightly.

Between lessons, Ellora found the time to pop over to the library. Every chance she got, she went in there and looked for books on the history of the Realm and of the Madori Orb. Melody kept insisting that knowing the history of the Realm wouldn't help, but Ellora followed her instincts.

On the way into the library, Ellora spotted a mop of dark hair that belonged to the boy who had been avoiding her lately. She felt a little twinge in her chest; she really didn't want to believe that Hunter could have anything to do with this, but she had to follow the signs.

"Ellora, how nice to see you." Wendy greeted her from where she was stacking books onto a shelf.

"Hey, Wendy! I was actually looking for Hunter Nash, I think he just walked in here. Have you seen him?"

"Hunter? No, he is in here a lot, but I haven't seen him today. Of course, I might have missed him." Ellora nodded in acknowledgement, before continuing to walk past.

Ellora decided to go and see if he had gone to speak to Oriel since she couldn't seem to find Hunter in the first few aisles. The door was closed, so Ellora backtracked and walked through the other aisles. She shook her head slightly and frowned; Hunter was nowhere to be found and Oriel's office had seemed empty.

Just to be certain, Ellora went over to Oriel's door once more and put her ear against the wood, listening for any sounds at all.

"I don't think she's in," Hunter said from behind her.

Ellora jumped into the air at the sound of his voice.

"A bit on edge, are we?" he asked, amused.

"Hunter," Ellora said. "You scared me."

Without another word, Hunter shoved his hands into his pockets and turned to leave the library.

"There you are!" Belle rushed over to her, as Ellora walked into the classroom that afternoon. She dragged her over to their desk and forced her down onto the stool by her shoulders. "I have something to tell you." She spoke in a low voice.

"Belle, Ellora, I trust you know what to do?" Master Graynor's voice came from behind them, making them jump.

"Yes, sir." They droned at the same time.

Belle watched him walk away from them before she spoke again. "I've been thinking about what you said, about the Orb. I decided to go to the library to do some research yesterday and see what I could find out."

"I've tried that so many times, Bee. I haven't been able to find anything," Ellora whispered.

"I don't think you looked in the right place. Really, Elle, your favourite book genre and you didn't even think to look in the 'Mythology' section?"

"Mythology?"

"Yes! I found a book on Aura mythology. There wasn't much in there that was relevant, but there was a page about a 'Madori Jewel'," Belle told her.

"Jewel? What is that, like another name for the Orb?" Ellora looked confused.

"No, I don't think so, Elle. From what I read, it looks like the jewel was made at the same time as the Orb. We should definitely look into this; it might help us out," she said before taking her place in front of the glass of water and closing her eyes to focus on creating that ripple.

"How are we even going to find anything else? You've already checked the library and you couldn't find more than that page. I couldn't find anything, either."

"True, but I was thinking maybe a different source." She smiled proudly. "I was talking to Melody earlier, and she told me her brother Jason took Aura History when he was in Third Form."

"Well, isn't that great for him. How exactly does that help us, Bee?"

"You know who taught him Aura History?"

"The Aura History teacher?"

"Our very own Mistress Maywether."

"What? Our Caeli teacher?"

"The very same!" Belle squealed excitedly. "She also teaches Aura History."

"So, maybe she'll know something about the jewel," Ellora said, as realisation dawned on her. Bee, you're a genius!"

"I know." Belle jokingly flipped her hair.

"And I have her later today for an extra lesson! It'll just be the two of us and I'll be able to ask her about it," she said, a new sense of hope fluttering in her stomach.

"Exactly!"

The girls stopped talking instantly when Master Graynor shot them a waning look, and they worked in silence for a few minutes before they talked again. Ellora hesitated for a second before asking: "What did you think of the new girl?"

"Ilisha? She seems lovely," Belle responded.

"Yeah, I guess so. But I don't know, Bee; there's something off about her."

"What do you mean? She literally seems like the nicest person on Earth," Belle laughed, clearly thinking Ellora was joking.

"I don't know. I just got a weird vibe," said Ellora. "I mean... don't you think she seemed a bit *too* nice?"

"A bit too nice to Hunter, you mean?" Belle asked, trying not to smile.

Ellora narrowed her eyes at her best friend. "What has *he* got anything to do with it?"

Belle raised an eyebrow knowingly and didn't break eye contact. Just before Ellora could reply, Master Graynor appeared in front of them. "Girls," he sighed. "Do I really have to remind you to do your work every lesson?" He stalked off, seeing them continue on in silence once more.

"All I'm saying," Ellora began before being interrupted.

"I know what you're saying, Elle. I'm just saying I don't really agree with you. She hasn't done anything wrong," Belle replied matter-of-factly.

"Yet," Ellora mumbled under her breath.

"I'm going to try this ripple thing again without draining all my energy like last time." Belle changed the topic of conversation, either not having heard Ellora's comment or not wishing to address it.

Ellora watched her best friend take deep breaths, like she always did. One by one, ripples danced across the surface and Ellora watched the beautiful display in awe. "You're doing it, Bee!" she cried in amazement, as Belle wiggled her fingers at the water. "How are you doing that?" Ellora asked.

"It's kind of hard to explain," Belle replied, still experimenting, flicking her fingers at the glass of water and watching the effects. "At first, I just focused really hard; pretended I was in the sea and the water was surrounding me. That's what I did last time, too. But this time, I pretended I was stepping into it, creating ripples with each step. Try it." She stood up, gesturing for Ellora to take her place.

Ellora clenched her eyes shut, remembering Asyra's calming song telling her to breathe. In and out, in and out, she tried, but she couldn't seem to focus. Finally, she pictured herself stepping into the sea. Nothing happened.

"I think maybe you're trying too hard, Elle. Look: soft, light touches." Belle demonstrated. They watched as the water danced in the glass, like a puppet under the control of Belle's fingers.

"Artemer, Keloa, what are you two doin—" Master Graynor started to ask, as he walked over to them and noticed the movements in their glass. "Belle, are you doing this?" he asked.

"I think so, Master Graynor," she said as she flicked her wrist to send a wave through the water.

"Try lifting some of the water out of the glass, Belle," he suggested, walking to the other side of the desk so he could closer examine her movements. Ellora watched as she twisted her wrist, so her palm was facing the ceiling, and slowly raised her hand upwards. Belle seemed so surprised when the water levitated out of the glass that she lost her focus completely and spilt the water all over the floor.

"Belle," Master Graynor began, as he swished his hand over the spilt water, pouring it back into the glass, "I would very much like to see you in my office this afternoon. Shall we say 4 pm?"

"Yes, sir," Belle replied.

CHAPTER FOURTEEN
Another Danger

At the end of yet another two-hour long class, a week later, Belle and Ellora spent their break walking through the gardens. "How am I going to ask Mistress Maywether about the jewel?" Ellora asked, flipping through the pages of the book about Aura legends that Belle had pulled out of her bag. "I need a way to ask without being too obvious about it; otherwise, she'll start getting suspicious and closing off. It would just waste time"

"Maybe you could ask about this history of the Realm," said Belle. "Like maybe ask her about the legend of the Madori Spirit. Or the Orb. That could get her to talk about the jewel."

"That's a great idea! Besides, she has a tendency to waffle on so I'm sure she'll talk about the jewel eventually, anyway." They laughed.

"Elle, listen, is everything okay between you and Hunter?" Ellora turned to look at Belle with an inquisitive look on her face, as soon as she asked the question. "It's just... before the Winter Break you were getting along really well, and now it's as if you don't even talk anymore." Ellora looked down, focusing on playing with the watch on her left wrist. Hunter had seemed to be avoiding her lately, and even though she felt uncomfortable at the knowledge he was hiding something, she would be lying if she said she didn't miss his company.

It was entirely possible that he ignored her the day she returned because he hadn't heard her, and it was also possible that the day he had been bleeding, it was because of a completely different reason. She had gone through the events multiple times in her mind, but something was nagging at the back of it.

Just as the girls were turning the corner near the West Courtyard, before she could reply to Belle, Ellora fell backwards onto the floor as something solid ran into her, crushing her beneath it. "Oh, Spirit, I'm so sorry," he fumbled.

"Hunter?" Ellora gasped, still trapped under him in an awkward position.

He scrambled up and onto his feet, a slight blush creeping up onto his face. Instantly, he reached out his hand to help Ellora up and, after hoisting her to her feet, also bent down to pick up the book that had flown onto the floor before thrusting it into her hands. "Sorry," he said, shifting between his feet, before attempting to rush off again.

Ellora narrowed her eyes slightly. "You seem to be in a bit of a rush; where are you off to?"

Hunter glanced at Belle and back to the floor again, muttering something under his breath which sounded like, to Ellora, that he was going to find their Madori Mistress, before marching off once more.

"Was it just me, or did Hunter seem ... *sad*?" asked Belle.

"Sad?" Ellora frowned. "You really think he was sad?"

She turned around, worried, to see where Hunter had run off to, and the worry disintegrated. Her jaw tensed immediately, and she narrowed her eyes just slightly. There was Ilisha, talking to Hunter. And he was smiling. And laughing. Ellora felt a pang of sadness – she hadn't even had a full conversation with him since the Winter break, but he was constantly talking to Ilisha. "He's *definitely* not sad," she stated.

Suddenly, Ellora felt a wave of calmness settle over her. She felt relaxed, as if she could fall asleep on the spot, and had to force her eyelids to stay open. A song prodded the mental walls around her mind, and Ellora allowed the sound to enter. "Ellora," Asyra sang. "Ellora."

"What is it?" Ellora snapped, still angry at the Madori spirit for neglecting to tell her about Oriel's possible death.

"Um, Elle?" Belle laughed nervously. "Who exactly are you talking to?"

"Oh, sorry, Bee. I just — I — there was a wasp," she blurted out awkwardly.

"A wasp?" Belle gave her a strange look.

"Yep, a wasp," she insisted.

"I need to talk to you," the gentle voice in her head whispered.

"Why?" She snapped the thought out of her mind.

"I will tell you in person; it's important. But don't tell Belle."

"Do I really need to come now?" Ellora felt exasperated and knew if she went to Asyra now, she would be late for the second half of today's Madori classes.

"*Now*, Elle." The voice was more commanding this time.

"Bee, I have to go find Mistress Oriel," she said.

"What? What are you talking about? Why do you need to find Oriel?"

"Just trust me, Bee. Please. I'll be back in our class in twenty minutes."

After a slight moment of hesitation, Belle replied. "I trust you. Go, I'll cover for you with Master Graynor," she said before walking back to their classroom.

Ellora hurried into the West Courtyard and looked around to make sure nobody was watching her before crossing through the door on the other side. "I'm here!" she called out, after firmly shutting the door behind her. "Asyra?" She made her way over to the patch of grass she had enjoyed sitting on last time she was there.

"Asyra?" She looked around at the lake, which looked even more beautiful in the sunlight. Now, everything seemed so much more welcoming; the light bouncing off the water was bright, and the leaves of the trees swayed gently in the breeze.

"Ellora." Asyra emerged from the water, spraying Ellora with a mist of water and making her jump up slightly, "how nice of you to come, my dear. I see you have made huge improvements in your meditation techniques." She smiled.

"Oh, as if I had a choice," Ellora grumbled.

"You had a choice, Ellora, and you made the right one."

"What's going on? I'm missing my Madori class right now and Belle can only cover for me for so long. What's so important?"

"Well, you may want to sit down; I have something serious to talk to you about." Ellora, slightly reluctantly, sat on the grass and Lucifer emerged from her pocket to rest beside her in the sun. "It's about your friend Belle."

"Asyra, please just tell me what's going on."

"I'm sure you've witnessed Belle Keloa's extraordinary mastery of the Madori Aura by now?" Ellora understood that must have been a rhetorical question, because Asyra didn't wait for her to respond before continuing. "Whoever has taken the Orb, it's *possible* that their motive is power. And if it is, it's likely they have *also* noticed Belle's unusual strength."

Ellora did not like where this was going.

"If this is the case, they may want her power."

"Want her power? It's not like she can just give it away," said Ellora.

"No, she cannot. But ... it can be taken."

"Taken?" Ellora shot up to her feet. "What do you mean by taken?" she demanded.

"Before I continue, Ellora, I have to tell you that this may not be the case. I cannot be certain, my dear."

"How can you not be certain?!" Ellora was getting angrier by the minute. "If my best friend is in danger of having her Aura stripped from her, I would really like to know!" she shouted.

"I'm telling you all I can." The voice in Ellora's head was more forceful this time, and Ellora actually felt slightly scared. She stumbled back, away from the figure in the water which had risen up to loom over her. "I just wanted to warn you." Her voice was soft again.

"Sorry," Ellora whispered. "I understand – you're not all-knowing." Asyra nodded her forgiveness sank back into the water a little, so she was no longer towering over Elle. "How can they take Belle's Aura?" Ellora asked.

"They could try to absorb it. I wouldn't normally think that this might be an issue, but if somebody is knowledgeable enough to know about the Orb, and how to take it, it's possible they also know how to absorb Aura. And if this is the case, everybody is in danger."

Ellora gulped. "Then, why Belle?" she asked.

"Belle Keloa is gifted. Not only could she be the first victim, but the effect would be most profound on her; the link between her Aura and her life will be severed."

"Severed?" Ellora stared, wide-eyed, at Asyra, who looked down on her sadly. "What exactly does that mean, Asyra?" She was getting frustrated at not being told the entire truth.

"Ellora, if Belle Keloa's connection to her Aura is severed, there is no guarantee she will survive."

Ellora stared at the Spirit in silence. Her face was expressionless, and her eyes were blank. Slowly, a look of fear crept over her features, but she thought of the frozen lake and took a breath, and then determination sharpened her eyes. "How do we stop this?"

"The only way is to get the Orb back. Whoever is doing this will need the Orb to absorb the Aura in the first place, so returning the Orb is crucial. Ellora, all I ask is that you keep your eyes open for anything or anyone else who could possibly be the culprit. I am sure you understand that time is of the essence," Asyra said as if that took the pressure off Ellora. If anything, it *added* pressure.

Once again, Ellora was convinced that a hot chocolate would ease, if not solve, most of the problems and anxieties swirling around her mind. She didn't even know where to begin with the Orb business and having just found out her best friend's life was at risk, she was feeling numb with fear.

Who could she trust? Maybe she could trust Mason. After all, he was a Prefect and he knew what was going on, so it wasn't like she would have to explain it all to him. Plus, she had only managed to see him a couple of times since the Winter Break and was missing his comforting presence.

Her train of thought was broken by a rumbling sound coming from around the corner, either from the library or the stairs, she supposed. Staying quiet, she seemed to be doing a lot of creeping around these days, she padded over to peer around the wall.

Hunter.

She gasped and swung back around, clamping her hand over her mouth; she knew he had heard her sharp intake of breath. She willed herself to calm down, to breathe steadily, but she knew now there was no way she could justify what he had just been doing. He had been trying to get out of the main entrance. Since Daphne's attack, Oriel had kept guards stationed around the castle at all times, but there was none by the door right now. And Hunter was trying to escape.

Her eyes clenched tightly, as if she could hide herself like that, when she heard footsteps coming her way. If Hunter found her, there was no telling what he could do. If Hunter was the thief, he would have the Orb, and he could do anything.

Please turn around. Please turn around. Please turn around. Ellora all but begged silently. She held her breath when the footsteps got closer. And closer. And closer.

A few more seconds, and he would find her. A few more seconds and that would be that.

"Hunter?" Oriel's voice called from a bit further away and Ellora's eyes widened. She had been saved. "Ah, there you are," Oriel spoke again.

"Oriel," Hunter replied in acknowledgement.

"I need to see you in my office," Oriel stated before leading the way to the library.

It was only when Ellora heard their steady footsteps disappear that she realised she was trembling. Her entire body couldn't keep still, and when she tried to stand up, her legs were too weak to support her.

She took a few deep breaths and allowed herself to visit the frozen lake in her mind.

"Elle?" A deep, familiar voice yanked her away from her trance. Ellora opened her eyes to stare into deep brown ones filled with concern. She looked around herself to see she was still crouched on the floor. For how long she had been there, she didn't know, but the corridors were still empty, so it can't have been too long.

She felt strong but gentle hands lift her by her arms, almost as if she was weightless, and everything came back to her. She couldn't hold it back anymore.

She blinked her eyes furiously, but it was no use; she could feel the wetness on her cheeks and down her face and her chin. Mason hugged her tightly as Ellora cried. She cried and she cried, and she cried.

She cried for Oriel and she cried for Belle. She cried for her parents. She cried for her baby sister. She cried for Hunter. She cried for Daphne. And she cried for herself.

She couldn't tell how much time had passed, or how in the Realms they had ended up in the staff dining room, but when she sat next to Mason, with a steaming cup of hot chocolate in her hands, she felt the tremors in her body start to ease.

She looked up at Mason to thank him, but her breath caught in her throat when he smiled sweetly at her. He leaned closer and tucked a strand of hair behind her ear. "It will all be okay," he whispered gently.

And in that moment, she truly did believed him.

"Ellora, did you hear me?" Clara prodded at her with her finger.

"Sorry, what was that?" Ellora shook her head. She had been thinking about her conversation with Asyra, not knowing how in the Realms she was going to save the Kingdom when she couldn't even create ripples in the water like Belle could do so easily. She had also come to a conclusion about Hunter: his Essence must have been Madori Essence if he could control the Orb. And nobody could know about her suspicions; he would have no need to harm anyone who didn't suspect him.

"I said, how do you feel about a girl's night tonight? We can watch movies and eat popcorn. Oh, and my mum just sent me my old version of that Human game 'Monopoly'; we could play a bit.

I don't think I have played since I last played with you about four years ago," she beamed excitedly.

"Well now, Clara, I'm certain there's a very specific reason why you didn't play again with Miss Sore Loser over here," Belle chuckled, gesturing to Ellora.

Ellora gave a faint smile, as she looked around her. Part of her thought she was imagining it, or she was becoming paranoid, but it seemed like people were staring at her. She caught the eyes of Henry Fischer, but he immediately turned around. She caught Xavier's eye too, but he merely smiled and waved awkwardly. What was going on? But she didn't have time to dwell.

She was listening to the conversation between her friends as if it was background music, but her thoughts were churning. If she failed, the Madori Kingdom would cease to exist. If she failed, *Oriel* would cease to exist. If she failed... Belle could die.

Ellora clutched her stomach when she felt a wave of nausea threaten to spill the very little she had eaten, on the floor. She stood up with the intention of getting to the bathroom, but an immediate wave of dizziness hit her. She reached out blindly for anything she could hold on to, anything that would keep her upright, her vision blurry and her hearing muffled.

"Elle?" Elle!" Belle's words were distant in Ellora's ears, as she felt her eyelids become heavier and heavier. Her body slumped against something soft and warm. She leaned into the comfort and relished in the familiar feeling.

"You are coming with me," a voice boomed and suddenly, she was back in the familiar house she recognised from her nightmares. She was no longer under the bed like last time; this time she was standing up and leaning against a wall.

"No, please!" Ellora's heart stopped at the sound of a child's voice. It was familiar. In fact, it was all too recognisable for Ellora, a voice she hadn't heard for years. "Stop!" The high-pitched cry created a knot in Ellora's stomach.

"Ophelia?" She sobbed. "Ophelia, where are you?" Her voice was trembling, and she could feel the wet tears pouring out of her eyes.

"Ellora, help me!" The owner of the voice was crying too, sobbing heavily.

"Nobody can help you now," the first voice echoed in the air. Ellora ran. She ran as fast as she could towards the sound of the little girl from her childhood. She ran one way and then the other, the voice seemingly coming from all directions.

"Relax, Ellora." There was another familiar voice. "Focus on your breathing, my dear. In and out. In and out."

"Asyra?" Ellora gasped out. "Asyra, my sister! She's in trouble. I have to help her!"

"In and out. In and out," the voice continued in regular intervals.

"You're not listening to me; I have to help her!" she screamed out. She tried to move, but it was as though Asyra's voice had her gripped in a vice. She couldn't even lift her arms.

She struggled against the force, but that did no good. She grunted and shouted as she tried to break free, but the pressure only became stronger.

Asyra's voice, which usually sounded soothing, now sounded eerie and venomous. But nevertheless, the song started to put her to sleep. Her eyes drooped closed, no matter how hard Ellora fought.

"Ophelia." Ellora tried to call for her again but only released a whisper of a breath.

"Elle!" The distress in Belle's voice caused Ellora to immediately snap her eyes open. "Oh, thank the Spirits." Tears flowed freely from Belle's eyes. Ellora looked around to see her friends dotted around her, all looking worried. Belle was crouched on the floor next to her; Melody was stood in the corner, by a bookshelf, nervously biting her nails; Clara was hovering by her feet; Dan was stood near Belle's limp figure, brows furrowed, and Oriel was touching the back of her hand to Ellora's face, checking for a temperature.

"Where am I?" Ellora choked out in a raspy voice.

"My office, Elle," said Oriel, handing her a mug of her sweet lavender tea. Ellora sat up, helped by Clara, who now seemed unable to stop pacing or shifting between her feet and looked around her. She realised she had been lying on the long sofa in Oriel's office. "We brought you here when you collapsed in the dining room; you were shivering, but your forehead was warm. I thought you were ill and was going to take you to the infirmary, but your friends here," she gestured to them, "insisted that would be the wrong thing to do. Apparently, this has happened before?" Oriel raised an eyebrow.

"I know you were just having a ... a ... dream, I guess we should call it, but it was so much scarier this time, Ellie." After a few moments, Belle was finally calm enough to speak. "I just didn't know what to do, and you just seemed like you were in so much pain." Ellora now realised that her muscles felt slightly achy, though she had no idea why.

"Is there anything on your mind, Elle? Anything you can tell us about what just happened?" Oriel asked her.

"We zhink zhey are linked to 'er emotions, Mistress Oriel." Melody's small voice came from the corner of the room.

"Yes, we do. But I'd rather not talk about it for now if that's alright." Ellora made eye contact with her Madori Mistress, telling her this was something she wished to discuss in private. It wasn't that she wanted to keep secrets from her friends, but she definitely didn't want Belle to know that Belle was in danger; it would help nothing. And she couldn't tell Dan without having to fill him into the situation. No, she would tell Melody and Clara when she had the chance, so they could help her look for the culprit and keep an eye on Belle, but for now, she would only tell Oriel. Besides, she didn't want to bring up Hunter with Dan in the room.

"Besides, I don't remember what happened in the dream," she lied.

Oriel understood her hint and simply announced that Ellora needed to rest, and that the others should go to their lessons since they now knew their friend would be all right. "I am going to personally make sure she is alright before sending her back to her routine." Everybody took this as a sign of dismissal and each hugged Ellora before reluctantly making their way out.

Thanks to the tea, Ellora was feeling much better physically. She curled her legs underneath herself on the sofa as Oriel positioned herself on the other side and turned to face her. "Do you want to talk now?" she asked and Ellora nodded.

She told her about what Asyra had said about Belle being in danger and watched, as a look of fear, then sadness crossed her Madori Mistress's face. "We can't let this happen," she said. "We have to find who it was."

"I agree. That's what I wanted to talk to you about this evening. I think..." Ellora took a deep breath. It upset her to even think it could be true, but if it was even a small possibility, she knew Oriel had to know. "It was Hunter."

Oriel's expression changed to one of disbelief. "Hunter?"

"I know, I don't really want to believe it myself. But Oriel, you have to believe me; he has been so different lately!"

"Ellora, it's not Hunter."

"But how can you *know* that?!" exclaimed Ellora.

The corners of Oriel's mouth quirked upwards only slightly, but Ellora caught it. "What's funny?" she demanded. Her tone was rude, but she didn't care; her best friend's life was at stake and Oriel was *laughing*.

"Ellora, nothing is funny. But I'm sure it's not Hunter. In fact, I just thought it was interesting that of all the people in the castle, you think it's *Hunter* working against us."

"What's that supposed to mean?"

"Oh, Ellora. Listen, I believe it will have to be Hunter's decision to disclose that particular piece of information. I will say, however, that I have known Hunter all his life. I know for a fact that he wouldn't do this. I do, however, think you should have this conversation with him; he has gone to great lengths to keep some things private in this school, and I should very well like to respect that. Please, don't worry. Look, I strongly believe with all of my heart that it isn't Hunter's fault, but if it will put your mind at ease, I'll look into it. Promise."

Ellora felt her heart lift slightly from the pit it had sunken into the moment she thought Hunter could have had anything to do with this. She knew her next step would be to talk with the boy, herself. She needed an explanation. Urgently.

"Thank you," Ellora replied. Even though she trusted Oriel completely, having her double-check would put Ellora's mind at ease.

"I think you are well enough to go to your class, wouldn't you say? You'll be able to catch the last hour of your Terrari Theory if you leave now."

CHAPTER FIFTEEN

Ophelia

Hunter hadn't shown up to their Terrari theory class. Ellora groaned internally when she noticed; she had been hoping to speak with him after the class about everything that had gone on, but she now realised it would be difficult enough to find im at all. After all, he ad already been doing a rather good job at avoiding her for the past couple of weeks.

She thought back to the Orb. The only thing reassuring her now was that the only way someone could leave with the Orb, would be through the castle door, which was almost impossible, especially since Oriel now had people guarding it.

"Elle, what happened earlier to make you pass out like that?" Belle asked. Ellora smiled slightly; she had been wondering how long it would take for Belle to ask.

"I spoke to my parents earlier." She was sad to see that lying to her friends was becoming easier. "So that's probably what it was." Nobody asked any further questions, as they all headed to the common room and settled around a large table. Dan suggested a game of poker and, when everybody agreed, jumped up to get a deck of cards.

Ellora agreed to join them for a couple of games before she left to go to her extra lessons and Belle went to another meeting with Master Graynor. She knew this would be the perfect opportunity to talk to Melody and Clara.

He dragged Belle with him, and as she heard their voices become more and more distant, she knew she had to tell Clara and Melody about the situation. "Guys, we have a problem," she said in a low voice, so nobody else could hear her. "It's about Belle. I don't want to tell her because it will only freak her out, but you're both aware about her Aura being ... *stronger*, aren't you?"

They nodded their agreements, leaning further forward to hear Ellora properly. "Well, Asyra called me today." They gasped and choruses of questions came from them both. As soon as Ellora continued to speak, however, they both slammed their mouths shut and leaned in closer, eager to hear what she had to say. "Belle might be in danger; whoever took the Orb might also want to take her Aura," she said in a voice that was barely a whisper.

"'Ow can zhey do zhat?" Melody asked.

"What will happen to her?" Clara shivered.

"They can do anything with the Orb if they're a Madori Aurum and, well, let's just say we have to stop them before that happens."

"What can we do?" Melody asked. Ellora noticed with an internal smiled that Melody looked somewhat like a warrior readying for battle in this moment.

"I think we should see if anybody else is being weird, like maybe hanging around Oriel's office, trying to find the key to the Gate room, or spending loads of time near the door. Or even just being secretive, I guess." Ellora answered, "But we need to remember—"

"Um, Elle—"

"Sorry, Clara, one sec, let me just finish telling you guys before Bee gets back."

"But Elle—"

"What? What is it?" Elle said, slightly annoyed at her friends for not letting her talk.

"'Unter just walked in," said Melody, wide-eyed. "And 'e is covered in blood."

Ellora whipped her head around and caught sight of Hunter limping into the room. She looked at the large rip in his trousers and the dark stain above his left ankle she knew had to be blood. Her eyes drifted upwards and she gasped when she noticed that one sleeve from his jacket and his no longer white shirt had been torn off completely and saw smudges of dark red spread across his torso. When she looked up and saw that his lip was split and bleeding, his eye was swollen and there was a deep gash in his forehead still oozing blood.

The second she looked into his eyes, he looked into hers. His eyes softened for a moment when they landed on hers, but they hardened again just as quickly, and they stood there for a moment, on opposite sides of the room, before Hunter broke the eye contact and turned, moving out of and away from the room as fast as he could with his damaged leg.

Ellora immediately broke into a run after him.

"Hunter!" she called. "Hunter!" He didn't react and continued to move away from her. "Hunter, please, I need to talk to you!"

As if she had pushed him past his breaking point, Hunter turned. She flinched when she saw the look of pure, unadulterated anger on his face. "Go and talk to your *boyfriend*, Ellora," he spat out. Ellora frowned; she assumed he was talking about Mason, but what did he have to do with anything?

"Hunter, I don't—"

"Save it," he snapped, but it wasn't as effective since his voice sounded hoarse.

Ellora felt like crying; she really didn't know what in the Realms she had done to make him so angry. "At least let me help you to the infirmary." She cursed herself inwardly at how trembly her voice had sounded.

"I can manage."

"Mistress Maywether." Ellora started to speak, when Maywether walked over to the desk during their private lesson to see her progress, "I was just wondering if you could help me with something."

"Of course, what is it, Ellora?"

"Well, I heard something about the History of the Realm the other day and I think it's really interesting, but I'm not sure just how true it is."

"Well, I'll try my best to help you." She sat down next to Ellora, clearly intrigued.

"I heard that each of the Kingdoms in our Realm have a Spirit that guards the Aura."

"It's true; that's what the legends say. And I believe them. Apparently, only the members of the Upper Council are invited to meet the Spirits of the Kingdoms. I've never seen a Spirit, myself, and I wouldn't even know where to begin to look for one, let alone what it would look like, but I suppose they're powerful enough beings that they can only be seen when they choose."

"What do they do? The Spirits, I mean."

"Well, it's said that each Spirit guards the core of the Kingdom. For example, the Incendi Spirit guards the core of the Incendi Kingdom and, subsequently, the core of Incendi Aura."

"What do you mean by the core?" Ellora asked the question to bait her teacher into giving the information she needed. She did feel slightly guilty to use her like this, but it was for the good of the Kingdom, really.

"Each Aura has a core that powers it. And the Aura powers the Kingdom, so without the Core, the Kingdom would, essentially, come to a stop." Maywether got up and walked over to her desk, rummaging through one of the drawers until she found an extremely large brown book that was so worn, Ellora was convinced it must have been used daily. "Like the great Lynchi-Obscuri War, see." She opened the book to a page with a folded corner and placed it on the table in front of Ellora, smoothing out the wrinkled pages. "In the war, their Cores were wiped out, and now nobody can access any Lynchi or Obscuri Aura."

"What happened to the Kingdoms?" Ellora asked, now genuinely curious.

"Well, you can still go to the Kingdoms, though not many do. The land is barren, and the War destroyed all of the buildings," she said, sadly.

"That's so sad." Ellora frowned. "What about all the people who lived there?"

"Many of them died." Ellora thought she saw tears in her Caeli teacher's eyes before she blinked them away. "But many of them were lucky and escaped. Some, especially those with children, escaped to the Human Realm and stayed there, wanting nothing more to do with our Realm. Even the Great Wykan left, refusing to come back to a Realm of death and destruction. Some people moved across Kingdoms, settling into a new life and trying to get over what had happened. But it affected them all greatly."

"The Great Wykan?" Ellora asked, intrigued.

"Yes, you haven't heard of him before?" Mistress Maywether asked, and Ellora shook her head in response. "The Great Wykan," she began, "was a sorcerer."

"A sorcerer? I thought that was a myth."

"Hardly. I'm sure, if you have never heard of the Great Wykan, you have never heard of the Kingdom of Magi." Once again, Ellora shook her head. "Magi was not a *type* of Aura, but a different practise. It was an art, you see, which not many had the abilities to perfect. The Great Wykan was one of the last of his kind."

"Did Magi Aura have its own core?" Ellora asked.

"In a sense," she answered. "However, not in the same way as the other Kingdoms; this one was more... *alive*, shall we say."

"Mistress Maywether, what do the cores look like?" Ellora asked. As interested as she was in Magi Aura, she had no time to waste.

"Well, each core looks different and is made from a different material. I, personally, have had the privilege to see the Madori Core myself when I first started working here. Oriel took me with her to see where it was kept, and it was just bewitching. There's no other way I could describe it.

"The books say it was made from the Silvernet flower," she said, turning to another page in the book. "You see, there used to be a small patch of flowers – Silvernet flowers – which used to be the core of Madori Aura. They were always in full bloom, no matter the weather or the time of year, and used to grow in a small area in the gardens, near the East Courtyard. In fact, they used to grow exactly where the fountain is now. But the Spirit of Madori supposedly felt they were too vulnerable, there.

"She asked Arellia, you know – the founder of our school, to take the flowers and turn them into a stone; an orb," she flipped the page to show an illustration of a woman picking glistening flowers. "The Spirit said that the Core could be kept safe that way; in the castle, guarded by the Madori Master or Mistress." She closed the book.

"What the books don't tell us, however, are the legends passed on through the generations. It is said that Arellia also made a jewel."

"A jewel?" Ellora tried to keep in her excitement.

"Yes. From the flowers that she picked, which she turned into a necklace that she hid somewhere in the castle. I suppose she was smart enough to realise that if the Orb was ever removed, the Kingdom would at least have some sort of power source. Unfortunately, nobody knows where this necklace could have been hidden, but the same way the Madori Orb can only be used to its full potential by a Madori Master or Mistress, I believe it is the same situation with the necklace."

"What can the necklace actually do? You said that its powers could be controlled?"

"Well, yes, in a way, I suppose. Because the jewel and the orb were made from the same source, they should, in theory, have some sort of a link between them. One would be able to locate the other, for example. But I'm sure it's just legend; if Oriel knew about it, she would have used it by now, given the circumstance—" She quickly clamped her hand over her mouth. "A slip of the tongue," she stammered out. "Don't think anything of what I said!" She chuckled nervously. "Now, enough chitchat; to work with you."

Ellora was sure she and Mason had decided to meet straight after her Caeli lesson, but ten minutes had gone by now, and he still hadn't shown up. She paced up and down the corridor. It wasn't like him to just stand her up like this without explanation. Although, with how kind he had been towards her earlier, she couldn't even bring herself to be angry with him.

She stopped her pacing when she heard two voices drifting towards her.

"-not worth your time, Hunter." Ellora knew that voice belonged to Ilisha.

"I just need to think about it," Hunter answered. Ellora swallowed hard at the sound of his steady voice. At least she knew he was all right, even if he was angry with her, although she couldn't work out why. She frowned, wondering if Oriel had told him of her suspicions. Surely not, though, since she had told her in confidence.

She knew undoubtedly that she had to speak with Hunter. When he had cooled off slightly.

Upon arrival at Master Rainclarke's classroom, Ellora found out that her lesson for that afternoon would have to be rescheduled for the next day. She didn't mind one bit.

Ellora rushed up to her girls' night, eager to tell them all what she found out about the jewel and wanting to know what Belle's meeting with master Graynor had been about. She knew that, even with all of the precautions Oriel had placed, it was only a matter of time and they had to come up with a plan.

She found them all dressed in their pyjamas, already gathered in Ellora and Melody's bedroom, with bowls of freshly popped popcorn, huge bars of chocolate, two large bottles of lemonade and a carton of strawberry juice. Melody had even pulled out a box of red, fish-shaped sweets that Hazel had given her. "'Azel said zhese were 'er favourites when she lived in zhe 'Uman Realm," Melody had explained.

When they were all settled in, with thick duvets and fluffy pillows draped across the floor, and TV from Belle's room set up, Ellora prepared to tell them about what had happened with Maywether. "We need to find it; it could help us find the jewel. We can protect." She paused slightly, glancing quickly at Belle before glancing back over to Clara and Melody, "Oriel. We can protect Oriel."

"We'll find it, Elle. Don't worry," said Belle reassuringly.

"We won't stop looking, but we need a plan," stated Melody.

"Well, we could hit the library," Clara suggested.

"Okay, but that can all wait till tomorrow. For now, I want to watch a film," insisted Belle.

Ellora, Clara and Melody all exchanged nervous looks, but considering that it was already late, they decided not to argue. Plus, they didn't want Belle to know she could be in danger.

"Aren't you supposed to meet Mason tonight?" asked Clara.

"I was supposed to meet him in between my extra Caeli and Incendi lessons. He didn't turn up," Ellora responded.

"What?!"

"'Ow dare 'e!"

"What a little Snorfuffle," Belle, Clara and Melody all said at once.

Ellora laughed. "It's okay, guys. He probably has a valid reason." She still couldn't bring herself to be upset with him. She would see him soon enough, anyway. And she knew all of the Prefects had been extremely busy lately, so she would give him the benefit of the doubt. "Besides, we were only going to meet for twenty minutes anyway. I'll probably see him tomorrow." And with that, Ellora pulled out Lucifer from her pocket, where he liked to spend all day, every day sleeping, and cuddled him close to her whilst her friends watched the film. All the while, however, Ellora was attempting to come up with a plan to track down Hunter.

Ellora's mind wandered as she mindlessly completed the tasks Master Rainclarke had set her for her extra Incendi lesson. They hadn't been able to discover any information about the jewel that morning in the library. Ellora had even tried to ask Oriel, which had proven useless as well since she knew nothing about it. They had all decided that their best bet would be if Ellora asked Asyra, so she had decided that she would go after dinner to see the Spirit and see if she had any useful information.

And, to make things worse, Hunter, who had turned up to breakfast with a black eye after the mysterious incident that had taken place the day before, had been avoiding her. She had tried to find him so she could have a proper conversation, but it seemed as though Hunter was incredibly good at hiding. She hadn't even seen Mason, so she had no idea why he had stood her up yesterday. She had seen Julia, but when she asked about Mason, Julia simply told her she had to leave and had walked away. Ellora had no idea what was going on.

Master Rainclarke must have sensed her lack of concentration on the tasks because Ellora startled so harshly she almost fell out of her stool when he spoke.

"Ellora, I can see you're not feeling up to any Incendi exercises today," he said gently, as he took a seat across from her. Ellora was still in awe that all other students found him scary; she thought he was the nicest one.

"Sorry, Master Rainclarke. I guess I'm just tired; I've had a lot to think about recently."

"Yes, Oriel told me," he said. Ellora looked up at him in concern. "She didn't give me any details, of course, but as someone who is *also* looking for the Orb, she did tell me the news about Belle."

"Oh. That."

"But let's not talk about that for now, Ellora. I'm sure it's consuming you just as it is me," he smiled reassuringly. "I would like to discuss something else, however."

Ellora looked at him curiously. "Sure," she answered.

"I'm worried about these episodes you keep having, Ellora. You passed out in the dining hall the other day and I know it's happened a few other times, too. I really would like to help you."

"I'm not sure you can." She gave a dry laugh, remembering her baby sister's pained cries for help she had heard in the last dream.

"Humour me," he said. "Can you tell me about them?"

Ellora thought about it for a moment, but she didn't need much time to decide; she knew she could trust Master Rainclarke and it wasn't as if telling him about the dreams could cause any harm.

"I don't really know what they are. I've been calling them 'dreams', but they're not dreams. They're something else –

something real." She paused to look at him and gauge his reaction. "I thought they might have been nightmares, but I don't think that's the case; when I wake up from them, it feels like it's actually happened, and I have to spend some time coming back to reality before I realise that it was in my head. Again. Every single time," she sighed. Master Rainclarke nodded but stayed silent to let her continue.

"We've linked them to my emotions. My friends and I, that is. Whenever I experience a strong emotion, I have one of these 'dreams'." She used air quotes. "It's not always the same. It's always the same place, and the same time – I'm always a child — but sometimes it's different parts of the dream, I guess. Like sometimes I'll see the start, sometimes I'll see different parts of the middle..."

"The end?"

"I've never seen the end." Ellora was surprised to realise. "And yesterday was different."

"How?"

"Well, I'm usually in the same room or heading to the same room, but yesterday I was in a different room. It was familiar, but until I woke up, I didn't realise how."

"What do you mean? What do you see in these dreams, Ellora?" he asked kindly.

"Well, actually, if you'd asked me that yesterday, I wouldn't have been able to tell you," Ellora laughed dryly, again. "I was aware that I was smaller. It was weird, everything seemed so big and I think that's why it took me so long to figure it out." She paused, trying to work out how to explain it all.

"I knew I was in a familiar place. Like I recognised it but couldn't place it – probably because of fact that I was so small. It's also dark there. All the time. So, I'm sure that made it difficult, too. I was also aware of how scared I was. And I mean ridiculously terrified out of my skin."

"And yesterday?"

"Well, yesterday I realised what was going on, in a way. I think my dreams ... or nightmares, or episodes, or whatever you want to call them, are actually memories."

"Memories?" Master Rainclarke seemed unfazed.

"Well, one memory, actually. I think it's been getting clearer since my Madori affinity was declared. It's the night Ophelia— my sister died. That's what I've been seeing," she stated. "Only ... it's different, now."

"Different how, Ellora?"

"It's different to how I remember. Everything's jumbled up and not in the right order. And some parts are just *completely* different. It's like a different memory completely. It's the same event taking place, I know that – I've known that since I heard my sister's cries. It's the same time, the same place, but it's just not the *same*."

"If I'm honest with you, Ellora, I already had my guesses that what you were experiencing was memories. May I try something?" Ellora wasn't surprised that he had already guessed since he had had next to no reaction when she told him.

"Sure."

Master Rainclarke adjusted his position on the stool slightly before he looked straight at Ellora across the table, into her eyes.

Ellora felt a weird feeling in her stomach, similar to butterflies, only it wasn't pleasant. And it only got worse and worse until she was clutching her stomach with pain. But she couldn't remove her eyes from his; somehow, her eyes were glued to his.

She felt something enter her mind, an intrusion. It felt similar to the way it did when Asyra called out to her but stronger. It tore down her walls. And then, she felt a sensation she had never felt before. The feeling of his mind entering hers reversed, as her mind contacted his of its own accord.

Suddenly, a sharp pain pierced through her head. She screamed. "Stop!" Finally, she felt the connection break and she snapped her eyes shut, burying her head in her arms and trying to ignore the ringing in her ears.

She heard a faint buzzing noise but couldn't make out what it was. Slowly, the sound became clearer and louder, and Ellora recognized the sound of her Incendi teacher speaking to her. "I'm sorry, Ellora. It's over. Sit up, come on," he said softly. She took a bar of white chocolate he was holding out to her, and then a plastic bottle filled with a bright blue liquid that could only be a sugar-filled energy drink.

She winced as another wave of pain shook through her head. "Look at me," he commanded. "Look at me, Ellora. I can help you." She slowly raised her eyes to meet his, eyes half-closed in pain.

As soon as she looked, the pain drifted away. She felt weightless as if she was floating on clouds, and her mind felt clear, empty. Slowly, she closed her eyes once more and let herself rest.

Ellora opened her eyes to find herself in an unfamiliar room. The ceiling was white and bare, and there seemed hardly any light in the room at all. She was lying on something soft, but she couldn't quite figure out what it was; it wasn't exactly comfortable, but it was definitely soft.

She blinked her eyes and rubbed her face, trying to adjust her sight to the dark room. She sat up slowly and found that her neck was sore, although she didn't remember hurting it. The last thing she remembered was Master Rainclarke.

She looked around the room at the bare, dark, burgundy walls. The room was mostly empty, but behind her, she found Master Rainclarke sitting behind a wooden desk.

"You're awake," he said, getting up from his seat and sitting in an armchair across from her. Only now did Ellora notice the glass coffee table lying in front of her. Without a word, he handed her another blue drink and a wrapped hard sweet. Without a word, she took them.

"What triggered your Madori Aura?" he asked, surprising Ellora.

"My Aura?" He nodded. "Well." She thought back, trying to remember the lie she had told her friends. "I was in the gardens, by the fountain, and—"

"The real reason, please," Master Rainclarke said pointedly.

Ellora gulped. "Asyra."

"The Madori Spirit?" His eyes widened slightly, but his tone stayed mostly the same.

"Yes. I was with her. For some reason, she can communicate with me. Neither of us know why. But she traced some sort of a pattern on my forehead with her finger. It was kind of like a squiggly line, I think."

"And then?"

"Then Oriel came. She told me about my affinity and that was that," Ellora said. She was confused as to why Master Rainclarke cared about her affinity so much.

"I see," was all he said.

Soon enough, Ellora couldn't take the silence anymore. "Master Rainclarke, what was that? That pain in my head and in my stomach. I've never felt something like that before. And I sure as Mistfall didn't like it."

"Language," he said in his teacher voice.

"Sorry," she replied.

"You asked what that was – confirmation."

"Confirmation of what?"

Master Rainclarke looked at her seriously. Ellora thought he looked quite sad, actually. He looked sorry. "Confirmation that your memories have been tampered with."

Ellora stared at him for a moment before replying. "What?"

"Tell me how you remember your sister's death, Ellora."

Ellora sighed, frustrated, but followed his lead, nonetheless-
. "There was a fire in the house. She died from smoke inhalation," she spoke quietly.

"What time was it?" he asked.

"What?"

"What time did the fire break out?" He insisted.

Ellora thought back and hesitated slightly. "I don't know, Master Rainclarke. I was eleven."

"Okay. For how long were you in the hospital?"

Ellora couldn't reply; she didn't know the answer.

"Which hospital did you go to?"

"Um—"

"Were your parents hurt?"

"I—"

"What caused the fire?"

She thought back and strained to remember the details, as he asked question after question. But for each question, Ellora couldn't come up with an answer.

"I don't know!" she shouted, finally at the edge of her patience. "It was eight years ago; you can't expect me to remember!"

"Ellora, even if it was eight years ago, I'm willing to be it was one of the most significant days of your life. You would never forget something as traumatic as that. Trust me. A night like that and you should remember every single detail; from the location of the fire, right down to the second on the clock."

Ellora looked down at her hands and twiddled the ring she was wearing around her finger. She didn't want to believe him; she didn't want to believe everything was a lie. But nothing made sense.

"Why would someone tamper with my memory? Who would do that?" she asked when she finally found herself able to talk again.

"I don't know, Elle." His use of her nickname sent a ghost of a smile across her face. "But I definitely want to help you find out. For now, I'm going to send you to your friends; I don't want to exhaust you and you've been here for almost an hour already. Our next private lesson is on Friday, and I'd like for you to tell me about every single one of your dreams. If that's okay with you," he added.

She nodded her agreement. "Sure. But ... Master Rainclarke, what was that?" she asked. "What happened to my head? What did you do?"

"That was my Aura calling to your Essence. You have an Incendi affinity too, Elle, not just Madori."

"How do you know that?"

"Because when I looked into your eyes, I channelled my Incendi Aura. I could feel it wanted to draw out your Essence – some of it, at least."

"Can it happen if you don't have the same Essence as somebody's Aura?"

"I guess it can. If two peoples' Essences or Auras greatly attract, it would be similar. But if they repel, it would be slightly less intense."

"Repel?"

"Well, yes, I say 'repel', but that's not quite what I mean. You see, the same thing happened with Oriel and I; how we met is a rather long story, but my Incendi Aura 'repelled' her Madori Aura, in a sense. This just meant our Auras work in harmony, side by side, not bleeding into each other. However, when they try to connect, they can cause big problems. It's usually students, who haven't had the correct training yet, who can have these problems. It's not always on purpose, but often their Auras can fight each other, is a way of saying it, I suppose."

"Sir, I still don't understand what my Aura has to do with my tampered memories," Ellora said, after absorbing what he had said.

"Well, you see, Ellora, whomever it was that tampered with your memories, blocked them off from the rest of your mind. And in the process of blocking off certain memories, it seems as though they also blocked off your Essence. It still flows through you, but it isn't connecting with your mind as it should."

"So, when Asyra unlocked, for a lack of a word, my Madori Aura..."

"She unlocked some of your memories."

Ellora tried to take in as much of the information as she could. She tried to think about what this could mean for her, but she was having a hard time concentrating and her head was pounding, so Master Rainclarke sent her to rest.

It was 5.30 when she got to her room. Dinner was in half an hour, but she felt exhausted. She crawled into her bed, covered herself with the duvet and closed her eyes tightly, hoping to drift off to sleep.

Unfortunately, that wouldn't happen.

Melody burst through the door with Clara, unaware of Ellora's presence. "I cannot believe zhis 'as 'appened," she said.

"Me neither. And worse, I can't believe they're blaming Elle. It *has* to be because of that Liviana girl. She's hated Elle from the start," agreed Clara.

"Oh, Spirits, what's that spoilt brat done now?" Ellora's muffled voice came from under the blankets.

"Oh, Elle, we didn't realise you were 'ere," Melody stammered. "Um, you were not supposed to 'ear zhat."

"Hear what?" Ellora threw off the duvet.

"Well, something's happened and that *hag* has been spreading rumours that it was all your fault."

"What has happened?"

"Well ... zhere is no water."

"What do you mean no water?"

"It's gone," Clara answered.

"What are you talking about? We live in the Madori kingdom," Ellora said. "We literally live in the *Kingdom* of Water."

"Just try it. Try to turn on the tap."

Ellora walked over to the bathroom and tried the tap. Nothing.

"What is going on?! How can we have a water shortage in the KINGDOM OF WATER?"

"Everyone zhinks it is because of zhe Orb."

"What, so they're now saying that I took the Orb?" Ellora scoffed in disbelief.

"Well ... Liviana is," Clara answered.

"Ah, Mistfall," Ellora groaned.

"Some ozher people 'ave been saying zhese zhings for some time, now, but nobody really believed it!" Melody was bursting with anger.

"So, what, we just aren't going to shower or go to the loo or brush our teeth or anything then?" Ellora tried to diffuse the situation.

"Oriel's trying to fix it. She said she's going to go straight to the water source and try to just *create* more," Clara said, propping herself down on Ellora's mattress so she could speak quietly to Ellora, not wanting to worry melody. "It's not so big of a deal since we can create more. It's just... it's stressing people out, you know? The idea that someone in this school could have the power to just evaporate the entire Kingdom's water source."

Ellora nodded grimly, but forced a smile when Melody walked over to them with a funny look on her face.

"What is a loo?" Melody asked. For a long moment, Ellora just stared at Melody and the confused expression on her face. Then, without warning, she laughed. "What's ... a loo." She gasped between breaths, laughing even harder than before. Clara looked over at her old friend, looking slightly concerned. But before long, she couldn't help it and fell over herself, laughing just as hard. The sight of the two laughing so hard set Melody off, too, and then the three were sprawled on the floor, laughing their heads off.

When they calmed down, they all lay on the floor for a while, clutching their sides and chuckling. And then, after some silence, Ellora spoke once more. "A loo is a toilet, Melody."

Another moment of silence fell across the room.

"It is going to be 'ard for Oriel, isn't it? To create a new source of water wizhout zhe Orb," Melody commented.

"I suppose so," said Ellora. "Hopefully, she'll find someone to help her." She didn't speak for a moment, before blurting: "Have either of you got any Lucozade or anything?"

"The Human drink?" asked Clara, confused. Ellora nodded. "I think I can get some from the kitchen; I don't have a clue why, but they've always got bottles and bottles of the stuff."

"It 'as so much sugar in it!" exclaimed Melody.

"That's the point," Ellora smiled. "The session with Rainclarke really drained me and I think I need some sugar before dinner to perk me up since I don't really have time for a nap. I just feel so unbelievably drained."

"I'll run down and grab it," said Clara.

"I can go," Ellora protested, but Clara insisted there was no need and that she looked like she needed the rest.

"So, are you going to see Asyra today?" Melody asked.

"Hopefully. For now, though, I just need to get through dinner. And with everybody thinking this is all my fault, I guess."

"Don't worry, Elle; we 'ave got your back," she smiled, reassuringly, and then cooed at Lucifer, who had just climbed up her shoulder.

It was an amusing sight to look at – Melody was such a small girl standing in a superhero pose, with a tiny orange fur ball napping on her shoulder. And yet, it made all the difference in the world to Ellora; she knew she could count on her friends.

CHAPTER SIXTEEN
Marble and Stone

By the time the girls went down to dinner, Oriel had recreated a water supply. Fortunately for everyone in the school, the chefs had Madori Aura on their side, and still managed to cook. Ellora was so lost in her train of thought when she walked into the dining room that she almost didn't notice how everybody immediately fell silent at her arrival. It was a couple of minutes after six she walked in, so the room and the tables were mostly filled, already. The students, and a few teachers, all stared at her in silence, watching her walk over to her friends at the table and take her seat. She kept her eyes down, feeling embarrassed, and remained silent.

"Hey guys," she said when the people around them talked again. "So ... that was weird." She attempted to break the ice with a nervous laugh.

"Yeah, it looks like the only people who don't think you're responsible are us. And most of the teachers," said Clara.

"Where's Dan?" Ellora asked Belle. Hunter wasn't there, either, but she had expected that by now. Dan told her that Hunter still wouldn't talk to him about what had happened but that he had been acting otherwise normal-ish. She vowed to find him sooner rather than later, whether he liked it or not.

"His mum called him a few minutes ago, so he's just talking to her in the library," said Belle.

Ellora walked out into the courtyard and, for only a few seconds, allowed herself to breathe in the fresh air. She needed it, after the whirlwind of a day she had had, and the weather was finally picking up now that Spring had arrived.

She strolled over to the door she knew was concealing a beautiful view. And an ancient Spirit. "Asyra? Are you here?" she asked when she reached the lake. "I need to talk to you."

"I'm here, my dear." Asyra's voice echoed. "What seems to be the problem? Have you found any leads?"

"What do you know about the Madori Jewel?" Ellora cut straight to the point.

There was a brief stretch of silence.

"Where did you hear about that?" Asyra snapped. Once again, Ellora felt the beginnings of fear of the Madori Spirit.

"It doesn't matter, Asyra. I'm just trying to find the Orb," she insisted. She watched Asyra carefully, watching her tense facial muscles and clenched fists, as she got closer and closer to the shore.

Finally, when Asyra's face relaxed, Ellora allowed herself to relax.

"I don't even know if it's real." Asyra sounded less angry, but she still wasn't as friendly or calming as usual. "Ariella may well have created it, against my wishes and in secret from me, might I add, but there is no way to know for certain. Unless you find it, that is.

"Even if she did create it, I'm sure that she used her Madori Mistress connection to the castle to make sure any regular person could find it. If you're going to find it, Ellora, you will need help. You will need the Madori Mistress."

"I just have no idea where to begin," said Ellora, who was still cautious of Asyra's mood.

"Well, my dear," Asyra began, and Ellora instantly felt at ease, hearing Asyra call her 'dear' again. "If there's one thing I knew about Ariella, it is that she was cunning. Too cunning for her own good and secretive. She would have hidden it somewhere nobody would have thought to look, and she would have known every possible hiding space there was."

"Somewhere nobody would think to look," Ellora repeated. "Oh, before I forget, can I ask you something?"

"Would it stop you if I said no?" Asyra joked, amusement glistening behind her eyes.

Ellora's lips twitched upwards. "Maybe. For a while, I was convinced Hunter had something to do with all of this, with the Orb and Belle and ... well, it doesn't matter. The point is, Oriel told me you know he is innocent. Right? You do *know* Hunter is innocent?"

For a small moment, an unexpected emotion flittered across Asyra's face. Surprise. But it disappeared and all that was left was amusement. "I am telling you, for a fact, my dear, that Hunter is not the culprit, nor is he working on the culprit. And, unfortunately, I believe that is all I am permitted to say."

"Permitted?" Ellora asked, taken aback by the blunt and undetailed, albeit helpful, answer.

"Oriel has asked me for a favour, and I have agreed. So, I will ask you not to ask me of Hunter again if you can help it."

And as what was clearly intended to be a dismissive gesture, Asyra turned around, showing her back to Ellora.

"Asyra told you zhat she is cunning, oui?" asked Melody. It had been an entire week, and they still hadn't figured out where the jewel could be. They were all sat with a tall stack of books in front of each.

"What's that?" asked Ellora, pointing at something in Oriel's office. She got up immediately and walked in, Belle, Melody and Clara closely behind.

"Good evening." Oriel greeted them with a confused look.

"Oriel, what is that?" Ellora asked, walking over to a painting on the far wall.

"A painting, Ellora. Are you feeling okay?"

"Asyra told me, the day that I met her, that Arellia was vain," Ellora mumbled to herself, examining the painting.

"Is this Arellia?" Belle caught on.

"It is. Seriously, girls, what's going on?" Oriel asked as they all crowded around the frame.

"Anyone else thinking what I'm thinking?" Ellora asked as she reached over to grab the portrait.

"That this is the perfect place to hide a small, stone-like object?" Belle played along.

"Like a jewel?" Oriel asked suspiciously.

"Exactly like a jewel," said Melody.

"It's stuck on something," Ellora grunted. "There's something back there." Belle reached around and unhooked the frame.

They all held their breath as Ellora finally removed the painting. The sight silenced them all.

"Zhere is nothing 'ere," Melody whispered, disappointedly.

"It's just a hook." Belle looked over at the wall for the object keeping the painting attached to it.

For a few moments, nobody said a thing.

"Unless," Melody suddenly muttered. She turned around and hurried over to Oriel's desk, rummaging around for something. When she turned back around, she had a knife in her hand.

"Um, Melody, what do you plan to do with that?" Clara asked nervously.

"Zhis really is zhe perfect place to 'ide zhe jewel," said Melody, before she sliced through the painting straight from the top left corner to the bottom right.

"Melody!"

"What are you doing?!"

"Stop!" Belle, Clara and Ellora shouted all at once.

"What?" said Melody, sadly. "I do not understand." There was nothing in the painting, either.

Everyone stared between Melody and the cut-up painting in shock.

The silence was interrupted by the sound of a laugh. It was Oriel. "Oriel, I ruined your painting! Why in zhe Realms are you laughing?" Melody asked in a thick voice, sounding as though she was on the verge of tears.

"Well, I never liked that painting much, anyway," she answered between laughs. "I've always thought it was a bit scary-looking."

After a long afternoon of thoroughly checking each of the other 72 paintings of Arellia around the castle, the group came back empty-handed. They were sure that they would find something; a safe or a small nook, maybe even the jewel itself attached to the back of one of the paintings. But they were disappointed. Ellora sat quietly, frantically rubbing at her hands. There *had* to be something they were missing.

On Monday evening, Ellora had gone to the library once again, but alone this time, to find some relevant books about the Aura School Founders. It was when she was walking through the shelves, looking for the right section, that she came across Mason.

"Mason, hey!" she called. She saw his shoulders stiffen slightly but walked over to him, anyway. "Where have you been? I haven't seen you in a while. I've tried to find you a few times." She leaned against the bookshelf next to him and smiled brightly.

Mason turned slightly to face her but wouldn't look directly at her. She frowned, feeling slightly insulted. "Ellora, hey. Sorry, it's been crazy busy what with the Orb and everything."

"Is something wrong?" she asked him. She remembered what Hunter had said about his being covered in blood. "Have I done something?" She was not a fan of how vulnerable she had just sounded, but she couldn't figure out why Mason would have anything to do with it unless she had done something wrong.

"No, you haven't done anything, Elle."

"Hunter told me—"

"I've got to go. Take care of yourself," he said gruffly, abandoning the book he was holding and walked in the other direction. Ellora watched him leave the library and frowned.

And just like that, she didn't feel like researching anymore. She *wanted* to crawl into her bed with a tub of ice cream. She groaned inwardly and slumped out of the library.

Ellora walked outside into the fresh spring air, hoping that a quick walk would get her head focused once again. But she tensed when she spotted the familiar head of inky hair sitting on a stone bench in front of the fountain.

She saw his hands waving in unfamiliar motions in front of him and, even though she had been looking for this opportunity for days now, she felt nervous. She walked over and stopped just behind him, leaning over his shoulder to watch the intricate gestures. She took a deep breath to prepare herself for this conversation.

One by one, each pink blossom from in front of him rose into the air, creating a swirling pattern. She was entranced by the intricate movements. He used the pointer finger of his right hand to gently flick the pretty pink blossoms up into the air and somehow elegantly wiggled the fingers of his left hand to keep the leaves swirling in the air. As she watched the movements, she felt multiple weeks' worth of tension ease from her body.

"Can I help you, Artemer?"

Ellora jumped slightly in surprise. "Oh," she blushed at her getting caught watching him and was, in that instant, very glad he was not facing her. "I was just watching you-I mean the leaves; I was watching the leaves." She mentally shook her head. "How did you know I was here?" Ellora asked.

"Please," Hunter scoffed, "you would make a bad spy – your sneaking skills are atrocious." He looked over his shoulder to glance at her before focusing back on the leaves. "And I could smell your vanilla shampoo the moment you walked out the door."

Ellora felt her face flush with colour again and raised her hand to her hair sheepishly. "I didn't realise it was that strong." After a long period of silence, she spoke again. "I'm glad to see you look fully healed. Healer Amare must have done a good job."

He let the leaves float back to the floor as he turned fully to see Ellora. "Is there something you wanted?"

"Yes. I wanted to apologise," said Ellora, looking down slightly. "I don't know if Oriel said anything, but I accused you of being the one to take the Orb, Hunter."

"What?" he asked, surprised, as he stood up.

"I know. I'm so sorry," Ellora said quickly. "I was just worried about it all, Hunter, you have to believe me; I really don't think it's you anymore. Well, actually, it was Oriel who convinced me otherwise, but—"

"What did Oriel say?" Hunter all but growled at her.

"She just said there was no way it could be you, and—"

"So, she *didn't* tell you why?" His face seemed slightly less tense now, but the line of worry between his eyebrows was still present.

"No," Ellora spoke in a voice not much louder than a whisper. "Hunter, what—"

Hunter didn't wait for her to finish speaking before brushing past her and marching inside.

Ellora sighed as she sat on the stone bench that Hunter had left and buried her face in her hands. She had hoped to get some sort of an explanation, some sort of help. That had definitely not gone as she had hoped.

When Ellora woke up at 7 am the next morning, she felt groggy. She had slept nine and a half hours, but she still felt unrested. After getting ready, she and Melody made their way downstairs to breakfast and sank into their seats, grateful for the hot tea in front of them.

She looked up as Dan walked over to them. "Good morning, ladies," he said cheerfully.

"Someone's happy today," Belle laughed.

"What's not to be happy about? I'm in the best Aura School in the Realm, I've got the best friends I could ever ask for, friends *and* the chefs have made French Toast today," he almost drooled over the food on his plate.

"Speaking of great friends," said Clara, "how's Hunter?"

"He still won't tell me what happened. It's really weird."

Since their weird conversation the day before, Ellora hadn't seen him again and she so desperately wanted to talk to him. She wanted his help, for one, and she wanted to know what was going on.

That same day, the most unexpected thing that could have happened, happened. Ellora, Clara, Melody, Belle and Dan were sitting at the table for dinner, when Hunter walked in. At the sound of his familiarly deep voice, they all turned and dropped their jaws to see him *laughing*.

He walked in, walking between Ilisha and Violet, waved them goodbye, and walked over to their table. "Hey," he said to no one in particular. They all stared at him in shock.

"'Hey'?" Belle spluttered.

"Not ignoring me anymore, then?" Ellora asked Hunter, still feeling slightly hurt at his cold treatment towards her. "You know, I just wanted to apologise to you." Again, he gave only a shrug. "Fine. Be that way," Ellora snapped. "And don't tell us why you were all bloody. Leave us worrying. Not that you care about us anyway, Hunter Nash." Ellora pointedly enounced every letter in his name.

"Worried," Hunter laughed. "If you say so."

And with that, Ellora could take no more.

She stood up quickly and walked around the table to stand directly in front of him, where he had stood up to reach for the jug of water.

"Yes," she said sharply, emphasising each word with a prod to his chest with her finger. "Believe it or not, we were *worried* about you. What, you think your *girlfriend* over there is the only one who cares about you?! Just because you can't find it in your cold, pathetic, COWARDLY little heart to even think twice about any of us does *not* mean we do not care about you, you ungrateful OAF."

Ellora was breathing heavily with her anger, her teeth clenched, and her eyes fixed hard on his. Silence surrounded her as their friends and the rest of the room watched them, mouths dropped open, eyes wide.

After a moment of looking at a blank, expressionless face, Ellora saw it turn into one of anger. No, not anger, rage. She flinched when Hunter grabbed the wrist of the finger still digging into his chest and shoved it away from him. With the white-hot fury in his eyes, Ellora was worried. It made her nervous, however, that she was worried she had upset him, rather than scared of what he would do.

"You think I don't care?" he whispered. She didn't know why, but the quietness of his words made her feel even more nervous. "You *really* think I don't care?" Sadness flashed in his eyes, but it quickly disappeared again to be replaced by that rage once more. Suddenly, he let go of her wrists and walked out of the room without a second glance.

Ellora, Belle, Melody and Clara were sitting in silence in the library. Sometimes, Belle or Clara would look over at Ellora, just to make sure she was okay, but she kept her head buried in a book, anyway.

She hadn't said a word since her argument with Hunter, and everyone seemed slightly afraid of her reaction. Even Lucifer had stayed on Melody's shoulder, for now.

"We could ask Wendy." Melody's suggestion broke through the tense silence, and they all turned to look at her.

"Ask Wendy what?" Belle asked.

"About Arellia," Melody replied. "We could tell 'er we are doing an extra project about 'er, or somezhing, and see if she as any useful information."

"Well, I guess if anyone has any information, it would be her," Clara added.

"I'll ask her," Ellora said, standing up and walking over to her desk.

"Hi Wendy," she said. "I just wanted to ask you something for a project. I need to find information about Arellia."

"Oh, I have a lovely book all about her."

"There's a book," said Ellora, arriving back at the table with her friends. "I've got the aisle and shelf number."

"I'll go and grab it, volunteered Clara.

Ellora was gathering up the books the four of them had already read so that she could put them away, before Clara came running back. Her face had turned bright red, and she was panting as if she had just run a marathon.

"Clara, what's wrong?" asked Belle.

"The statue," Clara gasped out, slumping into her seat. "I was looking for the book and then I saw this crowd of people heading towards Oriel's office. They looked really weird, actually." Clara side-tracked. "One was wearing a red dress and a red blazer, another was wearing a pink suit, and — it doesn't matter. Anyway, I overheard them talking about the statue out at the front of the school!"

"The statue of Arellia!" Gasped Ellora.

"Yes, but they were all discussing about how all the Aura Schools have a statue out in the front, but none are as beautiful as ours. And then I realised; we have two statues."

"You're right," Belle jumped up excitedly. "We have a second one in the East Courtyard! Why would Arellia put another statue in?"

"Probably because she is vain?" Melody caught on.

"And she must have realised that that would be a brilliant location to hide the jewel! Nobody would look in there," said Ellora.

"Amazing!" said Belle.

"Well, what in zhe Realms are we waiting for?" asked Melody. "Let's go to take a look."

"Not yet," said Belle. "It's only 5 pm. At the moment, people will be out there, playing football and stuff like that. I know that's where Dan is right now. We'll have to go after dinner; everyone will be in here because it'll be too cold. I suppose not being in the Caeli Kingdom is useful, for once; they would never have such a cold spring there. Anyway, that way, we'll be able to go without anybody seeing us."

"Sounds like a plan," said Clara.

"Should we tell zhe Madori Mistress?" asked Melody.

"Oriel's in a meeting, so I suppose we will have to tell her later. I wonder who those people are, anyway; I keep seeing them around," answered Ellora, who could feel her stomach churning at facing Hunter again in the dining room. But at least now, she had something to focus on.

"Were those the people that freaked out Rainclarke?" asked Clara.

"Yeah. Whatever they're here for, it can't be anything good."

Oriel never turned up to dinner.

The girls knew, whatever it was about, that the meeting she was in was important. But they also knew the Orb couldn't wait, so they investigated themselves.

"Do you zhink zhis could be it?" Melody asked in a hushed voice as they walked through the corridors.

"I hope so; I just can't keep lying to Dan," replied Belle.

Luckily, the Courtyard was empty – it wouldn't do to have the thief work out what they were doing and try to get away even earlier. The four tiptoed over to the statue as if worried a single sound could set off some sort of booby trap.

When standing around it, they stared. Seconds passed, and then more, and the girls stared some more.

"'Ow do we know what to do?" Melody asked, finally.

"Don't smash it!" Ellora, Belle and Clara immediately replied at once. Instead of blushing and feeling embarrassed, Melody laughed with them.

"I 'ave to admit, I was zhinking about it," she answered between laughs.

"There's nothing on the actual statue itself," said Belle, walking around the statue to examine it.

"Do you zhink zhere might be some sort of compartment?" Melody asked.

"It's worth a shot," said Clara.

And, so, they divided the statue into four sections – one each. Melody took the legs, Clara took the arms, Ellora took the torso and Belle took the head. They searched in silence, looking for some sort of nook where Arellia could have hidden the necklace, or a hidden compartment, even maybe a button or switch or level they could push to make something happen.

They found nothing.

"Ugh," Melody groaned. "Zhis is useless!"

"I think you might be right," sighed Ellora.

"Well, I guess it's a good thing we didn't take this to Oriel," Clara said, as they all walked over to and slumped onto a nearby bench. "This statue is nothing but a chiselled block of marble."

There was a moment of silence before Belle's head shot up. "What did you say?" she demanded.

"Um, it's good we didn't tell Oriel?" Clara said.

"No, after that," Belle jumped out of her seat and walked back over to the statue.

"It's just marble," said Clara.

"Bee, what's going on?" asked Ellora.

"You're right," Belle said quietly, almost to herself, her eyes fixed on the statue as her hands roamed over it. Anyone looking at her could tell how focused she was on the material in front of her. "This is just marble," she spoke louder this time, facing her friends again. "We have to go."

Belle was the first one through the door and back into the corridor, with Ellora, Melody and Clara jogging behind but struggling to keep up. "Belle, what is going on?" asked Melody.

"Where are we going?" Clara asked.

But Belle led them on without a word of explanation.

When they reached the library, Belle came to an abrupt halt and turned around to face her friends, who fell into each other after running to keep up with her. "Have any of you ever seen the statue of Malefic in the Incendi Kingdom?"

"Who?" asked Ellora.

"Malefic," replied Clara. "She was the founder of the Incendi School of Aura, kind of like Arellia. And I have seen her statue; outside the Incendi School. But only once."

"And what did you think of it?" Belle asked.

"Bee, are you okay? You seem a bit loopy if I'm being honest," Ellora interrupted.

"Trust me, Ellie," Belle replied seriously.

"Um," Clara hesitated. "It was a cool statue, I guess." She thought for a minute and frowned. "Actually, I was quite young when I saw it and I think I remember being quite scared of it."

"Exactly!" Belle clapped her hands in triumph. "The statue of Malefic, in the Incendi Kingdom, is extremely realistic, because it's made out of enchanted marble. It's creepy – it looks so lifelike and, in the case of Malefic, scary, because of her half-burnt face."

"Oh, I suppose it is zhe same for zhe statue of Cole in zhe Glassi Kingdom," Melody contributed. "I always zhought 'e looked so friendly because 'is statue's eyes always sparkle, just a little. You know?"

"And is the statue of Cole made of marble?" Belle asked, so excited she couldn't stay still.

"Oui!" exclaimed Melody.

"And I'm willing to bet the other Kingdoms have a marble statue of their Aura School's founder outside their school, too," said Belle.

"So why is it that the statue in our East Courtyard is made from marble," Ellora pieced together, thinking back on the first time she walked through the huge double doors to the building, "and the one outside the doors is made from stone?"

"Because Arellia is smarter that we gave her credit for." Clara smiled.

"She might be vain," said Belle.

"But she is as manipulative as can be," finished Melody.

"She must have known that nobody would even think to look for the jewel outside the castle, in plain sight," said Ellora.

"But to get out there, we're going to need Oriel," said Belle. "Besides, Asyra said only the Madori Mistress would be able to find it, right?" The other nodded, and they made their way to Oriel's office.

CHAPTER SEVENTEEN
Kristen

They had been waiting for about twenty minutes, now, just sitting on the carpeted floor just outside of Oriel's office. When they arrived, the girls had overheard some loud voices coming from Oriel's office and realised she was still in her meeting. So, while Clara and Belle had opted to wait in case the meeting ended, Ellora and Melody went off to get some food for Oriel, who they knew still hadn't eaten, and grab something for Lucifer to eat, as he had woken up from his nap in Ellora's blazer's breast pocket.

But even by the time they came back, they had to join Clara and Belle in waiting.

Lucifer startled and crawled back into Ellora's pocket when Belle jumped up from her spot on the floor and screamed. "Kristen!" she shouted at the top of her lungs, as the door to Oriel's office opened, and the group of oddly coloured people walked out. She ran over to the woman in front of the others, who was wearing a red blazer and matching red trousers, with a white top and white heels. She was tall, and Ellora knew she would still be tall, even without the heels.

Ellora looked over at the tall woman, who was smiling and had her arms wrapped tightly around Belle, and instantly recognized the familiar features: the straight golden hair, even if Kristen wore it longer, the happy blue eyes, the height. Belle looked exactly like her.

"Who's that?" Clara whispered.

"Belle, darling, I'm so happy to see you!" Kristen said warmly.

"Guys," said Belle, turning around. "This is Kristen – my sister, who also happens to be the Incendi Mistress. Kris, this is everyone."

"Ah, you must be Elle," Kristen said, giving Ellora a hug, too. "I've heard lots about you. And you must be Luci," she said in a babyish voice, coaxing Lucifer out of Ellora's pocket. "And Melody, and Clara, right?" she asked, turning to them. "It's lovely to finally meet you all."

"Likewise," said Clara.

"You, too," Melody replied.

"It's nice to finally put a face to the name," smiled Ellora.

"Listen, I'm incredibly sorry, girls, but I can't stay. I've been away from the school for far too long than I should." She frowned. "But I promise I'll come and see you soon," she said, mostly to Belle.

By now, the others had left, and it was only Kristen, Oriel and the girls remaining.

"Kris, what's going on?" Belle asked, worried. "I know you've been here a few times, and I'm assuming the others that were here are the other Upper Council Members. I know you wouldn't be here if it wasn't serious."

"It's nothing to worry about, Bee," Kristen answered, but Ellora could see the tension in her eyes. "Everything is going to be fine."

"Is it because of the Orb?" Ellora asked.

"You could say that," said Kristen. "Look, I really need to go. Sorry," she called behind her as she ran to get to the Gate room.

Ellora knew Belle wanted to run after her sister and get some answers, but she stayed.

"I've always wondered why we had two statues, but I figured it was because of how much Arellia loved herself," said Oriel. "Well, we have no time to waste. Let's get that jewel."

Oriel was the first to walk out of the library, followed by Ellora, then Belle, then Clara and Melody. The girls waited a few steps away as Oriel spoke to the guard on duty at the door. Ellora quite liked his uniform – he was wearing a long-sleeved, pale blue shirt with dark blue tie and matching trousers with suspenders. Although, she thought the tall, dark blue hats looked a bit ridiculous.

When Oriel was finished talking with him, the girls watched in awe as she made a few waving motions with her hands to the door. A beautiful blue glow travelled from the palms of her hands to the thick wooden door and then spread outwards, creating intricate little swirls and patterns. The glow spread slowly, beautifully highlighting each of the little shapes, until the entire door was glistening a light blue hue from top to bottom.

With a loud click that echoed around the room, the door was unlocked and swung open.

"Madori Mistress." A different guard came running over, with another following closely behind. Ellora had never seen so many guards before, she had usually only seen the one standing at the door.

"Officer Briar, what's wrong?" Oriel asked.

"Mistress, you must come with us at once. There had been a situation and somebody else is hurt," he said urgently, but still politely. Ellora thought how he spoke to her reminded her of how someone would speak to a queen. Although, that made sense since she was the Upper Council Member of the Kingdom, which pretty much amounted to a queen.

Oriel turned and looked at Belle, Ellora, Melody and Clara. "Girls, you'll have to investigate without me for now. I'll come back as soon as possible. Good luck." She turned back to the guard, telling him to lead the way before following after him.

"Well," said Ellora, "I guess we better get started."

The girls walked out in the air, which was so much colder than it had been half an hour ago in the East Courtyard, and over to the stone statue.

They inspected the statue in the same way that they had the last – Melody took the legs, Clara the arms, Ellora the torso and Belle the head.

"I can't find anything," said Clara. "I don't feel any buttons or levers or anything."

"Me neither," Melody sighed.

"Wait," said Ellora. "I think I remember seeing something in her eyes the day that we moved in." She crouched down slightly to look closer. "Yes, look!" she said, jumping up, when she noticed the familiar blue twinkle she saw on the first day.

"Oh, you're right!" cried Clara, looking over.

"But how do we get to it?" asked Belle.

"Guys, I zhink I 'ave found somezhing," said Melody. There was a SNAP and the blue twinkle became stronger, more like a light.

"Woah, what did you do?" asked Ellora.

"Zhere was a button, and I pushed it." Melody shrugged.

"Well, whatever you did, it looks like you've pushed the jewel forward. I think that's good," said Clara. "I think we just need to figure out how to open it up. Without smashing it," she added, quickly, with a laugh.

"Very funny," Melody retorted sarcastically. "Is zhis zhe part where we need Oriel?"

"Probably," said Ellora. "Unless we can just unlock it with our Madori Aura, maybe. Belle, it's a long shot, but why don't you give it a try?"

Belle nodded and moved to stand in front of the statue. Ellora, Melody and Clara watched intently, as she closed her eyes and breathed deeply. Ellora knew that she was going to the same mental place she always went to when using her Aura – the water.

She watched closely as Belle lifted her hands, her breath keeping its steady pace. She watched Belle's hands float over to the statue, resting on its head. She furrowed her brows as she watched Belle's fingers draw a squiggly symbol on the stone, the same symbol that had unlocked Ellora's Aura.

Another blue light spread across the statue and created cracks through the stone. Slowly, the blue light drifted over the eyes of the statue and created a small, square sort of shape. The shape pulled out from the rest of the statue, like a little drawer, and Ellora heard herself gasp, along with Clara and Melody.

"'Ow did you do zhat?" Melody whispered, her eyes wide and her accent sound just a little bit more prominent.

"Do what?" Belle flickered her eyes open and looked at the shock and amazement evident on her friends' faces. When she looked down, even she was surprised to see that a small, beautiful little, deep blue rock was nestled in a pocket of stone. "Wow."

"Wow is right." Was all Ellora could think of to say as she lowered her hands and retrieved the jewel from the statue.

The jewel was magnificent. It was one of the most beautiful things any of them had ever seen. And, yet, they had no idea what to do with it.

"We should probably tell Mistress Oriel," Melody suggested.

"You're right," agreed Belle.

The girls headed to Oriel's office, but the light was off, and the door was locked. They stayed there for a while, but when Oriel didn't return, Ellora suggested checking the infirmary.

Healer Amare told them that, although Oriel had escorted a Second Former who had severely burned the left half of her face to the infirmary, Master Rainclarke had come in with an emergency and she had had to go to the Caeli Kingdom. "She left you a note," Healer Amare said.

Ellora.

Something of urgency has come up and I must travel to the Caeli Kingdom. I know the four of you may need my help, although I have a sneaking suspicion that Belle may have helped you to the extent that you required.

I will explain everything when I get back. I fear there is more going on here than we first thought.

I will be back ASAP and will come to find you all, no matter the time.

Oriel x

They had all stayed together for the evening, so Oriel could easily find them when she returned, so they took the jewel back to Ellora's room with them.

"Luci seems to like it," giggled Melody, who was watching Lucifer play with the stone, pawing at it and occasionally trying to eat it.

"He can be its guard for the night, then," Clara chuckled. "Isn't that right, Luci? Isn't that right?" she cooed in a baby voice, tickling Lucifer under his chin.

Belle walked into the room wearing pyjamas and with her television in hand. "This will help to keep us awake."

"You're right," said Ellora, as she rushed over to help with the TV. "Hmm. I wonder if coffee will also help?"

"Do you zhink it is broken?" Melody asked when Clara and Ellora returned from the kitchen run. "It does not seem to do anyzhing."

"Well," said Clara, picking up the stone, "let's try..." she trailed off, as she vigorously shook the stone in her hands. "Nope, that didn't work."

"Maybe there's some sort of 'on' button?" Suggested Ellora.

"Hang on a second," said Clara. "Belle, you were the one who was able to unlock the jewel from the statue. Maybe you're the one who can use it."

"It's definitely worth a shot," said Ellora.

"Umm, okay, what do I do?" asked Belle.

"Take it," said Clara, handing her the jewel.

They all held their breaths as Belle took hold of the jewel. But nothing happened.

"Maybe you need to use your Aura?" Suggested Melody.

"Okay," said Belle. She closed her eyes and Ellora knew she was imagining herself in the water like she had told Ellora to do herself.

Slowly, Belle opened her eyes once more.

Nothing.

CHAPTER EIGHTEEN

A Ferri Aurum

Ellora woke up at 2 am to the sound of screaming. It took her a moment to fully wake up, and when she did, she realised the sound was coming from Belle.

"Belle, what's wrong?" she asked, urgently, shaking her.

"Move," demanded Melody, an unexpected command from the tiny, bubbly little girl. Ellora leapt back just in time to avoid the splashed water from where Melody had thrown it onto Belle.

"Agh!" Belle's eyes snapped open immediately. "WHAT WAS THAT FOR?!" she shouted.

Melody shrugged, "You were screaming."

Ellora turned around at the sound of the hushing voices coming from the beds – Clara was calming down Lucifer, who had been scared by all the loud noises and was now snuggled into Clara's sleeve, only his wide, little white eyes poking out in fear.

"What happened?" asked Ellora, turning around to Belle again.

"I don't know," she said, changing out of her sopping clothes into a pair of Ellora's own pyjamas. Ellora didn't mind, though; they shared most of their clothes, anyway. "I had some sort of ... weird ... nightmare ... thing."

"What was it about?" asked Melody.

"I don't know. I think I was in a cave or a tunnel or something. It was really dark. And dusty." Belle squinted her eyes as she tried to remember. "Someone was in there. And they were holding a blue light."

"A blue light?" said Clara.

"And then I was in the sea. Only, I wasn't alone – there was something in there with me. I remember seeing loads of red eyes."

"Zhis sounds creepy," Melody shuddered.

"And then I was near the fountain, I think. By the gardens. But I was cold. And wearing Ellora's trainers. And then I woke up."

"Sounds like a really weird dream," Ellora commented.

"I'm sure it was because of this stupid thing." Belle walked over to the jewel and snatched it from the ground. "I fell asleep holding it."

"Um, Belle?" Melody said, sounding nervous.

"Maybe it's cursed," said Belle.

"Belle." Clara tried to interrupt her.

"It's possible," continued Belle. "It could be a trap."

"WOAH!" Ellora shouted. "Belle, the jewel is glowing."

"It is," Belle answered, so surprised, her statement sounded like a question.

"It's flickering," said Clara. "What does that mean?"

"I don't know," said Belle. "But look. It stops flickering when I hold it in certain places, see?" She held it in the direction of the door, and the flickering stopped, but when she turned away from the door, it flickered more and more rapidly.

"You aren't going to like this," began Ellora sheepishly, "but I think it wants to take us somewhere."

"We were supposed to wait for Oriel!" exclaimed Melody, obviously scared.

"I know, but what if it's trying to take us to the thief? If whoever has the Orb is trying to escape now, we can't wait! Oriel said she would find us when she came back, so she must not be back yet," Ellora spoke urgently. If this was their last opportunity to catch the thief, there was no way in the Realms that Ellora was letting them escape.

"She's right," Clara sighed. "We can't let them get away."

"Fine," Belle grumbled her agreement, and even though Melody looked reluctant, she nodded her head.

"But I 'ave one condition," Melody said. "Lucifer stays ere."

The four creeped out of Ellora's bedroom, not wanting to awaken anyone. They were headed to the stairs when Belle gasped. "Do you see it?" she whispered, pointing at the floor by the staircase.

"See what?" asked Melody.

"The trail on the floor," Belle answered. "There's a trail of blue, glowing stuff on the floor and it leads down the stairs."

"Maybe you're the only one who can see it," suggested Clara. "It could be because you've got the jewel."

"Well, either way, I think that's the way we should go. Belle, lead the way," said Ellora.

"Why do you zhink it was not glowing earlier?" Melody asked in a whisper.

"I don't know," answered Ellora. "Maybe it's only glowing now because the Orb is on the move."

They followed the trail down the stairs, around the corner and through the corridor, until they reached the gardens. "Huh," Belle said. "That's weird."

"What 'appened?" asked Melody.

"This is just like my dream – I'm by the fountain and I'm in Ellora's trainers. They were quicker to get to than going back to my own room."

"Strange coincidence," said Clara with a frown.

"Bee, are we going into the garden?" asked Ellora.

"Huh," said Belle. "The trail ends here." They were standing directly in front of the fountain.

"But zhe jewel is still glowing," said Melody.

"I don't know what it wants," said Belle.

"Are you sure the trail is gone?" Ellora asked.

"Well, I can't see it anymore," Belle answered.

"It is time for some Aura, Belle," said Melody with a wink. Belle closed her eyes once more.

"Wait, I can feel something," said Belle. Suddenly, she opened her eyes again and hurried over to the fountain. "I just remembered something from my dream. Look, there are some weird marks on this side – symbols, or something." Ellora watched, as Belle closed her eyes once more and a blue glow accentuated the little carvings in the structure.

Suddenly, there was a loud CERLUNK noise, and a whirring sound came from under the ground. Belle and Ellora jumped away from the fountain and towards Clara and Melody, as it moved and twisted.

"Is it ... is it opening?" Ellora asked.

"I zhink it is," said Melody.

The top layer of the fountain sunk down into the ground, as half of the bottom layer swung to the left and the other half swung to the right. It almost seemed too crazy to be true – the pathway that the fountain had opened up to descended into a dark set of steps leading down into the Earth.

"Guys," Belle whispered. "The stairs are glowing blue."

Melody gulped loudly enough for them all to hear, and Clara shifted in her feet. Belle subconsciously stepped behind Ellora and Ellora took a shuddering breath. But, nonetheless, she stepped first. "No time to lose."

The further they walked, the narrower the path became. Eventually, even their single filed line could barely fit through the stony passageway and they had to turn and walk sideways. Ellora gripped onto the stones jutting out of the wall for support since it was so dark, and more than once, she got a painful cut on her palm she knew was bleeding.

"I can't breathe," said Belle, from just behind Ellora.

Ellora knew Belle was claustrophobic, but as far down as they had gone now, she knew it was better to keep going rather than turn around. "It's okay, Bee. Almost there."

And, sure enough, they shortly arrived at a large cavern, where the walls from the pathway seemed to widen and create a wide, empty room with six tunnels leading from it.

"There are two trails," said Belle, indicating two of the openings – one the second from the left, and the other the last one on the right.

"Two? 'Ow can zhere be two?" Melody panicked.

"Maybe the person who took the Orb didn't know which way to go," suggested Clara.

"Which trail is brighter?" asked Ellora.

"Um... this one is a bit stronger," said Belle. "Why?"

"Well, if someone didn't know which way to go, it's possible they backtracked, right?"

"Yes! So, it would create two layered trails!" Belle said happily.

"Well, what are we waiting for?" asked Melody. "Zhe sooner we are back in our beds, zhe better."

They only got about four metres into the tunnel before it got too small to walk through anymore. "We won't fit," said Belle.

"We will if we crawl." Ellora smiled apologetically. "I'm sorry, Bee, but you're going to have to go first because only you can see the trail, and if the path splits off again, we'll need you to tell us."

Belle took a deep breath, and Ellora could tell she was scared, but she went without a word, headfirst.

It felt as though they had been crawling for hours on the dusty floor before they finally emerged into another cavern. Belle moved faster the moment she saw that light.

When they got out of the tunnel, they discovered there was only one small platform they could stand on; they were surrounded by water. A deep, dark, bottomless pool of water.

"I knew we should 'ave waited for Mistress Oriel," Melody whimpered.

"There could be a hidden door or something," said Ellora. "Where does the trail lead?"

"Umm ... well, that's not right."

"What's wrong?"

"The trail goes into the water," answered Belle.

"I *really* knew we should 'ave waited for Mistress Oriel!" Melody whispered.

"Can we all swim?" asked Ellora. They all nodded their heads wearily. "Then we'll continue to follow the trail," said Ellora.

"Belle," Clara said. "Any chance you can use your Aura to see how deep it is?"

"Zhat is a good idea," Melody insisted, enthusiastically.

Belle nodded in response before closing her eyes. "It's actually quite shallow," she said in surprise before jumping in.

Ellora watched as Belle's head sank into the water. She saw ripples in the water, above where her best friend must have been swimming. And then, she saw the bubbles. The ripples stopped and the water became still. A still, empty block of darkness. Ellora stopped breathing momentarily, in fear, before the panic set in.

"Belle? Belle?!"

And then, a little ripple.

"Belle? Is that you?" she called out. Melody and Clara had their hands in the water already, trying to find her and pull her out.

As quickly as she had disappeared, Belle emerged once more. "You guys coming?" she asked, casually.

In unison, Ellora, Clara and Melody sighed in relief. "We thought you were drowning," Ellora said, accusingly.

"Drowning?" Belle looked confused. "I just went to see how far the water goes. There's a little passageway that I think we should go through that way." She pointed. "You guys thought I was drowning? I can *literally* control the water! Besides, look."

They all laughed stupidly as Belle stood up, the water only reaching her chest.

The water was murky, and Ellora couldn't see much when she dove in. The only thing she could see was the faint glow of the jewel. When they had been above water, Ellora had seen that it was growing even stronger now, but it just about shone through in the water.

Ellora followed Belle closely enough to be within touching distance, and every once in a while, she could feel Clara brush her hair with her arm from where she was swimming, and she could feel the movements of Melody's arms right behind her.

After around fifteen seconds of swimming, it was clear to Ellora that they still had much further to swim, and the thought instantly made her panic. She needed air soon, but they were still in the little tunnel Belle had found and there was no way she could get out, neither forwards nor backwards, in time.

Even knowing it was useless, Ellora swam upwards. She needed to find air, and she needed there to be some oxygen above her, above the water. She looked down, but she couldn't see the stone anymore. She was not only out of air, but she had lost her friends.

Her lungs were burning, now, without oxygen and her chest felt like it would split open. She frantically pulled herself along the rocks above her, trying to find some sort of opening or pocket of air, no matter how little it might be.

For a second, she thought about Lucifer and who would look after him when she was gone. She thought about her father and how he would be able to cope with the news that his daughter drowned, suffering a tragic, painful death. Or would he even know? Would they recover her body? She thought about her friends, Belle, Clara and Melody. She thought about Hunter and her last conversation, well – argument, with him. That would be the picture of her that would be planted in his brain forever.

Ellora finally stopped struggling. She let her body relax, feeling the heavy water drag her down to the ground, as she opened her mouth, finally unable to stop herself.

The coarse water felt like needles in her throat, and the pain in her chest got worse.

And then she was coughing. She was clutching her throat and coughing, gasping for the precious oxygen somehow surrounding her, even here at the bottom of this pool of water. Logically, she knew this didn't make sense, and for a split second, she even wondered if she was dead. But then, she was brought back to reality.

"GUYS!" It was Belle's voice. "Guys, are you alright? Speak to me, people!"

"Bee?" Ellora's voice sounded raspy and her throat felt gritty, but she could breathe and she could speak.

"Thank the Spirits." Belle's voice came again, but Ellora couldn't see her.

"I'm okay," Clara choked. Once again, from nowhere near her.

"Moi aussi," said Melody.

"Sorry about that, girls. I'm coming to get you," said Belle. "I don't know what I did, but I was thinking about how if we all had a bubble of air or something around ourselves, we would be able to breathe and speak and stuff. And then I thought we could use the air to communicate, like those walkie talkie things you used to have when you were younger, Elle. I remembered you telling me how you and Ophelia used to play with them."

Belle had reached Ellora, now, and grabbed her hand. Clara and Melody were behind her, also following along, but Ellora refused to let go of Belle and instead held on.

"Anyway, so I thought about all of that, and then it just … happened. Next thing I knew, I could breathe and speak again."

"Zhis is definitely some good information to 'ave," said Melody with a quiet little laugh. It was clear from the tone of her voice she was still scared, as she had been earlier, but was trying to put on a brave face.

And then, suddenly, the water cleared up. They could finally see. "Wow," said Clara.

"Cool," Belle echoed. The tunnel had opened up into an enormous water cavern, with tall stone walls and a bottom so far down, they couldn't even see it.

"Let's just get zhis over wizh," said Melody. "I still cannot wait to get back to my bed."

They continued to swim forward, unable to see a clear path to take but stopped immediately when a loud, thundering sound rumbled around them.

"What was zhat?" Melody whispered, a slight tremble in her voice.

"I don't know," Ellora answered. "But whatever it was, I don't think I want to know."

"Um, let's just keep swimming," said Clara.

But the deep sound echoed again, and they stopped in their tracks once more. They didn't know where the sound was coming from, but they definitely did not want to accidentally swim into the source. "We'll stick together," said Belle, pulling Ellora closer to her and moving closer to Melody and Clara.

"I think I know what's making the sound," Clara whispered in a voice so quiet with fear it almost sounded like the wind. Steadily and slowly, she lifted a hand up right ahead of them, to point at a pair of massive, glowering red eyes staring down at them. Another sound echoed around the cavern, but this time it wasn't a rumbling sound of movement. It was a deep, guttural growl.

"Nobody move," whispered Ellora, but it was too late. Melody was already swimming backwards as fast as she could, trying to get away.

Her screamed pierced the air surrounding them, as a thick, long, scaly tail swung up and hit her, like a bat to a ball. "Melody!" Clara cried as the small French girl flew, as if she was wearing some sort of jet pack, through the water and landed with a crash on a rock. Clara tried to swim over, but the tail smacked her, too, sending her back to Ellora and Belle.

"What in the Realms is that thing?!" exclaimed Belle.

Another tail coming swooshing towards them swim and they had to move backwards, even further away from Melody, to avoid being hit. Ellora whipped her head around, just in time to see a tail cutting through the water towards them and pulled Clara and Belle down with her to avoid it.

That was when she saw the head.

A huge, scaly, green head with evil red eyes and long, sharp teeth towered over them, with what looked like an eerie smile on its face. Ellora's heart plummeted at the sight.

"It looks like ... some sort of ... underwater ... sea ... serpent ... snake ... thing," Belle replied in a shaky voice. Nobody had the chance to reply because just when Belle was finished speaking, another tail came swinging towards them.

"What are we going to do?" Clara asked as they all leapt backwards, landing on a rock. "No way are we going to get around that thing!"

"First thing's first," said Ellora, as they jumped out of the way of another swish of the tail. "We get Melody."

Ellora didn't know exactly why, if it was the fear, or the intense situation, or the need to help Melody, but the three moved in perfect sync. Ellora leapt to the left when the next swing of the tail arrived, and Belle and Clara leapt to the right.

Ellora, however, clambered back to her feet as soon as she hit the rock and grabbed onto the tail before it retreated. The tail swung her from side to side, trying to shake her off, but Ellora dug her nails into the rough skin and refused to let go. She heard a roar of pain from the creature, but she kept her hold.

When the tail finally got closer to Melody, and Belle and Clara, who had made their way over to her in the confusion, Ellora leaped off and grabbed hold of Belle. "Melody!" Ellora shouted, trying to wake her up. Melody had hit her head, and there was a small trace of blood on the rock where she'd been thrown, but it didn't seem like a dangerous amount. "Melody, wake up."

Belle threw the four to the ground, keeping them pressed flat to avoid the tail as it swung once more.

"Quoi?" Melody's voice was like music to their ears.

"Thank the Spirits," said Clara.

"Right," said Belle, very business-like. "What's the plan?"

But before they could discuss, Clara saw something that changed everything.

"There's more!" she screamed. "More!"

The others turned to see three more pairs of glowing red eyes coming towards them from the left, and even more from all other directions.

"Wait," said Ellora. "Has it got nine heads?"

"Ellora Artemer, we're about to die and you're counting the number of heads?" said Clara.

"It *is* nine," said Ellora, ignoring Clara's comment. "Guys, this is a Hydra. I read about it in one of the Greek mythology books I borrowed from the library a few months ago."

"Wow, Elle. I never thought your love for mythology would save our lives one day," Belle said.

"Well, I'm not so sure about the saving our lives part," Ellora said. "But whoever took the Orb must have gotten past somehow."

"Belle?" Came Melody's voice. "Your ring – I zhink it is glowing."

Ellora looked down at Ellora's hand and, sure enough, there was the ring that Dan had given her. "Why is it glowing?" she whispered to herself.

None had realised it, but the water had become still whilst they were talking. Ellora looked up at the terrifying heads watching them, only to see that the glowing red eyes had become calm, yellow ones instead. "Guys," she whispered, afraid a single sound would set them off. "What's happened?"

"It looks like they're all enchanted by the redmer in my ring," answered Belle, moving her hand to the left and right, watching the heads follow in obedience. "It would make sense – I've read that many creatures can be entranced by powerful energy and if this stone is anything, it's powerful energy."

"This is our chance," said Clara. "Let's go!" She went first, leading the way for the others, who weren't far behind. They all held their breath as they swam, and Belle made sure her hand was up above her, in sight of all of the Hydra heads. But, as soon as they got close to the head in the middle, the eyes turned red again and they had to dodge several tails.

"It is not working!" cried Melody.

"Hang on," said Belle. "I've got an idea."

They took their positions on a rock far enough from the heads that they wouldn't attack them but close enough for them to dart through the opening when the time came.

"Ready?" asked Belle. They each nodded in confirmation. She took the ring from her finger and held it up high, watching the heads follow it like a cat with a laser. They watched as a bubble of air appeared around it. Belle sent the ring out into the water, throwing it as hard as she could. Controlled by Belle's Aura, the ring floated directly in front of each head, and their eyes turned yellow, once again. As fast as she could make it, Belle sent the ring down into the bottomless stretch of the water. And, just as she predicted, all of the heads followed.

"NOW!" cried Belle, as they all launched themselves from the rock and to the narrow little opening behind where the Hydra's heads were.

Ellora grabbed Melody by the arm and they swam together, with Belle and Clara just ahead of them. They got to the opening and Belle and Clara were trying to shimmy their ways in, when Ellora heard a grumble behind her. She turned slowly, seeing a glow of red behind her, and leapt into action.

"Go!" she shouted, shoving Melody into the tunnel before her, trying to help her in. She felt the warmth of hot breath on her foot and felt her limbs start to tremble from fear.

"Grab my 'and!" screamed Melody, reaching out to pull her in.

Ellora grasped onto Melody's arm, pulling herself along the rocks and forcing herself into the wedge in the rocks. But another force was pulling her backwards.

Before she knew it, her other hand was being pulled inside, too. But it was no use. The hydras were too strong, and she felt herself being dragged back out.

"I COMMAND YOU TO STOP!" Melody's voice bellowed through the water. "MY SUBJECTS, YOU BOW DOWN TO ME." Melody had let go of Ellora, now, and had emerged back into the water, her hands spread out in front of her. Her hair swirled around her and that feature caused Ellora to remember that Melody was a Ferri Aurum in training. Oriel had told her there is always a moment that makes the Aura in someone just connect with their body, allowing the body to properly harness it, and this must have been that moment.

Ellora wasted no time in climbing into the tunnel and pulled Melody along behind her.

CHAPTER NINETEEN
Another Bubble

They didn't swim for long before they finally emerged into a cave above them and climbed out of the water.

Ellora immediately collapsed onto the floor, panting, needing a moment to lie down and rest after the ordeal they had just been put through.

"What was that, then, Melody?" asked Belle.

"I don't know, I zhink somezhing inside of me just ... snapped."

"Well, whatever that was, it was pretty amazing," said Clara.

"Thank you, Melody," Ellora said, sincerely. "You really saved my life."

"Please," said Melody, "you pushed me into zhe cave before you; you saved *my* life."

"Um, guys, I hate to break this up," whispered Belle, "but do you hear that?"

CLINK CLINK CLINK

Ellora sat up as the sound echoed around the cave in which they were all camped.

CLINK CLINK CLINK

It sounded like it was coming from one of the tunnels leading away from the cave.

CLINK CLINK CLINK

Ellora turned her head sharply, trying to identify from where the sound was coming.

CLINK CLINK CLINK

Slowly and silently, Ellora stood up and motioned for them all to be quiet. She pointed at Belle and then pointed at the blue jewel in her hand, which was now glowing brighter than any of them had seen before. Ellora gestured towards the tunnels, trying to tell Belle to examine which tunnel had the strongest trail.

Belle closed her eyes for a moment, concentrating on the jewel, before she looked up again and peered down each tunnel, looking for the trail. Looking back at the others, she walked over to the tunnel on the right and gestured her hand in its direction.

CLINK CLINK CLINK

The sound was getting louder as the girls got further down the tunnel.

CLINK CLINK CLINK

Ellora's heart was pounding in her chest. This was it. They had done it. Belle would be okay.

The tunnel emerged into a light, open cavern after a few minutes of walking and the four froze. Ellora thanked the Spirits in her mind that the space was far enough from the water that whoever it was wouldn't have heard their chatting. Standing in front of them was a person dressed in a black hoodie, with the hood up, and baggie black trousers, clanging a rock against the wall like a hammer, the sound echoing so loudly around the room they couldn't even hear their own footsteps.

Ellora held up a hand, indicating to the others that they shouldn't move, and quietly walked over to pick up a sharp-looking rock from the floor. She gestured at a large, glowing rock on the floor near the thief, and she saw as the others' eyes went wide at the sight of a glowing, blue, sphere-shaped object shimmering and glittering so brightly that it almost seemed to flitter in and out of existence. Ellora felt herself drawn to the object, a feeling of immense power rushing over her as she stared. The centre looked as though it was made from a sort of turquoise material, encased in an icy blue barrier. The Madori Orb. Melody even had to cover her hand with her mouth to prevent her gasp from making a sound.

"Turn around," Ellora said quietly, holding the rock out in front of her as a weapon.

The figure in front of her froze immediately. Although she was already aware of the face, the minuscule sliver of doubt in Ellora was shattered, and she felt the briefest moment of relief go through her like a wave at the confirmation that the thief was not Hunter. But she felt another pang as she took in the familiar blonde hair.

"Drop the rock," Ellora spoke again, thankful that her voice sounded strong and didn't tremble like her hand seemed to in that moment.

The sound of the rock clattering to the ground from the figure's hand echoed around the empty room.

"Turn around," Ellora repeated. She prepared herself. She prepared herself to see the face of somebody she had trusted, somebody Oriel had trusted. She prepared herself to fight if she needed to. She prepared herself to snatch the Orb if she needed to.

But what she didn't prepare herself for was the sight of the complete hardness of the grey eyes that greeted her from under the black hood. Ellora felt her breath catch in her throat, swallowing deeply. She bit down hard on the inside of her cheek to stop herself from gasping or even yelling, as she felt like doing, at the girl in front of her. She fought the tears of betrayal she would not let fall. She tightened her hand on the rock and, even when she heard the gasps from behind her, stepped closer to the thief.

"Step away from the Orb, Julia."

"You know I can't do that."

"Julia, it's over. Don't you get it? There's no way out."

"You don't understand, Ellora."

"Then help me understand!"

"There are things going on, Ellora! Things you wouldn't understand. But you *need* to let me out of here. With the Orb."

"You know I can't do that, Julia."

"People will *die*, Ellora! Don't you see?! All of you! If you don't let me out, *you* will be personally responsible for the tragedies that are to come!"

Ellora froze for a moment. There was no way she could let Julia leave, let alone with the Orb. What tragedy was she talking about?

"I can't let you go," Ellora spoke defiantly. Julia had an empty look in her eyes that scared Ellora, but she didn't back off. She darted her eyes to the Orb, but even that quick glance was too long.

"ELLE, LOOK OUT!" Clara's voice screamed in what seemed like, to Ellora, slow motion. She looked up and saw the crazed face of Julia, as she lifted a hand almost as if in slow motion. There was a snarl on her lips, and water zoomed around Ellora like a whirlpool. The water was getting closer and closer, and Ellora had no idea what to do. At the speed the water was spinning, she would likely be torn apart. Ellora put an automatic hand up in defence, but she knew that it would make no difference.

"NO!" cried Belle.

Out of nowhere, when the water was about to capture her in its snare, it fell, and Ellora watched as Julia flew backwards into the wall. Ellora watched Belle walk forward, her hand up in the air, as Julia was held up against the wall, secured by a belt of water. "I dare you to try and hurt one of my friends again," Belle snarled and Ellora watched as the belt became tighter.

Before she did anything else, Ellora went over and picked up the Madori Orb, giving it to Clara for safekeeping.

"How could you do this?" she asked. "To the Kingdom, to Oriel? Do you know that Oriel would die if you had managed to get away with this?"

"It's all for the greater good."

"The greater good?! She would *die*, Julia," Ellora growled.

"Well, Ellora, you are clearly a blind, immature chid! You think Oriel's death is so important now, but you wouldn't if you knew the alternative. A life is just that. One life! *You*," she growled, nodding her head at Belle, "should count yourself lucky I ran out of time to drain your Aura. And *you*," she looked back at Ellora. "I can't believe you have stopped me, you absolute *idiot*. Of all people! And you're clearly deluded, the way you run around after Mason like a lovesick leitock. It's *disgusting*. Argh!" she shouted in pain, as Belle tightened the constraint.

Ellora could feel her blood boiling inside her, and she was *so* close to snapping.

"She is doing it on purpose." Came a small voice behind her, just loud enough for Ellora and Belle to hear. Ellora snapped around to see Melody, her face steely, glaring at Julia. "She is trying to make us drop our guards so zhat she can gain control. Do *not* let 'er." Ellora shared a glance with Belle, who nodded her head in a minuscule movement.

"Well, Julia, this *idiot* managed to stop you from escaping. How does that feel? Knowing you were bested by a *child*? And really, blaming timing on your lack of an attempt on Belle's Aura? Come now, tell us the truth. You were scared. That was the problem, wasn't it? You were scared of a *child*, Julia. Even when you had the Madori Orb, you knew you weren't strong enough." Ellora sighed in relief when her voice sounded unwavering. She took a slow, menacing step forward when her legs finally felt strong enough to handle movement. "And really, Julia, the water in the dining room? Bubbles? The fountain? Mere pranks, surely. Maybe removing the water source was a step in the right direction, but considering the fact that Oriel can create a new one, it was just a waste of time, don't you think?"

"That wasn't — Oh," Julia chuckled a malicious little laugh. "I see. What are you trying to do, make me confess? It won't matter. No matter what you do to me, we *will*—"

"We?" Clara spoke out for the first time. "Who's we?"

Julia's eyes flashed in fear, recognition of what she had just said. But she kept her mouth shut.

"Who is 'we', Julia?!" Ellora bellowed.

The small smile on her face was the end of Belle's patience. She enveloped Julia in a bubble and sent her straight to the ceiling.

"LET ME DOWN!" Julia's words were muffled by the thickness of the bubble – good planning on Belle's part.

"How are we going to get out?" asked Clara. "No way can we drag her back the way we came." She gestured up at Julia, who was still pounding against the walls of the bubble.

A nagging voice at the back of Ellora's mind gave her an idea. "Give me a minute," she said.

"Asyra?"

No response.

"Asyra?"

Silence.

"Asyra, are you there?"

"Ellora? What's the problem?" Ellora had never been so happy to hear the Madori Spirit's voice in her mind.

"Oh, thank the Spirits. I need your help. We found the Orb."

"Oh, you did?! Ellora, you must take it straight to Oriel. She had just returned and I can sense she is weak."

"Yes, but I don't know how to get to her. We are stuck in some sort of cave. I think it's under the school somewhere, but we've been through so many turns that I can't tell you where. We went under the fountain and had to battle a Hydra, Asyra. But we did it."

"Ellora, I'm so very proud of you. How in the Realm did you manage?"

"With a lot of help."

"Okay, listen my dear. Time for congratulations will come later. For now, it's fortunate that I know which cave you are talking about. I had all but forgotten about it, however. It didn't occur to me that a student would know. In fact, it's lucky your thief didn't know how it *really* works – I'm sure she was trying to get through the wall?"

"Yes, how did you know?"

"Those who know about the cave don't all know that only a Madori Mistress is able to open that wall. It leads to a path straight to the Mainland, and if someone were to get through, they would be gone forever."

Ellora gulped.

"Listen, my dear. To the right, there is another wall. Tell your friend Belle to unlock it."

"Unlock it? What do you mean?"

"Just trust me. That wall will lead you back to the castle."

"Belle," Ellora spoke out loud this time. "Time for some more of your magic."

CHAPTER TWENTY

, An Unexpected Stay

W hen Ellora and her friends had emerged with Julia following behind in Belle's bubble, Oriel had immediately run up to them to make sure they were okay. Ellora had watched as her eyes had teared up when she saw who the thief had turned out to be, but she had let Master Rainclarke take care of that while she led the girls back to her office for tea and explanations.

"Oriel," Ellora said, after they had recounted their night. "There was something weird that I noticed Julia say before we brought her out. She said 'we'."

Oriel's face went pale. "We?" she asked. Ellora nodded. "Thank you, Ellora. We will deal with that. We will have to interrogate her. She will be kept at Mistfall."

"Mistfall?" Clara asked, her eyes wide.

Oriel nodded. "In the Human Realm, criminals can be sent to prison. Here, we do not take such risks. Especially with powerful Aurums. No form of prison would be impenetrable. She will be sent down to Mistfall."

"Oriel," Melody piped up from the corner of the room. "Zhere are so many zhings zhat do not make sense. Pour example, what 'appened to zhe water source? Julia was about to claim zhat was not 'er doing."

"Yes, Melody. Thank you for bringing that up," Oriel said. "As I said in the letter I wrote, there is more happening here than we first thought. Now, I didn't want to tell you all about any of this but seeing as Belle is going to be my Madori Mistress in training and you have all already gone through so much, I only feel it right that you know."

"What?" Belle asked, her mouth gaping open.

"Yes, Belle, I apologise I meant to speak to you about this properly, but it is plain as day that you are destined to be the next Madori Mistress. Do you accept the position?"

"Of-of course!" Belle beamed and Ellora beamed back at her.

"Now, I fear there is something dark walking among us, girls. Daphne's attack had nothing to do with the Orb. Well, at least, not directly."

"Oriel, what do you mean?" Ellora asked, feeling slightly fearful.

"The reason why I had to run out last night was because of a problem in the Caeli Kingdom. It was... raining," Oriel replied. She stopped there to let the girl absorb the information.

"Raining?!" Clara exclaimed.

"But it never rains in zhe Caeli Kingdom!" squeaked Melody.

"I know," Oriel said, in what Ellora was sure was an attempt at a reassuring voice. "There is something else going on here, and I am determined to find out what. I believe it also explains some of the other things that have been happening here."

"Does zhis mean zhe pickatoos were also affected because of zhis?" Melody asked.

"And the strawberries?" Clara asked.

"Yes, it would appear so," Oriel replied sadly. Ellora looked at her now and noticed the changes in her Madori Mistress since she had last seen her only a few hours before. Dark bags drooped under her eyes, her face was pale. She almost suggested getting some food before Belle spoke again.

"Oriel, what about… Daphne?" Her voice was barely louder than a whisper. The room went silent as all eyes anxiously snapped to Oriel.

'Yes, I think her attack was also linked to whatever is going on. Or… *was* going on. It seems as though Daphne stumbled onto Julia when she had the Orb, and Julia used the Orb to erase her memory. And I also think she tried to use the Orb to harm her, without finishing her off, thankfully. That's why we couldn't find the assailant. I think Henry Fischer saw something similar the night that Mason came to find me. Once again, his memory was altered so, although he was terrified, he couldn't remember why. Listen girls, I am telling you all simply as a courtesy. Please, do *not* go out looking for any more clues or putting yourself in danger." Oriel's eyes looked so exhausted, so desperate, that Ellora had no choice to agree.

"On the condition that we all go and have a bite to eat; I'm starving, and the sun came up a while ago, so I'm sure we've already missed breakfast," she said. Oriel gestured for her to lead the way.

The walk to the dining room was short, and silent, but everyone was so caught up in their own thoughts and worries nobody even seemed to realise.

Ellora jumped when she almost walked into someone, immediately apologising.

"You should pay more attention to where you are going!" Liviana spat in her face before sniffling and storming up the stairs. Ellora stared at her wide-eyed, as she realised the Princess had been *crying*. She took a deep breath and continued her journey; she would worry about *that* later.

A week later, life was returning to normal. Although Hunter had mysteriously disappeared and none of the teachers would share any information about it. Belle had started her Madori Mistress Training and Ellora was busy with her extra lessons. She was even continuing to see Master Rainclarke to work on her memories.

She was on her way to a session with the Incendi Master, when she bumped into someone. "Mason, hey!" she said before he could run away again. She knew she needed to talk to him about what had happened nevertheless, especially when she remembered what Hunter had told her.

"Listen, can we talk?" she asked, placing a gentle hand on his arm in a somewhat friendly gesture. She had been doing a lot of thinking since that night in the tunnels. Thinking about Hunter. And that was when she had realised that she hadn't thought about Mason even *once* since that night. In fact, she hadn't thought much on him since the Winter Solstice.

She frowned when Mason shrugged her hand off his arm. Reluctantly, he looked at her, his shifting and nervous eyes refusing to meet hers.

Ellora gasped when it hit her, Liviana crying, Hunter and Mason having a fight, Hunter refusing to tell her what was going on, Mason's guilty looks.

"Did you cheat on me?" she whispered, feeling her heart drop into her stomach. She had already planned to break everything off with him, but that someone she had trusted could do this to her really hurt.

Mason snapped his eye away from her and attempted to walk in the other direction.

His reaction told her everything she needed to know.

"Coward," whispered Ellora.

Mason froze in his tracks and turned slowly around to face her.

"I am *not* a coward." He stated through gritted teeth. "I am the Prince of Japan." As he spoke, he slowly inched towards her, like an animal stalking its prey. All traces of guilt were gone from his eyes, and Ellora could tell from the anger that had replaced it that she had hit a nerve.

"You're not special, Mason," Ellora said, refusing to cower back. "You're a spineless little wimp." Ellora could see the rage on Mason's face getting harsher, but she refused to surrender. "Imagine having *you* for a King – how are you going to rule a country if you can't even tell a nineteen-year-old girl that you cheated on her."

"Don't you dare talk to me like that. *I'm* the one your little bodyguard tried to tear apart. Don't you dare start feeling sorry for yourself."

When he finished speaking, Ellora had to clench her teeth to prevent herself from screaming. How could the sweet, wonderful Mason she had met all those months ago even think about talking to her like that? But then she realised, with a twinge to her heart, that other people had realised; even Julia had known. How could she have missed this.

"Oh, really, are you the victim, now, Mason? Are you really that self-absorbed that you care for and think about absolutely nobody but yourself?" A crowd was gathered now, watching their spectacle, but Ellora didn't care. "You know what, Mason? You're just a stuck up, immature, arrogant little jerk who doesn't deserve the light of day." There was silence as she turned to leave, but Ellora paused and turned back around. "Your highness," she spat out viciously.

Mason was clearly speechless, as she brushed off his coat and tried to leave with his head held high, like the Prince he was, but Ellora could see his nerves at the evil stares he was receiving from others around them.

Ellora walked into the library like a girl with a mission. And her mission was to find Hunter.

His raven-black hair wasn't difficult to spot in the small sea of students, and she purposefully made her way over to him. Only, when she arrived, she found herself unable to come up with anything to say.

"Artemer." Hunter looked up at her and inclined his head in a short nod of acknowledgement, before looking back at his book. Ellora nodded back and shifted between her feet and playing with her fingers.

"I broke up with Mason," she blurted out.

Hunter looked up at her slowly with one eyebrow raised. "Indeed?"

"I — it's just that — will you come on a walk with me, Hunter?" Ellora couldn't remember the last time she had felt so nervous, but there was still an air of tension between them from the last time they had spoken or shouted, and Ellora was determined to clear it.

Hunter looked up curiously at her before abruptly shutting his book and standing up, placing it back on the shelf. "I suppose we do have a lot to discuss."

Their walk started in an uncomfortable silence, but Ellora had no idea where to begin. Finally, when they reached the fountain outside and headed for the gardens, she could take it no more.

"Thank you. For what you did to Mason, I mean." Her voice was quiet.

"Nobody deserves to be treated like that," Hunter answered.

"I'm sorry you got hurt in the process."

"I'm sorry *you* got hurt in the process."

Another silence.

"How did you know him, anyway?" Ellora asked, looking over at the boy. He was walking with his hands behind his back and his eyes focused directly in front of him, but at her question, he glanced at her briefly out of the corner of his eye.

There was yet another silence, before Hunter sighed deeply. "I will tell you, Ellora, but only if you swear not to share this secret." He looked so serious that for a moment, Ellora thought he might have been joking. But the look in his eyes told her he was dead serious.

"Of course," she answered.

"There is a lot you don't know about me, Ellora," he began. "Mason and I, and Liviana for that matter, essentially grew up together. They would constantly be visiting my home in London. You see, Nash is not really my surname. Oriel is a good friend of my family, so she allowed it to be changed so I could avoid any sort of special treatment, but my surname is Winnashire."

Ellora's mouth dropped open, and she closed it when she realised she must have looked like a fish. "Winnashire?" she asked. "Winnashire?" she repeated. She almost couldn't believe him. "So, your parents are—"

"King Archer and Queen Louisa of England, yes, and my baby sister is Princess Sapphire of England."

Her eyes were still wide as she stared at him. This boy, with the sharp jawline and silky black hair, was the very same boy, the thin, smiling boy she had taken a fancy to when she was a child. There was absolutely no way she could ever admit her old crush on the Prince of England now.

But, looking at him more closely now, she really saw some similarities. The mysterious, dark eyes, the hair, although was now a lot smoother and softer, was as dark as night. Of course, he was now so much taller than he had been. Ellora was willing to bet she would have been just as tall, if not taller than, him back when they were children, but now she had to look up at him, tilting her head backwards.

"Urm, right. Your highness, then," Ellora said jokingly and stepping away, only just having realised she had inched closer to him.

"Absolutely not. This is why I don't tell anyone." Hunter all but growled.

"Hunter, I was joking!" Ellora reached up and placed a hand on his shoulder before he could walk away. He looked at her strangely but continued walking with her when she removed her hand.

"Yes, well, Mason, Liviana and I essentially grew up together; Mason and his family visited my home on almost a daily basis when I was very young, and even Liviana would come once a week. Each castle has a Gate in it, you see. Although, I stopped wanting to see them as I grew older and saw them for what they really were."

"Royal pains?" Ellora suggested, repeating what he had said at the Winter ball.

It surprised Ellora when Hunter released a short chuckle. "Yes, exactly," he said.

They passed a few more minutes in silence, but it was not uncomfortable this time.

"Can I ask something else?" Ellora asked warily.

"I don't believe I could stop you if I tried." Ellora smiled brightly when she realised Hunter was joking with her.

"I suppose you're right," Ellora answered and waited a beat. "On the day... when Daphne..." She swallowed thickly at memories of the night.

"I suppose you are asking why I was hurt on that night? And why I was bloody? It is a fair question. I've heard you have met Asyra. She had also told me about the Orb, and I was in the library to do some research, when I heard a yelp. Of course, I ran to see what was going on and found Daphne being... well, you know. I tried to pull that...*thing* away." He grimaced with disgust.

"What thing?" Ellora asked, swallowing heavily.

"I don't know exactly what it was. It wasn't really anything tangible; it felt like... energy."

"Oriel thinks Julia used the Orb to hurt her. Maybe it was the energy from the Orb that you felt," she suggested.

"It probably was. I tried to fight it."

"And you got hurt."

"Obviously. I tried to help Daphne, but when I heard you come in, I knew you would help Daphne. I tried to chase down the energy, thinking it was a person. I thought it was somebody who had bought some sort of enchantment to keep themselves hidden. I thought... if only I could catch them. But I was too weak."

"Hunter, weak is the last word I would use to describe you." Ellora frowned at the sadness in his eyes, but continued, nonetheless. "You have to tell Oriel what happened, Hunter."

"I did," Hunter replied, a dark look in his eyes.

"How did you know Asyra?" she asked, changing the subject.

"My grandfather, the late King Arnold, was the Madori Master than trained Oriel, you know. I used to come here all the time when I was a child and grandfather even introduced me to Asyra."

Ellora smiled up at him, and they continued in silence once more. When they had completed a full lap of the gardens and were back in the warmth of the castle, they stood awkwardly.

"I'm sorry I suspected you, Hunter. I really am."

"I know." Hunter smiled. Ellora returned his warm smile.

A high-pitched scream filled the air and made Ellora jolt up from her dream. She looked up to see Master Rainclarke looking worriedly at her and realised that the scream had come from her. Before saying anything, he thrust a mug and a chocolate bar into her hand.

"What do you remember?" he asked.

"Ophelia was calling for me, again. But there was no fire this time that chased me out of the house," Ellora responded. "Someone was definitely chasing me, though. My parents were unconscious in the living room, I remember that. And there was someone else there with them. I don't know who he was, but I definitely recognised him from somewhere. He had white hair, really long white hair, and he was leaning on a long cane. I woke up when he looked at me."

Rainclarke placed his chin in his steepled fingers, leaning his elbows on his knees. He seemed to have come to a conclusion of some sorts but seemed reluctant to tell her. Finally, he sat up and Ellora knew he had reached a decision.

"Someone has definitely tampered with your memories, but I am not inclined to believe that it was your parents."

"I didn't think so either, sir, but who else could it be?" Ellora asked.

"A good question," Master Rainclarke said. "Ellora, I think we should stop our sessions for the time being."

Ellora sat up quickly. "Sir?"

"I need to do some research," he said. "We can continue in the coming academic year if you would like." At her nod, he continued. "We also need to find a way to unlock your Incendi Aura."

Belle had been so busy with her training, and Ellora had been so busy with her extra classes that their timetables never seemed to match, and they hardly ever saw each other. One of the first times Ellora got to properly spend time with Belle since she had started her training was in the early summer, on Ellora's birthday. "Bee, I know you love the library, but I *really* don't want to spend my birthday there," Ellora protested as Belle dragged her towards the big double doors.

"I know, Elle, it'll only be quick I promise I just need to get something."

"Okay, fine, but—"

"SURPRISE!"

Ellora's mouth dropped open when she saw almost her entire form gathered in the library with banners and decorations everywhere. Even Wendy, Oriel and Master Rainclarke were smiling at her from the back.

"W-what?" Ellora stammered, feeling tears form in her eyes. Since Ophelia had died, she hadn't liked celebrating her birthday much; it reminded her too much of her sister. And so, it had been many years that Ellora had done something big, but that her friends had done all of this for her warmed her heart.

"I can't believe you did all of this for me!" she exclaimed as she walked into the party with Belle.

"Well, I thought it would be a good idea. Besides, we could all do with a bit of fun, don't you think?" she asked, looking over to their friends, to Daphne, and to Oriel.

"I got you something," said Hunter, appearing at her side when she was alone and staring out of a window at the back of the library.

"What?" Ellora looked up at his with her eyebrows furrowed.

"Well, today *is* your birthday, isn't it?" he joked, sending her own words back at her whilst gesturing around him.

Ellora chuckled softly. "I suppose it is. Thank you." She took the small, red box from Hunter's hands. She opened the box easily to see another box, turquoise coloured this time, inside, with the words 'Persephone's Chocolate Bon Bons' written across the front in gold.

"Hunter!" She gasped, as she removed the small box. "These must have been so expensive; these are so rare! I can't accept this," she insisted, but Hunter merely shrugged.

"You like them, don't you?" A shadow of worry danced across his face as he furrowed his brows.

"*Like* them? Hunter! They are my absolute favourites!" she exclaimed, automatically wrapping her arms around him in a hug. Hunter stood stiffly at first but slowly put his arms around her shoulders and patted her back twice before he let go.

"I can't *wait* to show Clara."

"Promise me you will come and visit soon?" Belle asked Ellora, tears in her eyes. It was time for everybody to leave for the Summer break, but Belle would be staying behind to continue her training. Hunter was staying too, for his extra training, but Oriel had insisted Ellora go home for at least some of the holiday; she had, after all, been working harder than any other First Former for the past year.

"Of course I will, Bee. I'm even trying to convince Oriel to let me come back early for some extra training. Spirits know I don't want to be at home," Ellora replied. And, as if on cue, Oriel appeared from around the corner. She walked over to them and gave Ellora a warm smile.

"We will be in touch, dear, but please, Ellora, at least spend *some* time relaxing. You have had far too stressful a year. I'm going to force this one to talk a few days off, as well," she said, nodding towards Belle.

"I will, Oriel. Promise." Ellora smiled.

"Good. Then maybe I will consider your coming back earlier, Ellora. Expect a letter from me in the next few weeks." She gave Ellora a pat on the shoulder and left the girls to it.

"You'll keep me updated, won't you?" Ellora asked her best friend. She was the last one to leave the school, as she had prolonged it for as long as she could. Even Dan's parents had picked him up earlier.

"I will, Ellie. You'll be back here in no time."

"Yes, I think you're right, Bee. I believe I will.

Afterword

Thank you so much for visiting The Aura Realm and the Madori Kingdom with me; I really hope you enjoyed Asyra's Call. It truly means the world that you would take a chance on a small indie author like myself.

Reviews mean the world to us, as authors (especially independently published authors), so if you did enjoy Asyra's Call, I would be incredibly grateful if you could leave a quick review!

THANK YOU

I would first like to thank you — my readers. I truly do appreciate all of your support, your reviews and your messages. I cannot thank you enough for taking a chance on a new writer like myself. I truly hope you have enjoyed your trip into The Aura Realm, and that you will return soon.

To my friends and family: There are an overwhelming amount of you to thank. I know for a fact that each of you know how grateful I am for your love and your encouragement. I really don't know how far I would have come without you.

Isha, thank you for reading the first chapters I ever wrote. I can't imagine they were all too easy to read, being the first draft and all, but you gave me such overwhelmingly positive feedback and encouraged me to keep going. Without you, I could never have finished this book.

Gina, what in the Realms would I have done without you and your love for Honey Cheerios? You really helped me so unbelievably much that I really don't think I would be anywhere near publication without you.

Ellie, you were my first ARC reader and I know I have already told you countless times that your feedback meant so much to me, but I don't think I can tell you enough. You really gave me that last push I needed to go ahead and publish, so thank you.

There are so many people I would like to thank for supporting me and this book's journey, that I think it would actually be impossible to name you all. I will have to end by saying an overall Thank You: to my friends, my family and my readers. I love and appreciate every single one of you.

ABOUT AUTHOR

Maya Unadkat is a multi-genre UK-based author of young adult fantasy and romance novels. She is a student at Royal Holloway, University of London working to acquire her Bachelor of Arts degree in French and Spanish. When she was just sixteen, she discovered her love and passion for writing and when, at age nineteen, she was hospitalised due to appendicitis, she decided to begin working on her first novel. She hasn't stopped writing since. Her passions include stories, chocolate and Jane Austen.